MacKenzie

GOD'S AMAZING GRACE
UNFOLDS IN STORY

The Unfolding

By

JIM AND TERRI KRAUS

BARBOUR
PUBLISHING

To our son, Elliot

© 2003 by Jim and Terri Kraus

ISBN: 1-58660-859-2

All Scripture quotations, unless otherwise indicated, are taken from the HOLY BIBLE, NEW INTERNATIONAL VERSION®. NIV®. Copyright © 1973, 1978, 1984 by International Bible Society. Used by permission of Zondervan Publishing House. All rights reserved.

Scripture quotations marked KJV are taken from the King James Version of the Bible.

This book is a work of fiction. Names, characters, places, and incidents are either products of the author's imagination or used fictitiously. Any similarity to actual people, organizations, and/or events is purely coincidental.

Acquisitions and Editorial Director: Rebecca Germany
Editorial Consultant: Ramona Cramer Tucker
Art Director: Robyn Martins
Layout Design: Anita Cook

Published by Barbour Publishing, Inc., P.O. Box 719, Uhrichsville, OH 44683, www.barbourbooks.com

Our mission is to publish and distribute inspirational products offering exceptional value and biblical encouragement to the masses.

Member of the
Evangelical Christian
Publishers Association

Printed in the United States of America

One

Chicago, Illinois

PINK LIGHT SPILLED OUT onto the street and pooled in squares on the sidewalk. The neon sign above blinked with a soft static crackle every ten seconds, proclaiming WASH-DRY-FOLD-WASH-DRY-FOLD-WASH-DRY-FOLD. Its intermittent glow washed a cheerful tint over the street-corner bench upon which Annie Hamilton sat.

Crossing her legs, Annie glanced over her shoulder. There was no one inside the laundromat—*her* laundromat. A long row of stainless-steel washers and dryers stood shoulder to shoulder along the west wall of the building. For a minute, she considered going inside to lock the door to her office. But then she shrugged.

Not much of value there to steal.

She took a deep breath, inhaling the scent of Lake Michigan, only eight blocks to the east. It was a clean scent, a liquid, rolling scent that always pleased her.

Annie always enjoyed sitting on "her bench" on the sidewalk in front of the *WASH-DRY-FOLD* laundromat. But it was even more of a special treat when the spring air was newly warm and the moon grew bright and gibbous. Tonight was just such a night.

Annie took some small pleasure in telling people she was the owner of the *WASH-DRY-FOLD*. She even collected their expressions and their curious, stumbling responses. Her favorite reply so far this month had been from a tidy little Korean man, a recent immigrant to both America and the Lincoln Park neighborhood: "You mean someone own this? This not public property—like park or subway?"

A car slowly rolled past. Annie turned to look. No one would describe the traffic on MacKenzie Street as busy; only during the morning and afternoon rush hours did a pedestrian need to look both ways. At night the street stilled further. Neighbors sitting on their stoops would invariably glance up when a vehicle passed by and would often wave since most traffic was caused by people who lived there and not by those passing through.

MacKenzie Street lay three blocks west of North Lincoln Avenue, which lay three blocks west of Lincoln Park. The park was bordered on the east by the lake, so MacKenzie was an easy walk to the water. It was a short street, less than a mile in length. Much of the area around MacKenzie and Dickens—in fact, most of the Lincoln Park neighborhood—had become gentrified and sophisticated over the six years that Annie had lived above the *WASH-DRY-FOLD*. The newly moneyed and "yuppies" had not yet fully discovered MacKenzie Street. So from Annie's vantage point, the neighborhood remained, at its core, bohemian in style and working class in attitude. She liked that combination.

Annie sighed contentedly and inhaled again. She knew the air might not be as clean as say, Wisconsin, but she was not in Wisconsin and knew she couldn't hold her breath the couple hours' drive it would take to get from the Windy City to the dairy state.

She shook her head, smiling. Why was it that such strange comparisons always popped into her mind?

The screened door creaked open behind her, and she turned, startled.

Hermes Diegos, one of her regular customers, slipped into the laundromat carrying a green duffle bearing his name scrawled in black marker. She knew the duffle dated from his time in the military.

The door slammed with a noisy clatter. The hand-height metal bar over the screen was loose, rattling when the door opened and clacking when the door shut. Annie knew which screw had fallen loose—it had done so twice before. She made a mental note to repair it in the morning. She knew her business was not chic or fancy, but she was determined it would be as clean, tidy, and well repaired as she could manage.

Shouldering the canvas bag she'd been given for donating fifteen dollars to the Friends of Lincoln Park benefit eight years ago, she stood, stretched, and climbed two steps to open the screened door. Virtually every time she opened that door, a smile came to her face. That screened door was the reason she lived where she lived and did what she did.

At least it was part of the reason.

When she had first considered purchasing the laundromat business, she had taken careful note of its screened door. Somehow the sound of its coiled spring and squeaking wooden frame brought back a flood of memories from her childhood summers at her grandparents' cottage in Wisconsin—of businesses that operated without air-conditioning and security systems, like the ice cream store and the shoe repair shop. Whenever she touched the wooden frame, she felt renewed, almost returned to that period of sweet innocence. It was as if the door were a portal to a simpler time, a time without worries.

"Hello, Hermes," she called, smiling. "You're here late tonight. Overtime?"

Hermes nodded with almost every word she spoke. She knew he struggled with English. English was not the first language of many of her customers. So she spoke slowly now and took care with each word, forming them with no high or low inflections.

"Overtime, *si*. Work is good," Hermes said with great cheer. "They ask. I work." He nodded and waited.

"Do you need change?" Annie asked.

Hermes shook his head quickly. "No. I have much quarters." He proudly extracted a fistful of coins from his pocket. Then his face tightened in concern. "You close soon? I should come tomorrow?" He gestured at his duffle.

"No," she said, her tone soft and kind. "It's not late. Please. I have work to do in my office. You do your washing. You have plenty of time."

He grinned at her and dragged the heavy duffle toward the economy-sized washer. Annie knew he would stuff every item into one full load—colors, whites, darks—all of it mixed together.

Opening the door to her office, she tossed her bag to one side. Its contents made a metallic noise as it fell. Walking behind the old walnut desk, she pulled out her heavy 1940s-style office chair. She didn't feel like sitting because sitting meant paperwork, her least favorite part of the job. But she wouldn't feel right walking upstairs to her apartment, leaving Hermes all by himself. So she sat down and gazed around her.

Although she'd quickly fallen in love with this place and its historic façade, its truly redeeming quirks had only shown themselves to her slowly, over a period of days and weeks after moving in.

One endearing characteristic that Annie so loved was the building's odd assortment of entrances and egresses. She could enter the laundromat through the robin's-egg blue front door or through a thick door that faced the back alley. She could get to her apartment on the second floor through a separate paned door on the street, or she could use the door behind her in the office. There was also a stairway that went from the basement to the second floor without making a stop on the first floor—most likely the original entrance had been boarded, bricked, and painted for decades. And in a pinch, Annie could climb the dumpster out in the alley, jump up a foot, and pull down the fire-escape ladder that led to the metal grate and balcony by her kitchen window. She had done that only once—the time she had lost the key around her neck when a wave had knocked her over while swimming in Lake Michigan one hot and windy day last August.

Just then a faint meowing sounded from the other side of the narrow door behind her. Annie leaned back in her chair and scrabbled for the brass doorknob. The door had not been locked, and she chided herself once again for forgetting any semblance of security. The brass handle turned and rattled as she pulled the door open.

She already knew who was on the other side.

A puddle of gray fur, like a large and animated dust bunny, waddled in. It placed its paws on the top of the bottom drawer and offered a most pitiful cry.

"Well, well, little Petey. Did you miss me?" she crooned.

She picked up the ancient cat and plopped him on the desk. The cat stared first at Annie and next surveyed the entire laundromat. Then he promptly fell to his side, demanding attention.

"If you hadn't come with this place," Annie teased, "I would have dumped you into the lint bin a long time ago."

Petey the Cat purred in response and rolled onto his back.

Annie scratched at the fat tomcat—or former tomcat—and wondered if she had any food left for him. If not, there was a twenty-four-hour convenience store a few blocks down on Armitage. The cat food there was expensive, but at midnight, she didn't feel like walking the six blocks farther north to the Treasure Island grocery on Fullerton near DePaul University, even though it was a warm spring evening. If she was out of food for the cat, she would be forced to buy one can at the inflated price, but one can only.

As she patted the cat, she caught a glimpse of her reflection in the glass wall of the office. The darkness outside robbed the clean glass of its clarity, making it opaque, almost mirrorlike. She could see lights outside, but only if she concentrated, ignoring the closer, colorless images.

She turned her head to the left, then to the right, holding her chin up just so. With her free hand, she smoothed her hair. The humidity of the laundromat had made her long auburn curls even tighter. She again thought of cutting it short. But the last time she tried that style, she had felt like a red-haired Chia Pet. She gathered her curls and, using both hands, slipped an elastic band around them, forming a thick ponytail.

Not all that bad for forty-one.

Annie knew no one would describe her as a raving beauty, but she imagined her more charitable friends would claim she was "pretty, in a peasant sort of way." She wasn't sure what a peasant looked like, exactly—earthy, perhaps, with a bit of solidity and firmness. Yes. She felt solid most of the time.

It was a hard-won personality characteristic, based on a lot of years of being alone.

She grinned at her reflection. She liked herself best when she smiled.

Solid. Firm. Good stock.

She laughed.

Then, unbidden, the thought came: *Much like the selling points of a muskmelon.*

She let her hand graze her jaw line. The skin was not as firm as twenty years ago—or even ten years.

But, then, what is the same as twenty years ago? Not much.

Annie pushed Petey the Cat out of her way, turned away from her reflection, and began to sort through a stack of mail that had been on her desk since the previous day. Most of it was solicitations for credit cards and financial planning seminars.

I get added in to the Lincoln Park demographics, she thought. *Little do they know how inappropriate both solicitations are.*

Once sorted, there were only five envelopes that required her attention. Three were monthly bills, and one of them was the gas bill. She hated opening that one. It was always huge—often far more money than she had paid for her first car. A laundromat used a lot of gas. And water, but the water bill would not arrive for another week.

The bills she slipped into a brown accordion folder. No matter what date they arrived or were due, she paid the lot of them on the ninth of every month. That was another difficult and distasteful task.

Then she turned her attention to the letters. One was from

the church she attended off and on, asking her to consider making a pledge for their building campaign. She slipped it in the slot behind the bills. She would consider the plea, but not until after the ninth.

The last letter was a formal proposal from the Westlake Maintenance Company. Daniel Trevalli, the company's representative, had visited her and her laundromat three weeks prior, taking pages of notes and recording the serial number of each washer and dryer she had on the premises. Until now she had done her own maintenance on her machinery, occasionally calling for additional service when the problem was beyond her own limited, "refer to the owner's manual" education. Westlake promised her lower costs and prompt service for a one-year, single-fee contract.

Annie didn't open the proposal; she simply held it in her right hand. She remembered the dark-eyed Daniel, dressed in a neat service uniform, with his name stitched over the breast pocket. He had joked and laughed and asked her so many questions. Because his dark hair was thinning a little, that meant he was most likely close to her age. But she'd never been good at guessing ages.

She stared at the return address. Daniel had not been wearing a wedding band. As much as she resisted the temptation to scrutinize every man's left hand, it was a fact of her life. She was sure everyone her age and still single did exactly the same thing.

"It's not a desperate act," she once explained to a friend from college. "It's just that I'm curious. And it gives me a frame of reference." Her friend, who was also single, had only nodded knowingly.

Annie sighed and placed the letter back on the desk. She would open it in the morning when her head was clearer. She was quite certain Daniel had not included any personal greetings, so there was no real urgency in the opening.

She stared back out the window, out to the street. She watched Mr. and Mrs. Halliston pass by—a couple who had lived in the building three doors down for over forty years. She waved and Mrs. Halliston waved back. Mr. Halliston merely continued walking. He had acknowledged very little these past few years.

She jumped at a tapping sound, her hand fluttering to her heart.

It was Hermes. His friendly face was nearly pressed to the window glass of her office. He was waving. "I done. Clothes all dry."

Annie smiled. She knew his clothes still had to be damp, probably wet actually, yet he would save fifty cents by hanging them inside his small apartment, draping them over every available piece of furniture. He was frugal—something she definitely understood.

"You close now," he said. "Go to bed."

She walked with him to the front door. "I will, Hermes. You must get rest now too. You cannot work twenty-four hours a day!"

He grinned. "If they ask, I work." His words rang with hope.

Annie watched him walk down the street and turn at the

corner, heading west on Dickens, toward the expressway. There was a laundromat closer to where he lived, Annie knew. She had gone there once to check the competition. Their dryers lasted only half as long as hers for the same amount of money. She understood why people like Hermes walked the few extra blocks. She would have done the same thing herself.

Now she flipped the switch that controlled the three rows of overhead fluorescent bulbs. She left the neon sign on all night, having been told that it took more electricity to turn it on and off than to just let it glow. Taking the key from her pocket, she turned it in the front lock. She pulled the door twice to make sure the dead bolt had engaged. Then she locked the back door and headed up to her apartment via the door and stairway in her office.

Petey cried and circled her legs, darting up a step, then back down. Annie nearly stumbled at the top.

"Are you trying to kill me for the insurance money, Petey?" she asked. It was a familiar routine for both of them.

The pantry did, thankfully, hold one last can of cat food. Petey circled and meowed as Annie opened the can and filled his dish. He sprinted over and slid neatly into the wall. Then he sniffed at the food, meowed once more, looked up at her, and walked away without tasting a bite.

Six years ago Annie never would have imagined she'd be sharing her home with a cat. She simply wasn't a cat person. But she had grown to love Petey. Yet this one feline peculiarity nearly drove her to distraction. If there was ever a time she could dislike the animal, it was at this moment. So Annie just growled back at him, "It's good food! You ate it yester-day. And that's all you get today."

She fussed and fumed as she set a kettle on to boil. She knew a cup of herbal tea would soothe her nerves. But instead of getting a tea bag, she measured out a spoonful of instant coffee into a mug. She checked the refrigerator for half-and-half, then remembered using the last of it at lunch.

"It will have to be skim milk instead." It was almost enough for her to reconsider the herbal tea.

Almost, she thought, *but not quite.*

She carried the mug of coffee to the spacious front room. The glow from the street lamp was enough to light her way. She missed experiencing darkness. It never got truly dark in the city. The only real and true darkness, she'd discovered, was to be found on an overcast, moonless night up in the north woods. How well she remembered such nights from youth camp, when darkness was so dense she could feel it engulfing her hand and body as she walked through it. Yet she had never been afraid of it. There was a peace in the darkness too—a peace she hadn't often felt in her growing-up days at home.

In her apartment was a pepperbox, built so the large win-dow jutted out street-side from the building. There a scatter-ing of throw pillows lay on a wide, cushioned window seat. On the seat was a quilt neatly folded, which she had bought at a huge flea market out in Kane County, west of the city, early that spring. It was a "crazy quilt," a dark swirl of blues and blacks and browns and burgundies, with yellow hand-sewn stitches in a meandering pattern—like an abstract piece of art from the turn of the century. Annie wasn't sure if it was as valuable as the seller had indicated. But it truly didn't matter, for she simply loved the colors and mood of the old fabrics. She tucked a throw pillow under her head and behind her back and draped the quilt over her legs. The air was warm, but Annie simply liked the sensation of being blanketed. . .all covered, snug, and cozy.

She set the coffee mug on a mahogany table to her left. From her perch she could see headlights in a sparkling profusion from Fullerton Avenue, three blocks to the north of her. She could watch the approach of the occasional car as it made its way down MacKenzie Street.

Young couples would be out strolling on a night like this. Annie, alone and in the darkness, would be invisible to them as they walked below her. She would make up stories about who they were and where they had been—to dinner at a romantic little bistro, to a play at the theater, at the movies, or simply out for a walk along the lake. Sometimes she would recognize them. Being the owner of the neighborhood laundromat had its benefits. Annie knew at least as many people in the area as did the ward's alderman—perhaps more.

A pair of headlights made their way down the street. When the vehicle slowed at the corner, she could see the silhouette in the glow of the streetlight. A cross between a small pickup and a step van, the vehicle displayed on its side the bold graphics of a rental company.

The driver must not have been certain of the destination

because the vehicle slowed again, and Annie could see a head peering from the driver's window. The vehicle crept on another few feet, then stopped. For a long moment, nothing happened.

Then yellow hazard blinkers flashed into the night. A young man, no more than twenty years old, got out from the driver's side and made his way to the stoop of a three-flat brownstone on the other side of the street from Annie. A *FOR RENT* sign had been in the window for many weeks. The vacant apartment was the basement unit. A light switched on in the first-floor window.

It was Tony Korzak's building. He and his wife, who barely spoke English, lived in the first-floor apartment with their three boys. Annie knew them, but not well.

After a minute, the young man bounded back to the truck and slapped open the rear door. He brought out a large cardboard box and headed straight to the door beneath the stoop of the brownstone—the main entrance to that basement apartment.

Annie watched as he made another dozen trips back and forth. The cargo was mostly boxes, some luggage, a lamp, a small table, a couple of chairs, then finally a single twin-sized mattress and box spring. In no more than twenty minutes, the job was finished, and the young man stopped, lit a cigarette, and slammed the truck's door shut.

Finishing her coffee, Annie was about to get up and head to bed. She had watched the same scene with regularity over the years. Young people moved in, young people moved out. It was only the older people who stayed put.

She grinned. *I must be an "older people" now.*

The lights in the truck snapped on and the passenger side door opened. In the warm glow of the streetlights, Annie recognized the figure to be that of a young woman—perhaps in her early or mid-twenties. Shoulder-length blond hair, long legs—*willowy* was the term that came to mind. Annie would have liked to have been described as "willowy" even once. But that would never be.

The willowy young woman walked alone to the sidewalk. Turning back to the young man, she talked with him for a few minutes. He flicked his cigarette into the street—a habit Annie despised. Then he held out something in his hand and dropped it into the outstretched hand of the young woman. The object glistened in the light.

It must be the key.

Why hadn't the young woman helped carry anything into the apartment?

That's odd, Annie thought. She could come up with no story to explain it.

A minute later the young man jumped into the truck and drove away. By the time the truck passed, the young woman was already taking the six shallow steps down to the door of the basement apartment, 2108 MacKenzie Street, Lower Level.

Annie watched for another moment. She could see only a shallow glow from the front window. Then it became dark.

Annie took a last drink from her coffee—now grown cold—and stood up and stretched again, hearing a ripple of crackings from her back. She shuffled to her bedroom, knowing that in the dark, Petey, with murderous intentions, would often lie in the middle of the hall, in the shadows. So she shuffled instead. That way she would only kick him softly and not trip.

But tonight Petey the Cat had fooled her and was lying on her pillow, emitting feline snores as he snuggled alone on the downy whiteness.

Two

ANNIE COULD USUALLY IGNORE the clattering noises of early morning garbage trucks and the squeal and rumble of city buses. She could even ignore the jackhammers of construction from the condo building project three streets to the south.

But Petey the Cat was the one thing she could not sleep through. For weeks now, precisely at 4:00 A.M.—almost as if he wore a wristwatch—Petey would begin leaping and pouncing on imaginary victims that stirred beneath the thick down comforter on Annie's bed.

In the predawn gray, Annie would awaken to the curious, tensing wiggle as Petey rapidly shifted his haunches back and forth, lowered his shoulders, flexed his clawless paws, and leaped at her foot or arm or elbow. Occasionally he would attack her hair, which would cause Annie to toss about in sleepy anger, often grabbing at a pillow to swing with a somnambulistic flailing.

Afterward Petey would sit in the doorway of the bedroom, his face exhibiting either feline contrition or surprised indignation. Annie was never sure which.

This morning the cat did not attack her person. Instead he sat on the open window opposite the bed and batted at the cord and tassel of the window blind. The irregular *clatter* and *thunk*, Annie decided later, was worse than his direct assault. She sat up in bed and resisted the urge to shout at this infuriation. But she knew her voice would easily carry to the street below. She did not want to garner a reputation as an odd, spinster woman. . .or the neighborhood "cat lady."

Annie blinked her eyes and stared at the clock. She needed glasses and knew it but refused to admit to requiring them just yet.

If you simply choose not to notice a subtle failing. . .then there is no aging.

Yet even as she thought the words, she knew they were not true. Picking up the alarm clock, she held it close to her face.

"Five o'clock. Not bad, Petey. A full hour later than yesterday. I can see why you came with the laundromat. No one in their right mind would have paid money for you."

The cat batted the cord again and nearly fell from his perch. Annie's laughter was throaty and deep, causing the cat to stalk away, suffering from what Annie hoped was feline embarrassment.

Instead of shuffling into the kitchen for coffee, per usual, Annie grew inspired. She dug into the back of the closet and found her running shoes. She had purchased them nearly three years ago, but they were still almost like new. Because they were horridly expensive, Annie never wore these special shoes for just a walk. They were reserved for her nearly non-existent jogging program. She pulled on a baggy pair of gray sweatpants and a battered gray sweatshirt.

Petey attacked her shoelaces as she sat on the kitchen floor, tying them just so. She slipped her house key—the key she hung on a leather thong on the back of the kitchen door just for times like this—around her neck.

Once on the street, she leaned against her bench and began to stretch. Somewhere Annie had read that for every five minutes of running one did, one needed to spend at least a minute in stretching—both before and after the run. She consulted her watch.

"Five-ten. I should stretch until five-twenty. Then I could run for thirty minutes, stretch some at the end, shower, and be back on the job before six."

Annie rarely opened the laundromat at six, but on Wednesdays, she had three regular customers who worked the night shift. The trio would stand outside the locked front door, waiting for the "official" opening at 6:30. Last winter she had first become aware of their early hours as they waited like slowly developing snowmen, with snowflakes covering their hats and shoulders. Since then, Wednesday opening time had been set back to six o'clock.

Just then, in the flinty gray of the morning, Mrs. Alvarez, a compact older woman, bustled around the corner and nearly collided with Annie, who was midway through a complicated calf-loosening routine—and only a minute into her stretch.

"Annie!" Mrs. Alvarez called out cheerfully. "What on earth are you doing?"

"I'm going running."

Mrs. Alvarez offered her a look wavering between compassion and incredulity. "This early? Only crazy people run when it's still dark outside. You're not a crazy person, are you, Annie? You don't look like a crazy person."

"I don't think I am," Annie replied with a smile.

Mrs. Alvarez shifted the two large grocery bags she carried in her arms and tried to inch the shoulder strap of her large canvas purse farther up her shoulder. The bags rested against Mrs. Alvarez's ample bosom like boats at a mooring.

"Here—let me help," Annie said and took one of the bags from the older woman.

"No, no," she countered. "You're running."

"That's alright. I can help you carry these. Where are you going so early? Your daughter's?"

Mrs. Alvarez leaned close to Annie. "She's proud, my daughter," Mrs. Alvarez said in the tone of a conspirator. "But she and her husband, they don't make a lot of money. Rent is high. He works hard, but there never seems to be enough. I slip a bag or two of groceries inside her front door every so often. I don't tell her they are from me. She doesn't ask. This way I know the little one has enough to eat."

Mrs. Alvarez's daughter, Rosa, lived two blocks farther south on MacKenzie in a very small and very tidy home, squeezed in between two large four-flats. Rosa was a beautiful girl, and her infant had the most luminescent eyes Annie had ever seen.

"I'll help. And I'll be quiet," Annie said as she shouldered the heavy bag. "Walking is exercise too, you know."

ග   ග   ග

On the way back, Mrs. Alvarez insisted they stop at the Quality Bakery on Armitage. "I have to get you something as a reward. That bag was heavy. My arm was in pain. So I have to get you something. I see to it that good deeds do not go unrewarded. It's the right thing to do, you know."

Annie's healthy inclinations evaporated in the thick, sweet aroma of the German bakery. Trays of delicately golden, crusty rolls begged to be slathered in butter and jam. Annie's eyes must have given her away.

"You want rolls? I'll get you rolls. You deserve a treat, Miss Annie. You don't treat yourself as often as you should. I can see that. Everyone can see that."

Before Annie could resist, Mrs. Alvarez was forcing a bag of warm rolls into her hands. "For your breakfast. It is good to treat yourself for breakfast."

Annie felt overwhelmed in Mrs. Alvarez's hug as they reached the laundromat. Before they parted company, the older woman paused, inclined her head across the street, and whispered to Annie, as if they might be overheard. Annie wanted to giggle—the two women were the only inhabitants of the deserted street.

"The basement flat? They rented it? Someone moved in there? When did this happen?" Mrs. Alvarez asked.

Annie chuckled inwardly. There wasn't much, she'd learned through the years, that Mrs. Alvarez did not notice. After all, the only sign of the change in occupancy was that the FOR RENT sign was missing from the first-floor window. But Mrs. Alvarez had remarked on more than one occasion that the basement apartment would be hard to rent—not enough windows, she claimed—unless the renter was desperate.

"Last night. A young woman. I think she's by herself," Annie said.

There was a keenly arched eyebrow in reply.

"No, no," Annie answered quickly. "She looked normal to me. It might have been her brother who helped move her in."

Mrs. Alvarez sniffed. "As long as she is not one of 'those women'. . .you know what I mean."

"No. I'm sure she's a nice person," Annie continued. "Mr. Korzak is a nice man. He would be careful. He must know she is a good person."

"Mr. Korzak is from Lithuania," Mrs. Alvarez responded. "You know how they are." She gave an all-knowing shrug. "They know the value of a dollar. The longer an apartment stays empty, the more money is gone from his pockets. Money talks louder than morals, my dear Annie."

Annie glanced at her watch. It was five minutes until six. The run would have to wait until tomorrow.

"And don't tell my daughter a word of this, Annie—I mean, the groceries and all. You promise me?"

"I promise, Mrs. Alvarez. Not a word."

Annie sat on her bench and stared at the basement apartment across the street. She saw a light come on. It shined dully through a small square of glass-block windows.

She must be an early riser, Annie thought. *I hope Mrs. Alvarez has nothing to be worried about. For her sake and the new woman's.* Annie herself wouldn't want to be on the wrong side of Mrs. Alvarez's ire.

Annie tried to quiet the voice inside her that seemed only to speak up when trouble was on the horizon.

She seemed like a normal young woman. She really did.

And yet that small voice was not mollified into silence. Only when her three worn and tired early morning customers shuffled into view did Annie break off her reverie about her new neighbor.

§   §   §

Annie had been kept busy all day—busier than usual. Two machines malfunctioned. One she repaired easily. The second resisted all her efforts at bringing it back to life. As she taped up the OUT OF ORDER sign on the dryer—a task she hated to do—she reminded herself, once again, to check the maintenance contract that lay on her desk in the office.

She wasn't sure why she had been so hesitant to sign the document. But after today, she was certain a long-term contract was best for the business. Even with one machine down, she would lose money during busy periods. Worse, repairs always turned costly—and too many broken machines tarnished the image of the place.

Twilight—the time of dinner preparation—settled in over the neighborhood. Only two customers still waited inside for their laundry. Both were young men who leaned against the washers, waiting for the dryers to stop, looking slightly inconvenienced at having to be in a laundromat.

Annie nodded to the two, then stepped outside to the street, leaving the smell of lint and bleach and freshly folded sheets inside. She pulled her sweater around her shoulders and sat out on her bench. It was not that the air was truly chilled, but that the laundromat was so warm. A large air conditioner was installed over the door, full of rattles and hums when operating. But she wouldn't think of switching it on until June.

An air conditioner is as expensive as running a dozen dryers full-time, she had once calculated. *Besides, people don't come to a laundromat to get cool, do they?*

She crossed her arms, holding a corner of her sweater in each hand, as if preparing to knot the sweater around her.

From the corner of her eye, she saw the door to the basement apartment in Mr. Korzak's flat open. A young woman slipped out. She stepped up to the sidewalk, glanced both ways, and hesitated—as if deciding in which direction to take an evening stroll. Then she set off north, toward Fullerton Avenue, with great purposeful strides.

She does look normal. At that distance, Annie found it difficult to guess at the girl's age. However, she was pretty, with long blond hair, worn straight and parted in the middle.

Without thinking, Annie brought a hand to her neck and grabbed at the mane of hair she had corralled with a tight scarf. All day in the laundromat—in any weather—and her hair developed a mind of its own, twisting in auburn abandon.

I wonder where she's going?

No more than fifteen minutes later, the young woman returned, carrying a plastic bag from the Treasure Island supermarket. Annie was surprised. She had never left a supermarket without spending over fifty dollars and carrying at least four rustling bags. But this young woman, new to an apartment and new to a neighborhood, evidently had her entire supply of "stocking-up-on-the-staples" food contained in one small bag.

From above Annie heard a plaintive cry. She winced. It was Petey the Cat. He had wedged himself under the open window and now pushed against the screen. It was a practiced maneuver. Once seeing Annie, he began a plaintive howling, as if he had not eaten for a week or enjoyed human company for even longer.

"Quiet, Petey!" Annie said loudly in his direction. "I'll be up in a minute."

The cat heard her voice and howled all the louder.

Annie stood. The young woman from across the street had almost reached the door of her flat. Annie hated having to talk with a cat in front of other people, especially strangers, so she turned and offered a wave and a smile to the stranger. The young woman first looked at Annie, then up to the second-floor window and the cat, then back to Annie. She offered a half-wave and a half-smile in return. As if expecting Annie to call to her, she paused before slipping inside the door, now hidden in shadows.

The cat howled again, as if being tortured by rogue CIA agents seeking to gain security codes for some new top-secret feline weapon.

Annie turned back again and hissed a second clipped, "Quiet!" How she wished the cat would only admit its hard-headedness and understand English like every other animal she had ever owned. Had she missed her chance to meet her new neighbor?

§   §   §

The highlight of Annie's evening consisted of feeding Petey. It wasn't for lack of things to do in a city like Chicago, where something was happening all the time. But most activities required companionship.

After high school her closest friends had gone on to any number of colleges across the country and were now either married with children and/or living in another state. Annie had met some interesting people while attending the

downtown campus of the state university. But the environ-
ment at a large "commuter" school wasn't very companion-
able or conducive to forming close relationships; most had
remained merely acquaintances. In the past several years
she had gone back to take a few more art courses, one at a
time while keeping up with running the laundromat. But
by then the student population had become younger and
younger by comparison, and Annie had found few class-
mates with whom lasting friendship was feasible. The few
singles she knew from church were either dating someone
or often away on job-related travel. So most nights it was
just Annie and Petey the Cat.

This night Annie selected a different flavor of expensive
food, which the cat promptly and defiantly ignored. Such
ingratitude and specificity infuriated Annie to a higher level.

"Then you'll just starve to death, you ungrateful animal!
I am not throwing good cat food away again. There are cats
in Europe starving right now."

Despite his refusal to eat, the cat seemed no worse for
wear and looked as if he were gaining weight, rather than
losing it.

For her own dinner, Annie took a microwavable "complete and balanced" dinner from her freezer, heated it, and
ate it standing over the sink. If she had been truly hungry or
in a hurry, she could have eaten the entire meal in no more
than five bites. She had considered herself above the lonely
personal resignation it took to resort to microwavable entrees
as a primary food source...until she'd discovered such a dinner

choice was quick and required no advance planning. The route from the freezer to the microwave was so easy, so well marked, so convenient to navigate. Fast food or sitting in a restaurant by herself was seldom her choice.

Tomorrow I'll go to the store and buy a bunch of beautiful fresh vegetables and make a nice hearty soup. Enough of this convenience food. Soup is good. I can do soup.

In the past few minutes ten customers had shown up, dragging in bags and baskets of laundry. Their numbers made it a busier night than normal. Annie knew she did not have to be downstairs. In fact, at a recent trade-show gathering of laundromat and dry cleaner businesses, she had learned that most owner/operators simply came in the morning to unlock the doors and once again in the evening to remove the coins and lock up. Annie would have felt awkward if she had done that. It would be like having guests at home and retreating to a private room—or, worse yet, leaving the house altogether.

She hurried back downstairs, leaving Petey in a sulking hulk by the back door. The customers, most of whom were regulars, greeted her with smiles and nods when she stepped out of her office. Then, as if rehearsed, they retreated into magazines, headphones, cell phones, or private conversations.

Annie wasn't needed. She knew she shouldn't feel hurt, but a part of her did.

The air was warm and humid inside, enhancing the sharp smell of detergent. She looked about, saw nothing that required attention, and, instead of returning to her office, stepped outside again.

Her bench was empty, as it most often was. She walked around it, sat down, and stared across the street at Mr. Korzak's flat and the two flowering crab apple trees he had planted at each corner. The trees had burst into a gigantic snowball of tiny white blossoms, and in the breeze the petals would scatter like a spring snowfall. Each offered only a few days of exquisite beauty, then returned to a hearty, utilitarian green.

From somewhere south of her, perhaps as close as the next block, came the scent of Koreanspice viburnums, with their heavy, petulant fragrance, almost intoxicating in intensity. Annie always wished, at times like this, that she had some open earth, instead of only asphalt and concrete, to plant some shrubs or trees.

Maybe I'll buy some big planters this fall—when all the garden stuff is on sale. I miss tending to a garden. Images of herself, her mother, and her grandmother bending over the flowers, peas, and beans of a riotous garden briefly flashed through her mind. It was during those young childhood summers that everything about the world had seemed so peaceful, so right. How little did any of them know then what would soon go so wrong.

Annie was staring south along MacKenzie, wondering who had planted the viburnums last year without her noticing, when a person suddenly materialized in front of her. Her hand jumped to her throat in surprise.

"Oh, I'm sorry," the stranger said, her voice as soft as a child's. "I didn't mean to startle you."

Annie looked up. It was the young woman from across

the street—from Korzak's basement apartment with too few windows.

"Hi," was all Annie could muster in response.

"I saw you sitting here earlier," the stranger continued. "I figured you lived here. Do you? I mean, not on the street. . . but, like, here."

The young woman gestured with her right arm, a graceful sweep that encompassed and included the entire MacKenzie Street neighborhood.

Annie drew in a sharp breath. "Why. . .yes. I do. I mean, I don't live here on the bench or anything. Up there," she said and pointed behind and above her. Just then Petey chose to howl again through the open window. "That's Petey. He's my cat. At least he is for now."

The young woman giggled. "He sounds a little angry."

"He hates the service and the accommodations. I'm sure he could do better. I could be persuaded to let him try."

The young woman extended her hand. "I'm Taylor. Taylor Evans."

"Annie Hamilton."

The young girl's handshake was a lot stronger and more determined than Annie would have imagined. And Taylor was younger than Annie had thought. Maybe twenty, not much more. Even less, perhaps. As Annie aged, everyone began to appear woefully younger and younger. Even the new policeman, a red-haired Irishman who walked the beat on MacKenzie three times a day, appeared to have just exited junior high.

The young woman was a natural blond, Annie quickly decided, and her skin had a fresh-scrubbed glow. It was not a look Annie was used to seeing in the city. On MacKenzie Street there were Poles and Lithuanians, Hispanics and Germans and Greeks—but not many young women who looked like they would be comfortable on the back porch of a farmhouse, carrying a pail of freshly gathered milk.

"Is the Treasure Island the only supermarket around here?" Taylor asked. "It seemed kind of expensive. I tried to ask Mrs. Korzak, but I don't think she understood me—or maybe I just didn't understand her."

That's why her grocery bag was so light.

Annie offered Taylor a reassuring smile. "It's the biggest store around. And it's open twenty-four hours. I guess that's why the prices are high. You have to wait for specials if you shop there."

Taylor nodded and Annie continued. "There's a bakery on Armitage that's good and not as expensive. And two doors down from the bakery is a vegetable store—the old-fashioned kind. The owner is from Greece, and the prices are good. If you don't mind the walk, over on Clark Street is a discount grocery. Not nearly as nice as the Treasure Island—but it's a lot more reasonable."

"Clark Street? Where is that?" Taylor asked, looking about as if she might be able to see it from where she stood.

Annie stood. She had misjudged the young woman's height. Annie towered over Taylor.

"You go north on this street for two blocks," Annie

explained, pointing up MacKenzie. "That street is Webster. Then you walk east—toward the lake—for two blocks. That's Clark. Go north on Clark and you're there. It's an Aldi store. You can't miss it."

"The lake is that way?" Taylor asked as she jabbed her finger to the east.

"It is. Only a ten-minute walk. There's a nice public beach at North Avenue."

At mention of the beach, a curious look came into Taylor's eyes—wistful at one moment, sad at another, and maybe just a little angry, like a child overlooked by parents who haven't noticed their offspring has gone missing.

"I don't think I'll be going swimming," Taylor said briskly. "But thanks for the directions." She consulted her watch.

Annie saw that Taylor was wearing a class ring—it must have been from her high school. She was much too young to have graduated college.

"Listen, Aldi is closed now. They don't keep late hours. But I was going to shop there tomorrow," Annie said. "You could walk with me and I could show you the way. I have one of those old-lady pull carts for groceries."

Taylor stared at Annie. Her expression seemed to soften. "I couldn't ask you to do—"

"Nonsense. I was going anyway. About nine o'clock? That's not too early, is it?"

"No. That would be so nice."

Neither spoke for a moment, then Taylor nodded, as if

uncomfortable with the silence. "Tomorrow morning then. Thanks. It was nice to meet you." And she stepped away.

Annie watched as the young woman crossed the street. She did not turn back. She simply disappeared into the basement apartment.

She is not from around here—I'm sure of that. She has the hint of an accent.

Annie peered into her laundromat. A few customers remained. She turned back and stared at the bottom floor of Mr. Korzak's building.

She seems very nice though. And very young. Very, very young.

The lines on Annie's forehead deepened as she pondered. There was something troubling. . .or disconcerting. . . about this young woman. It was not a bad troubling or an evil disconcerting—but it was something, Annie was sure.

She sat back on her bench and crossed her legs. From above her came the howled yelp of an angry house cat, again pretending to be trapped between the window and screen. Annie shut her eyes and sighed. She decided to ignore Petey this time.

There was another yelp, even more heart-wrenching than the first. It was so convincing that a couple across the street stopped their walk and looked about, until the husband saw the cat and pointed at Annie's second-story window. The two began to turn around with rapid movements, as if searching for some official sort of authority to notify of this obvious case of animal abuse.

Annie stood up and hailed the couple across the street.

"It's okay. He's my cat. And I think he's hungry."

The couple waited, lips firm and drawn, and did not move until Annie walked inside.

ⓢ   ⓢ   ⓢ

The next morning Annie insisted that Taylor add her three bags of groceries into Annie's self-described "old-lady" grocery cart.

"No one can walk all this way with three bags of groceries," Annie explained, "unless they buy very small and very expensive groceries."

Taylor held her hand over her mouth as she giggled, as if ashamed of the musical sound of her laughter.

"Like a bag of caviar," Annie explained. "I think I could carry that for more than six blocks."

"Caviar?"

"You know," Annie replied. "Fish eggs. Expensive fish eggs."

Taylor made a face convincingly close to appearing as if she were actually ill.

"I take it you've never tried it."

Taylor shook her head, and her blond hair followed the sweep of her neck. "My father. . .I mean. . .I know people who fish use it as bait. . .I think. Fish eggs. Not caviar. Not if it's as expensive as it sounds." Suddenly the young girl grew silent, as if she had expended too many words, and stared at her feet.

The Unfolding

Once again Annie wanted to ask Taylor where she came from and how she had found herself alone in the basement apartment of Mr. Korzak's three-flat. Annie really wanted to ask—but listened instead to that insistent voice inside telling her to remain silent.

She will tell me in her time—if there is to be a time, Annie told herself. Words popped into her head: "*A time to tear and a time to mend, a time to be silent and a time to speak. . .*" The words were haunting and familiar and called up memories of Sunday school lessons in a damp church basement.

The two women stopped in front of the laundromat. Taylor reached down and gathered up her groceries. Annie had been secretly gratified to see the young girl had indeed bought a bunch of staples—soup, sugar, saltine crackers (two boxes), milk, tea, bread, peanut butter and jelly, unsalted butter, three small packages of hamburger, celery, lettuce, bottled dressing, and a package of double-stuff Oreos.

"Thanks so much," Taylor said. "I don't think I would have found that store if you hadn't taken me. Chicago is just so big."

"No problem. Like I said, I had to go shopping as well."

"You know, everyone back home says people in Chicago aren't friendly. Well, that just isn't true."

Annie was again a heartbeat from asking but bit her tongue.

If she wants to tell me, she will.

Taylor did not move just yet but shifted her bags from one hand to the other.

Annie smiled again. "I guess I should get to work," she said and nodded toward the laundromat.

Taylor appeared puzzled. "You work at the laundromat?"

Annie prepared herself to collect another response concerning the revelation of her ownership of the place.

"No. Well, I do, sort of. I own it. And I live in the apartment upstairs."

Taylor's grin spread across her face. "That is the coolest thing I have ever heard. You own it? Like, all by yourself? You don't take orders from anyone else? No parents or anything? That is so totally cool."

Taylor's unfettered enthusiasm was so contagious and unexpected that Annie felt herself grinning too. "Yep. All mine, all by myself."

"That is so cool." The lines around Taylor's eyes sharpened. "I really envy you, Annie," she said softly.

Then she hurried toward her basement apartment, leaving Annie wondering if there had been a hitch in Taylor's final words.

Three

ANNIE KNEW WHERE THE book was—on the top shelf on the bookcase in the second bedroom. She kept it there because that bookcase and that shelf were out of sight. The book had been a gift from her parents—when they were happy and when Annie was certain that the world would forever remain that way. But the world did not, and now the gift was wrapped with unsettling memories.

However, it was the only Bible in her possession that included an extensive index and cross references. She ran her finger down the alphabetical list. She stopped, checked the number, and flipped the gilt-edged pages.

The book was Ecclesiastes. Verses six and seven confirmed her initial guess.

A time to search and a time to give up,
a time to keep and a time to throw away,
a time to tear and a time to mend,
a time to be silent and a time to speak.

But none of those words felt like the verses she heard in her head, however appropriate the words were to today's situation.

Looking up on the page, she spotted the more familiar refrain:

A time to weep and a time to laugh,
a time to mourn and a time to dance,
a time to scatter stones and a time to gather them,
a time to embrace and a time to refrain.

She stared at the words for a long time, feeling both intrusion and regret. It was a familiar feeling. Talk of embracing always brought wistfulness to her soul. It had been a long time since Annie had felt any embrace.

Annie closed her eyes. From below she heard and felt the familiar rumble of dryers and washers and the muted conversations of her regulars.

Without counting, she knew her last official date was nearly a decade in the past. It had been a good relationship, they had enjoyed each other's company, he laughed easily, she was content.

And yet, when he asked her to follow him to California,

she said no. She helped him pack and waved as he left. And then that was all.

Why didn't I go with him? What was so important here?

The circle of questions was all too familiar. Murmurs of the past had intruded into her life too many times. She knew she couldn't change the past, that she had to move on. But sometimes it was difficult. Sometimes she simply felt lonely— like on days like today.

Annie squeezed her eyes more tightly shut to force the images of the happiness that could have been hers out of her awareness.

Maybe I'll talk to Pastor Yount this weekend.

Annie had spent years avoiding church, spending Sunday mornings walking by the lake or holed up in her front room, lying on the sofa with the *Chicago Tribune* scattered about her.

She remembered when she had first visited the church and first listened to Pastor Yount. She had found comfort in his words and some small measure of hope. Slowly, one week at a time, she had become a regular there.

Maybe I'll ask Taylor if she wants to come with me.

Annie sighed.

As if she knows me well enough to say yes.

Struggling to push the emotions away that threatened to overwhelm her, she leaned forward in her chair.

A time to tear and a time to mend, a time to be silent and a time to speak. What "time" was this in her life? Time to take a chance—but if so, on what? Or on whom?

Just then Petey, who was picking his way across the living room, moaned as if he found each step somehow distasteful. He jumped up on the window bench, circled twice, and simply fell over on his side, his gray coat catching the afternoon sun like a furry net.

She glanced at her watch. It was only half past two.

Was this what she wanted her life to be like forever? Annie stood, suddenly impatient, anxious. Setting the Bible back on its accustomed shelf, she hurried down the back staircase into her office and rummaged through the contents of her desktop.

The letter was where she had left it.

She opened it, scanned it once again, and dialed the number. Her heart began to beat faster. She knew why and tried her best to ignore it. She refused to act like a silly schoolgirl when she was a mature woman.

But there's always hope. . .the chance for a different kind of future.

"Daniel Trevalli, please," she said into the phone. "I would like to discuss the proposed contract he drew up for me. This is Annie Hamilton."

There was a pause.

"Yes, I'll wait."

Catching her reflection in the glass window beside her, she noticed that the flesh that once seemed firm—even a few days prior—now appeared to sag ever so slightly.

A time to. . .

Annie tightened the muscles in her jaw, then shook her head at the useless effort.

§　　§　　§

After she had spoken with Daniel, Annie quickly hung up the phone. She pivoted her desk chair away from the window to the laundromat, not wanting any of the customers to see her flushed cheeks.

Daniel Trevalli remembered her, he said, because of her laugh and her bright green eyes.

She knew those words were flirting words and that they had no real business being included in a discussion of a maintenance contract. But then again, there they were. Annie had heard words like them so seldom in the past years that they felt odd and strained but so very delicious. Now she relived each part of their conversation.

Daniel had stated several times that she could sign the contract and mail it in. "But if you want to hold it until I come, that would be fine. I could be there tomorrow to fix what's broken. I hope that's soon enough."

With her breath catching in her throat, Annie had said, "Tomorrow would be fine." She had added, in a hushed tone, "When I mail important documents, I'm never positive they actually get to where they are going."

Daniel had laughed and asked about having something

important to tend to in California. "Would you hand-carry the paper there?"

Annie had giggled. "I don't do business with anyone in California."

"Take a chance, Miss Hamilton," Daniel had said, his words smooth and soft. "Life is much too short to be that worried. Take a chance. You could be most pleasantly surprised. The worst that can happen is that you have to spend another thirty-seven cents on a stamp. Am I right?"

Annie had smiled as she nodded into the phone.

They had talked for six or seven minutes, then Daniel claimed another call was holding for him and that he would see her tomorrow, between noon and three.

Annie had thanked him and told him she would keep the contract in her office until he came.

Daniel's laugh echoed in the phone as she let the receiver down.

"It's just a service contract," she said aloud to no one in particular. "Just a service contract."

But his laugh continued to ring in her heart.

ॐ   ॐ   ॐ

Annie loved to walk along the streets of Chicago and explore every bit of her neighborhood and its outskirts. In the space of twenty blocks, she could carry herself from some of the worst examples of urban planning—from large-scale urban apartments that were cold, sterile, and so incredibly inhospitable and dangerous—to elegant blocks of old brownstone mansions that still graced the Gold Coast, the streets around Lake Shore Drive. With their carved, etched, and beveled details, the mansions exuded great yet subtle shadings of wealth and money and power. The windows seemed slightly frosted, so a passerby could almost, but not truly, see into the world of golden shades and warm, glowing chandeliers.

In contrast, the windows of the housing projects she also passed might be protected with a sheet or blanket or plywood or left absolutely and totally bare, so anyone could see the cold reality inside with no distortion.

Annie loved the space in between those two extremes—not the extremes themselves. The projects, with their despair and anger and their institutional, sparse coldness, frightened her. The mansions, with their guarded and coiled wealth, intimidated her. They reminded her too much of the coldness of her childhood home. . .and of her father. But all the spaces and all the people who lived in between those two bookends of her neighborhood felt as if they were family.

There was the Steriopolis's on Division, with a third generation learning the business of dispensing the best hot dogs on the north side. In the Olympia Restaurant, brothers Peter and Thomas, besides serving hearty, solid food, created elegant chocolate fantasies. There were antique shops, resale shops, secondhand clothing shops, upscale boutiques, neighborhood taverns, rock-and-roll bars, restaurants, convenience stores run by Koreans and staffed by Bosnians. In any one block she could encounter the traces of a dozen different nationalities.

There are hundreds and hundreds of stories behind the doors on these streets, she thought as she walked along.

Annie's ramblings took her up and down the alleys as well as the main streets. It was during her walks that she "collected." She did not search for things in a specific way. She stumbled upon them, as if serendipity brought her path and the objects' location together. These collected bits and pieces and materials would be used in her creations and shadowboxes.

Much of what she found wound up on her worktable or stored beneath in milk crates and clear plastic shoe boxes. These objects, in aggregate, appeared worn and without beauty. But Annie had a way to select and display and place and arrange colors and textures together—a broken, rusted, metal spring, placed just so on the background in a shadow-box might then magically appear to be both sad and joyous and full of intrinsic, industrial beauty and grace.

Annie did not fully understand how she did what she did and seldom fully thought about the process. All she knew is that when she saw something discarded, it would radiate to her not what it was, but what it might become. She could see the jewel beneath the dust and the dirt and the fingerprints. Was it, perhaps, because that's the way Annie saw herself?

Annie sold her work at the myriad open-air art fairs that dotted the neighborhoods on the north side of Chicago in the summer. Last year she had astounded herself by asking seven-hundred-and-fifty dollars for a small shadowbox— and had actually sold it for that amount, with no haggling or negotiating. The new owner had gladly written the check, and Annie had felt only a trace of sadness as he'd carried it out of view.

Last summer had been a good year; Annie had sold dozens of pieces, including a few larger ones. She had made enough to purchase new materials, canvases, and shadow-boxes without dipping into her savings. This summer she hoped for a small profit. It would be enough to satisfy her.

The pleasure for Annie, the reason she did what she did, was for the "seeing." The money was merely incidental. It was rescuing the doomed from the abyss, she once giggled to herself. Whatever she used was once lost but was now found and beautiful and had purpose again.

This day she found little to collect. She refused to root through dumpsters or trash cans. She would only select items that possessed a story as to their discarding, a tale of woe or surprise. Annie needed to know how that object came to rest in that specific alley at that specific time, being found by this specific person.

One of the women from the church had bumped into Annie as she was on one of her meandering searches and had said, when Annie tried to explain what she was doing, "Oh, it's like a metaphor to a deeper spiritual search." Annie had blushed at the remark, never thinking what she did had any deep meaning. If anyone ever asked, Annie told them that she simply enjoyed walking, looking, discovering, and uncovering. She called it "unfolding." She was not certain what she meant, but it seemed to satisfy others.

Now, discouraged, she turned the corner at MacKenzie and Webster. She had been certain the day held a greater promise. The light and buoyant mood she found herself in after talking to Mr. Trevalli was in danger of evaporating completely.

The laundromat was on her right. The lake was to her left. Across the street was Mr. Korzak's three-flat.

She heard Daniel Trevalli's words again. . .*take a chance*.

Crossing the street, she took the three steps down to Taylor's apartment and tapped. She heard the sound of someone rushing toward the door; then it flew open.

Taylor's expression made it obvious she had been hoping for someone else. "Oh. . .it's you."

Annie must have looked crestfallen.

"No. . .Annie, I didn't mean anything. I just thought. . . my brother said he might come down sometime—and I guess I thought it might have been him. I'm sorry."

"I thought you might like to come to dinner tonight. Nothing fancy. I'm. . .I'm making soup. Do you like soup? I have some great rolls from the bakery."

Taylor's face brightened. "I do like soup. I really do. What time?"

"Time? Oh. . .maybe six o'clock? Would that be okay?"
Taylor said it would.

As Annie said good-bye, she wondered if she had
enough time to make soup from scratch.

It was 4:30.

It will have to be a quick, non-simmering soup—that's all.

§   §   §

At six o'clock Annie opened the door, greeted Taylor, and
retreated into the kitchen to attend to last-minute soup-
preparing details.

"Make yourself at home," she called out. "Dinner is almost ready."

Taylor's footsteps were hesitant, muted even, since she
was shoeless and clad only in thick wool socks. Annie could
hear Taylor's slow progress through the living room.

A large mirror hung over the nonfunctioning fireplace.
Annie had found it in an alley behind Division Street, leaning
by itself, unbroken, against a utility pole. She had seen in the
reflection a dumpster, a fire escape, and the blue sky over Lake
Michigan. It was enough to make her carry the heavy, awkward piece twelve blocks, stopping every hundred yards to
massage her aching arms. The mirror now reflected Taylor
back into the kitchen. Her hands were crossed in front of her,
as if she were frightened of touching some forbidden object.

Annie watched as Taylor circled the couch, leaning

forward at her waist to stare hard at the few art pieces and shadowboxes Annie had kept for herself. All the while Petey the Cat intertwined her legs in loose, loopy circles. Guests in Annie's apartment were unusual, and Petey had evidently decided this stranger needed an intense investigation.

On a table by the fireplace Annie had placed six old foot-high letters, made of sheet metal. She had rescued them two years earlier from a building on Lincoln Avenue that was being demolished. Taylor's fingers now traced the outlines of the letters, as if she were blind and her fingers were revealing which letters were what.

"Are you hungry?" Annie called.

Taylor jumped at the question. "Yes. . .I think I am. I haven't. . .had much today."

"I hope you like vegetable soup. I sort of threw it together at the last minute. I know the rolls are good, though. Mrs. Alvarez bought them for me."

Taylor took her seat at the vintage porcelain-topped table in the kitchen. She smiled at Annie.

"Do you. . .you mind if I say grace?" Annie asked. She found herself drawn to traditions of her childhood. Traditions like praying before meals, before bedtime, and going to church on Sunday.

"Sure. I guess," Taylor said slowly. "I mean if you want to, go ahead. At home we did. My father and brother went to church some—not all the time. My father is pretty busy. He said church was good, but that he wasn't a fanatic about it."

So Annie kept it short and ecumenical.

"Did you do all the boxes and paintings?" Taylor asked.

Annie nodded.

"They are so cool. I've never known a real artist before."

Annie held up her palm. "I'm no artist. I just like finding things. Overlooked objects, really. People don't look closely enough. There is beauty and truth in everything. If something has worth, then the intrinsic value and truth will show through."

With her own words came memories for Annie. Memories of her mother, who used to tell her the same thing. . .until the devastating day when her mother was no longer there.

"Wow, I guess you're right," Taylor replied, even though Annie imagined the young woman was simply agreeing so as to be an accommodating guest.

"Did you study art," Taylor asked, "in college?"

While she ladled out the soup, Annie replied, "I did. A few courses. My father didn't see any use in it. He wanted me to be an elementary school teacher. That's what I got a degree in. He said that a woman—if she's not getting married—had better have a stable career to fall back on."

As she spoke, Annie blinked her eyes, wondering why that painful truth had been so easy to share. It had been decades since that bit of parental advice had even come to her awareness.

"Did he think you weren't getting married?" Taylor asked.

Annie eyed the young woman closely. But the scope of her question conveyed no subtle undertones, no devious digging for a deeper revelation. It was the simple question of a transparent young woman.

"I don't think he thought I would—"

"I don't want to pry," Taylor said quickly. "It's okay not to answer. I mean, you hardly know me."

"It's okay. I came close once. To being married, that is. I had just graduated from college. But it didn't work. We were too different. He lives in Des Moines now. The last I heard he was married with three children and drives a minivan."

Annie hoped her words sounded dispassionate and impersonal, but she knew that anyone could hear her decades-old regret reverberating through.

Taylor busied herself with the soup. She took great pains to carefully tear each roll into quarters and dip it into the thick broth, bringing it to her mouth with apparent pleasure. "This is really delicious. Is it hard to make?"

Annie giggled. "Everything goes into a big pot. Toss a couple of bouillon cubes in and add some seasonings. Cook it for just an hour or so, and you've got soup!"

"However you did it, it's delicious. Better than my mom's, that's for sure."

Annie smiled at the compliment. "Are you looking for work, Taylor?" she asked. "If you're looking for a job, I know a lot of people in the neighborhood. I could ask around."

Taylor looked up. Annie saw pain in her eyes.

"No. I'm not looking for a job. Not yet. I mean, I'm not going to be working right away anyhow."

The young woman's eyes went back down to her soup and remained there, as if she were considering her next words very carefully. The silence grew longer until Annie realized that whatever words Taylor was holding inside would not be uttered tonight.

Finally Taylor glanced up with a pleading expression, as if to ask that no more questions be asked at the moment, for there was a fear of answering them.

"Well, then," Annie said cheerfully, "I can take you with me on my walks around the neighborhood. It's good exercise. And I can show you all the hot spots and cheap eats."

Taylor tried to smile. Her left hand sought out a small rise in her belly. Annie told herself that Taylor simply carried a few too many pounds on her frame. She thought there might be a hint of a Wisconsin accent in her words—but only the barest hint. Annie could hear the tinge—and it brought back memories of summers on her grandparents' farm in Wisconsin Rapids. Annie knew that farm girls were less likely to be model thin. It was all that butter and cream and corn-fed beef.

At least that is what the folks in Chicago told themselves about their neighbors to the north.

But Taylor's subtle hand gesture spoke more than a thousand words. Annie blinked. Could it be? Her deduction was much too simplistic, she thought. But she also knew immediately, without truly realizing the implications, that there was more to Taylor's story—much, much more. Yet the young woman would not, at least this day, share with Annie the details of that story.

A time to be silent and a time to speak. . . The words kept running through Annie's head.

"Yes, Annie," Taylor said softly, "I would like to walk with you. Are you going out tomorrow?"

Annie smiled reassuringly. "Yes. I was planning on it. Around nine?"

"Nine is good. I'm sure I will have been up for hours by then. Should I come here?"

Annie nodded and told her that would be fine.

Four

THE NEXT MORNING, AFTER her walk with Taylor, Annie found herself doing what she said she would never do—primping for a serviceman. In the past, she and some other of her unmarried friends would make fun of secretaries who dressed better—or more provocatively—on the day either the UPS man or the Xerox repairman was scheduled to visit their offices. Her group of unmarried friends had slowly and steadily grown smaller in number, and now a thoroughly chagrined Annie stood in front of her full-length mirror, debating what to wear and how to do her hair.

All because Daniel Trevalli was scheduled to come to the laundromat.

She glanced at her watch. "He said between noon and

three. I have a full hour to obsess about all this," she said out loud.

Catching sight of her almost worried and tight expression, her mouth scrunched up in a wizened, surprised circle. Laughing at her anxiety, she reached in and found a khaki skirt and her standard denim shirt. However she did take time to iron them and spent nearly twenty minutes on her hair. She almost succeeded in taming the curls by using a blow-dryer and a product in a purple bottle called "The Ultimate Straight and Natural Spritzer."

"Now, what do I do to look natural—like I haven't been waiting for him for hours?" she asked Petey, who had been drawn into the bedroom at the sound of the hairdryer. It was a sound he had not often heard.

Petey had not supplied any answers, so Annie went downstairs, sat at her desk, and sorted through the same stack of bills, junk mail, and catalogs for nearly an hour.

Annie was startled by a rapid tapping at the window—the window that faced Dickens. She saw his smile first, as if Daniel Trevalli was truly glad to be here. She rose and walked to the front entrance, hearing that voice inside admonish her, *That must be the same smile he gives every one of his customers.*

"Annie Hamilton," he announced as he walked inside, "you have made the right decision. Both Daniel Trevalli and Westlake Maintenance make good on their promises."

She smiled broadly.

"I said between noon and three. . .and it's only fifteen minutes after twelve. Not bad, right?"

"Not bad," Annie replied. "Do you need the contract. . . before you start work?"

When Daniel rolled up the sleeves of his shirt, Annie noticed he had nice arms.

"Nah. I'll get to the actual fixing first. We can talk contract afterward. Maybe even have lunch. Have you had lunch?"

Annie told him she hadn't.

"Perfect. That will give me all the motivation I need to work fast. I'm a big believer in having the right motivation," he said, then scanned the machines. "The one with the sign—that's your bad boy?"

Annie nodded.

"Well, let Dr. Danny take a look."

Annie followed him to the dryer. "I hope I didn't damage it any more by trying to fix it."

"I'm sure you did no such thing, Annie Hamilton. And I'm sure I'll have it better than new in no time."

He opened his tool chest. A surprisingly huge array of tools was tucked inside in almost clinical order and neatness.

"Do you need anything else, Mr. Trevalli?"

"Annie Hamilton—it is not Mr. Anything. You call me Daniel. . .or better yet, Danny." He winked at her and she tried not to look away.

"We'll save Dr. Danny for later," he said more softly.

For a moment Annie was unsure exactly what he meant. Did she look that needy?

Then he continued, "After I get the patient fixed, that is."

She stood back, her arms folded loosely across her chest,

and watched as Danny quickly disassembled the base plate and pulled out the timing mechanism. From his tool kit, he extracted a voltage checker and touched the wire leads at one point, then another, and another. In less than five minutes, he peered up at her, his grin wide and triumphant.

"Here's the problem. The fuse between the timer and the main relay—sort of a fuse to a fuse—went bad. It didn't blow, which is why you didn't catch it. But the wire is bad. Wouldn't trip right."

He popped the small fuse out with a special tool and slipped a new one in. He had been right. Annie had seen the fuse; from appearances she had assumed it was working correctly.

"Good as new," he said, slipping the unit back to the rack, screwing it back in place.

"That was quick. I was expecting a bigger job," Annie said.

"Big or little, Annie Hamilton, you don't pay any more with Westlake. That's the beauty of extended service."

"Oh," she said, "that reminds me. I have your contract—it's in the office."

He snapped the base plate back onto the clips and slapped his toolbox closed. "Don't hurry. I did promise you a lunch, didn't I?"

She stopped and turned to face him. "You did, actually."

"Then let's go. I'm sure you know of a good neighborhood place."

Immediately she began to compile a list of possibilities.

Clancey's was too expensive. Nick's, over on Lincoln, might be too intimate.

R. J. Grunts—yes, she thought. *That would offer the right mix of good food and room for conversation.*

As she wrestled with her choice, a beeper on Danny's belt went off—shrill and annoying. He grabbed it out of its holster and stared at it. He scowled as he watched a scrolled message blink across the screen. Scowling even harder, he pressed two buttons and snapped the pager back in.

"Annie Hamilton, will you forgive me? Please? There's a laundromat up in Evanston that just lost an entire bank of dryers. I'm the closest tech to the job. If it were one dryer, I would call in off-duty. But a whole bank? I can't ignore that, can I? Can I take a rain check for lunch? I was really looking forward to it. I really, really was."

Annie hoped he was telling her the truth, because she chose to believe him. "Sure, Daniel. I understand. You'll be through here again. My machines break down with great regularity."

Daniel tilted his head back and laughed. "I like you, Annie Hamilton."

She hoped he meant that. He gathered up his tool kit, slipped the contract into his breast pocket, and waved twice in farewell—once at the door and once as he turned the corner on Dickens.

She stood and stared out the window as the battered white panel truck with *Westlake* on the side pulled quickly into traffic.

"He married?"

Annie jumped.

Mrs. Lang, an older Italian woman with a thick bush of white hair tied into a bun at the back of her head, was standing right beside her. Now the woman tapped at the window and pointed. "That good-looking fellow. He's Italian, right? He married?"

Mrs. Lang had married a German steelworker who died ten years into their marriage by falling off the building next door to the Sears Tower. He had left her with five boys, no debt, and a fierce independent streak.

Annie shrugged. "I'm not sure, Mrs. Lang."

"I didn't see no ring. And I know Italian boys. Have five of 'em myself."

Annie nodded. "I know, Mrs. Lang. They're all good boys."

Mrs. Lang offered a knowing smile in return. "They break hearts, my boys. Too good looking. Italian and German. The combination is a killer."

Annie watched as the Westlake truck veered around a slower bus and zipped north, out of her sight.

"So, he going to call you? Or you be a modern woman and call him?"

"Mrs. Lang," Annie complained, like a daughter to a mother, "I hardly know him."

"Women these days. . . I see them calling men all the time. My boys—women call them all the time, day and night. You call him, Annie."

Annie did not know how to politely refuse. "I don't know, Mrs. Lang."

"You call, Annie. That one looks like a good one. You call. You wait much longer, you're going to dry up and shrivel away. You can't do that. You're not getting any younger—none of us are getting younger. And you need kids. Right? You ain't got much time to waste, Annie. You call him."

Mrs. Lang meant well, but Annie really hadn't needed the reminder of time passing. She felt the ticking of the clock every day.

Just then the dryer fell still, and Mrs. Lang hurried over to extract her clothing before any wrinkles could set in. "You call him, Annie. He's a nice Italian boy. You won't be sorry."

Annie lifted her eyebrows in mute surprise.

"Don't become like that crazy spinster cat lady down on Wells Street—the one above the dry cleaners. You know the one, Annie. You're too pretty for that."

As Mrs. Lang rattled on, Annie would not admit it to anyone, but she was actively considering taking the older woman's advice.

But how might I get Daniel's home phone number? she wondered.

⑨   ⑨   ⑨

It was a Tuesday, a warm and breezeless Tuesday. Taylor had now been in Chicago almost a month. She and Annie did not walk together every day of the week, but almost. It was rare for them to skip even a single day. Annie surmised that Taylor waited inside the front door, staring out the window, until she saw Annie's front door open. By the time Annie made it midway across the street, Taylor was already climbing her front steps, smiling and waving.

Just as she did today. Annie did not tell her how much she enjoyed these walks. None of Annie's friends—her contemporaries—had the flexibility that Annie had. She was the only one who could take an hour-long walk in the middle of the day if she chose. Annie could have invited any number of customers along—customers she now considered her friends. Yet all, almost without exception, were older—much older—and more prone to give advice and pronouncements, rather than listen to Annie talk of culture and art and boys. . .or men, actually. Men, until recently, had never been much of a subject for Annie.

Taylor changed all that.

When Annie had told her, a month ago, of Danny's first visit and his words and actions, Taylor had literally jumped up and down, holding Annie's hands, offering a quiet screech of happiness. Annie felt as if she were back in high school, such was Taylor's excitement.

Today they walked north, paralleling the lake, along Halsted Street. At first Taylor had been puzzled at walking through the alleys. But when Annie explained her mission and what she was searching for, Taylor enthusiastically joined the quest. She would point out objects and shove cans to one side, as if she played bird dog to Annie's huntress.

The air grew warm and their steps slowed.

"Want to stop for a latte?" Annie queried. "There's a nice

little neighborhood coffee shop around the corner."

"Latte? Is that like a coffee?"

"You've never had one?"

Taylor shook her head.

"Well, then," Annie said, "let's get you indoctrinated."

As they entered the small store, the warm scent of coffee percolated about them.

"Is latte coffee?" Taylor asked again.

"It has coffee in it," Annie replied. "Can we have two lattes, medium please?"

Taylor blinked a few times. "Can. . .can you make it without coffee? I mean, caffeine. Can you make it without caffeine? I'm not supposed to have that."

The clerk nodded, then called out, "Two medium lattes—one regular, one decaf."

Annie helped with the two coffees and sat at a table by the window.

"I'm just glad we have an alternative to Starbucks in the neighborhood."

"Starbucks?" Taylor asked.

Even though Annie was continually confounded with how much Taylor didn't know of big-city culture, at times she wondered if the girl feigned her ignorance just to see Annie's reaction.

"I take it you didn't have Starbucks where you lived before," Annie said.

"Nope," Taylor replied. "It was a pretty small town."

Annie had asked very little about Taylor's past, but slowly

the young woman had revealed a few details. Per Annie's guess, Taylor *had* grown up in Wisconsin, in a small town way up north that she was sure Annie had never heard of. When Taylor mentioned it once—Mercer, just north of Manitowish—Annie admitted she had never heard of either of them.

"So," Taylor said as she added three packets of sugar to the latte, "have you heard anything from Dr. Danny?"

Annie did her best not to feel awkward. "No. We talked last week. I had to call him at his office because another machine went down. He asked about lunch again. I told him to call me when he's in the area."

"Is he coming over to fix what's broken? I want to see him," Taylor pleaded. "Would you call and tell me when he shows up?"

Annie felt as if she had slipped through a portal in the time-space continuum and found herself back in Mr. Wansour's eleventh-grade English class, comparing notes on boys with Anita Della Donna.

"He can't come this time," Annie replied, noticing Taylor's crestfallen expression. "He said he was subbing for the tech on the west side and they would have to send another tech out for me."

"Bummer," Taylor said. "But was he friendly? Did he sound interested?"

Taylor made Annie repeat the entire conversation—twice—and pressed repeatedly for the real emotion behind both of their words.

Before Taylor's arrival, it had been years since Annie had talked like this—intimate girl-to-girl—and it had been nearly as long since she had a reason to talk like that. She both enjoyed it and felt terribly conflicted. She had a life, nice people around her, a business, and a hobby/avocation she was passionate about, and yet, according to Taylor, it was of no concern unless there was a man involved.

Annie surmised that many of her older customers/friends/neighbors would share that sentiment. "A woman is not really a woman without a man," the outspoken Mrs. Lang had once pronounced. Annie had pointed out that Mrs. Lang had been without a man for nearly a decade and had led a productive, satisfying life. She was a strong person, a good person, a positive woman—all without a man. But Mrs. Lang had made her position clear: "I ain't without a man. I'm a widow. That's a big difference, Annie."

Taylor sipped the last of her latte. "I like it. I like this a lot. I bet it even tastes better with real coffee."

Annie had her own guess as to why Taylor couldn't drink caffeine, but they had never talked openly about it. Annie was merely waiting for Taylor to share what she needed to share when she had to share it. So far, Taylor's life was but a shadow to what Annie had told her.

As they stepped out of the store, Annie told Taylor of the fights that she'd had with her father when she was beginning college and how they had not really spoken for years now. As she spoke of their final, pivotal confrontation, Taylor listened intently.

Taylor kept repeating softly, "I know how you feel. I know how you feel."

Annie was certain that she did not. But it was nice to have some empathy, all the same.

They walked in silence, the two of them, up Halsted. They slowed as they passed a vintage clothing store. In the window were a few pairs of frayed bell-bottom jeans and a shirt that looked as though it had been tie-dyed at home in a galvanized bucket using Rit dye.

"Isn't that the coolest stuff?" Taylor said, pointing.

Annie did not reply. She had actually worn outfits like that in high school, never realizing how bizarre and truly unattractive they had been.

At the end of the next block, Annie saw a familiar face. Scarf tied around her head, the woman was striding quickly down the street, holding two mesh bags at her side.

"Mrs. Alvarez!" she called out. "How are you? I haven't seen you for weeks."

Mrs. Alvarez appeared startled for a moment, then grinned when she saw Annie.

"How are you?" she said, all the while eyeing Taylor, who stood a few steps back, almost as if she were hiding. "I have been at my baby brother's—in Elgin. His wife just had their fifth. And her high-society mother is just too busy to come and lend a hand. As if I could ever imagine telling blood that I'm too busy to help. The nerve of that woman!" Mrs. Alvarez's words dripped in anger.

Mrs. Alvarez nudged her head in Taylor's direction.

Annie took the hint.

"I'm sorry. This is Taylor Evans. She's the girl who rented the apartment from Mr. Korzak."

It was obvious Taylor felt scrutinized. She ducked as if she were searching out a place to hide.

"Taylor," Mrs. Alvarez said pleasantly enough, extending her hand, "I am happy to meet you."

They shook hands, and Mrs. Alvarez held on for a moment.

"Taylor," she continued, "you are very young to be on your own. How old are you?"

Annie winced at the direct question. Mrs. Alvarez was not known for her tact.

"I'm. . .I'm. . ."

The old woman held on tightly to her hand.

"I'm seventeen."

Annie arched her eyebrows in surprise. She'd known Taylor was young, but seventeen? The reason it felt like she was back in high school was because one of them still *was* in high school!

The older woman, not letting go of Taylor's hand, drew her even closer. Mrs. Alvarez cocked her head to the side. "And when are you due?"

Taylor blinked several times. Her lips moved silently, then she said aloud in a whisper, "September. September first." Then her eyes widened. She brought her hand up to her mouth. Yanking her grasped hand away, she began to run north along Lincoln, heading in the direction of her small, dark, basement apartment on MacKenzie.

"What did I say?" Mrs. Alvarez asked loudly and shrugged. "She's pregnant. Anyone can see that. People ask, don't they?"

Annie knew, deep down she had known for weeks, but she had never acknowledged the pregnancy in front of Taylor. She had been waiting for Taylor to share the news with her, when she was ready. However, when Taylor wore tighter clothing, as she had today, that small rounded belly was obvious. A few too many candy bars never settled in quite the same place. Annie should have known that someone would bring the truth out into the open. Would it have been better if Annie would have talked with Taylor about it first?

"No, you didn't do anything wrong, Mrs. Alvarez. She's just. . .emotional right now," Annie said. "I have to see if she's all right."

And with that, Annie took off running.

§   §   §

Annie did not even knock. The front door was unlocked and she slipped in, calling out Taylor's name.

Mrs. Alvarez had been correct. The apartment did not have enough windows. It was dark and smelled of old rafters and musty closets not receiving light or fresh air in decades. The front room contained a tiny television and a love seat that might have been purchased at Montgomery Wards a couple of decades earlier. A lamp sat crookedly on a cardboard box. The next room was the kitchen. It was small and spartan, with only two wobbly chairs pulled up to a short counter. The refrigerator was harvest gold, and the cabinets were faced with almost black doors. A fluorescent fixture, pull chain dangling, glowed weakly from the center of the ceiling.

The next room, Annie surmised as she walked through, *must be the bedroom.* She heard the muffled sound of sobbing. Tapping at the door, she called, "Taylor? It's me, Annie. Can I come in?"

"Go away."

Annie did not listen. She edged the door open. Resting directly on the floor was a crooked lamp and a simple mattress with only a box spring under it. The comforter, a gay and childlike print with pink and yellow flowers, should have graced the bedroom of a little girl, with a dozen dolls arranged in order of emotional significance on its ruffled shams. Instead a scattering of magazines fanned across its surface.

Annie knelt by the side of the bed. She reached up and stroked Taylor's long blond hair. "It will be all right, Taylor. It will be."

Taylor turned, sobbed again, and embraced Annie in the fiercest and neediest hug Annie had ever felt. Taylor's teary breath grew hot on Annie's shoulder, now muffling the sobs.

"It will be all right, Taylor," Annie whispered as she held the young girl close.

"I am so scared," Taylor gasped between her sobs.

"About being pregnant?"

Taylor leaned back. Her eyes were red with tears. She sniffed loudly. "That too. It's everything. I hear noises all night long and I can't sleep. I don't see the sun until the afternoon. And I don't know anyone here besides you. I don't know what I would do if I didn't know you."

With that, Taylor burst into a new flood of tears. Annie embraced her tightly once more.

Mrs. Alvarez was right. The only person who would rent this place is someone very desperate.

Very desperate indeed.

Five

TAYLOR DID NOT SPEND another night in Mr. Korzak's basement apartment. That afternoon, after her condition was officially unmasked and discovered, Taylor had cried and sobbed for what, to Annie, seemed like hours. When the young girl finally gained the barest measure of self-control, Annie had her gather up her essentials and pack another change of clothing, plus pajamas, and insisted she accompany Annie back to her apartment.

"I have a third bedroom, Taylor. I don't even use it for storage. It's basically empty. There's an extra bed in there, the room has windows, and a bathroom is just down the hall. Please. You can't stay here by yourself."

Taylor, still sniffing, looked once around the darkened

room and nodded, her reddened eyes brimming with tears again.

§   §   §

It was clear Mr. Korzak was upset over losing a paying tenant since his Lithuanian speech filled with what was obvious invective. However, he was mollified back into English when Annie paid him rent for a second, unused month's worth of occupancy.

Taylor's transition into Annie's third bedroom was easy and comforting. It had taken the two of them no more than an hour to haul all of Taylor's meager belongings across the street and up the flight of stairs. A few pieces of furniture they had left, to Mr. Korzak's obvious pleasure. Now he could advertise the apartment as being partially furnished.

Mrs. Alvarez apologized to Annie again and to Taylor. Her apology appeared heartfelt and earnest. Mrs. Alvarez might be blunt, Annie confided to Taylor, but she had a heart as big as Lake Michigan.

At last Taylor finally admitted the severity of her circumstances—she had only $750 left and no idea of how she would have survived on her own, while having to pay $500 a month in rent.

Annie insisted that Taylor make an immediate appointment at the free clinic south of the Lincoln Park area and just east of the Cabrini Green housing projects. The hours were not convenient, the clinic was tricky to get to using public transportation, and it was hard to get an appointment, but the services were free to those who could not afford it—and Taylor could definitely not afford it.

§   §   §

Even though Taylor had moved in, Annie still did not press her on the details of her life and how it was that she happened to wind up in Chicago, alone and pregnant. Knowing she was with child was enough for Annie.

Both Mrs. Alvarez and Mrs. Lang, true to their kind but interfering natures, badgered Annie for details, insisting she find out the why and how and where of Taylor's background.

"If a girl like that stayed with me," Mrs. Alvarez insisted, "she would have to tell me everything. Maybe she has a dangerous background. Maybe she's running from the police. You could get in a lot of trouble harboring a fugitive like that, Annie."

Annie simply smiled at her friends' barrage of words. "Taylor will tell me when it's time. If it's ever time."

Mrs. Lang shook her head, making clucking noises with her tongue. "Annie, that girl is under your roof. She owes you the truth, don't you think?"

While both women pressed hard and often for details, when they saw Taylor, such gossipy bravado would disappear in a mist of grandmotherly concern. They would ask after her diet and morning sickness and aches and pains and gently lay hands on her rounded belly, making pronouncements as to the sex of the baby. Each selected one of the two sexes available and repeated their insistence that theirs was the correct selection. Mrs. Alvarez knitted a sweater with a pair of pink booties and hat. Mrs. Lang bought a similar outfit in blue.

Annie could tell that Taylor lapped up the older ladies' mothering, like a kitten laps up spilled milk, with great eagerness and innocence.

She watched as people circled Taylor, joyful at the new life growing inside the girl. Annie was happy she could provide shelter and comfort for Taylor, but at the edge of her awareness was also something akin to jealousy. It was hard to admit that even to herself, but watching yet another friend come lay a hand on Taylor's cute little belly, Annie tasted a familiar bitter taste at the back of her throat. She knew she would never be in Taylor's position. . .or at least that's what she assumed. Even if her personal, childbearing expiration date could be measured in years and not months, just where might the father of Annie's child and her possible husband be hiding?

Annie forced those thoughts and unfulfilled dreams to the back of her mind and tried her best to focus in on the joy that swirled around her new roommate.

§   §   §

On a Sunday morning, almost a full month after Taylor had moved in, Annie woke early. On Sundays she kept the laundromat closed until twelve-thirty in the afternoon. That could have provided her one day a week to sleep in unfettered and unencumbered by guilt.

Yet for the past three years, instead of sleeping in, reading the thick Sunday edition of the *Chicago Tribune*, and drinking a full pot of coffee by herself, she had been attending a growing neighborhood church on Webster Street, a short walk from the laundromat. If anyone had asked just why she had begun attending, she might have told them it was because she was raised going to church with her mother, and it felt like coming home. Or she might have said that the pastor reminded her of a favorite uncle and his sermons were interesting. Or she might have said that the music was good or it might be a place to meet a man or any of another dozen logical reasons.

But the truth of it was that she really didn't know why. One Sunday morning she had watched dawn come to the city. She had gone out and walked and walked that day, with no destination in mind, and had somehow found herself on the steps of Webster Avenue Church. The beauty of its Gothic style had beckoned to her. She'd stopped on the steps as the stirring doxology was sung and as the rich notes of the old pipe organ had come pouring out the open doors. She had slipped in and not said a word to anyone. And afterward she had slipped out just as silently.

The next Sunday she'd returned—and had been doing so with almost total faithfulness since.

While every reason she might give to an inquiry might be partially valid, the only true reason, she had to admit, was that she was lonely. Despite her neighborhood friends and her art and her work at the laundromat, she was lonely. It was a deep and dark loneliness she could find no balm to cure.

Going to church helped, she thought. At least that's what she told herself every Sunday as she rose and prepared for the service.

This morning, as she had for the past three Sundays, Annie gathered her clothing and dressed quietly, hoping she was not disturbing her guest. Taylor had been suffering through what appeared to be terminal morning sickness—at least it seemed that way to Annie, who had an aversion to such things as vomiting.

Even as a child she had dreaded field trips. If someone on the bus became ill, Annie would be the sympathetic next in line. So with the laundromat open, Annie had reason to be downstairs during those precarious morning hours. But on Sundays, she did not have to leave until 8:00 A.M. Twice now, on Sundays, Annie had almost felt as green as Taylor.

Today, however, appeared to be different. Taylor was at the kitchen table as Annie sneaked past with her wrinkled dress in her arms.

"Did I wake you?" Annie asked. "I'm sorry."

Taylor smiled and offered a half-wave. "No. I got up hours ago. I thought it was going to be a usual morning of barfing. But nothing happened. I actually feel good. I even had toast and tea."

"That's good news," Annie replied.

Taylor stared at Annie. "Where are you going?"

Annie hesitated only a second. "To church." Such hopefulness dawned on Taylor's face that Annie quickly added,

"Would you like to come with me? It's less than a ten-minute walk. Are you up to it?"

Taylor shrugged. "Sure. Is it, like, a real dressy church? I don't have much that's real dressy."

Annie smiled. "No. It's not dressy. People even come in blue jeans."

"They do? That's so cool. But I think I'll wear those khakis with the elastic waist that you bought me. I don't think my jeans really fit me anymore."

A half hour later both of them set out for church. Taylor was attractive enough to turn heads, and with the beauty of her childlike face and her promising rounded belly, the pair of them got more looks and stares and smiles than Annie imagined she had gotten alone in her entire lifetime. They both took a pew near the back, although Annie generally sat closer to the front. But Taylor might be struck by any number of urges during a prolonged sitting spell, so discretion was advised.

After the service Annie introduced Taylor to several people she knew from her visits there. There were smiles enough, Annie thought, but some seemed to be frozen in place, especially after Taylor turned full silhouette. When Annie made no mention of a husband, of course, being polite and welcoming, no one in church asked.

During the following week, however, Annie fielded a score of phone calls, questions, and "advice" from her church acquaintances.

"Does her husband know she's living with you?"

"Don't get too close. . .she could take off and stick you with all her hospital bills."

"She seems like a nice girl. . .but, Annie. . .what about all the responsibilities?"

Annie had merely smiled or mumbled responses into the phone. She had tried to remain polite and careful. She knew they meant well and were concerned for both her and Taylor. After all, Taylor was an unmarried mother-to-be. But Annie already knew some of the risks. So why, she asked herself, did everyone else feel the need to point out those risks, unasked? How many of them pointed out the risk of a second helping at the church potluck dinners to all those in the congregation carrying more than a few extra pounds on their frames? Imagine the consternation and hurt feelings had she been the one to do just that!

๑   ๑   ๑

The following Wednesday morning, Annie stepped up the back staircase. Although she was trying her best to be quiet, the stairway creaked and groaned with sounds worthy of a horror movie.

As she turned the doorknob slowly, she heard the familiar and most uncomfortable sounds coming from Taylor's bathroom.

She hurried into the kitchen to boil water for a cup of herbal mint tea with ginger. Mrs. Alvarez had pressed a handful of tea bags into Annie's hands, and both women were surprised when the tea seemed to provide a great deal of help.

Taylor stumbled out into the kitchen, a damp washcloth on her forehead and another draped around her neck.

"I thought they had passed," Annie said.

Taylor shrugged and tried to grin. "I hoped so too. The book says they can come and go the whole way through pregnancy. Nine months of morning sickness. Doesn't seem like a fitting punishment."

Annie noted that Taylor seemed to find the worst-case scenario in any situation and focus on that as an eventuality, rather than hoping for the best.

"I'll have tea and toast for you in a minute."

"The mint and ginger tea?"

Annie nodded.

"Good. That does seem to help. Did I thank Mrs. Alvarez for it?"

"You did."

Taylor dabbed at her forehead. "You all have been so nice to me. I don't know what I would have..." Her face tightened.

Annie knew that the tears were close. She pulled a chair next to Taylor and embraced her. It was a familiar pattern and a comforting one to both of them.

"I wish I could have stayed home," Taylor whispered. "I am such a loser."

"You're not a loser. Not at all. You just...you just made a mistake, that's all. Everybody has made mistakes. Only you got caught. I guess it happens."

Taylor looked up. "You mean that?"

"I do."

"Have you made a mistake like this, Annie?"

Annie's arms tensed. She wasn't sure what Taylor was asking, nor was she sure how she would answer it truthfully.

"A mistake like this? Like when you can't go home anymore and life is so totally screwed up and everything is just the biggest bummer you could ever imagine?"

Annie leaned back, took a napkin from the holder on the table, dabbed at the tears on Taylor's face, and tried to fashion an answer that would not make her feel guilty.

"Taylor, I have done things. . .things I am not proud of."

"But I mean like this," Taylor said and spread open her hands, as if to frame the life within her.

"No," Annie replied quietly. "I've never done that. I've never been in your situation."

"He said he would be there," Taylor said.

"Who?"

"Derrik. He's the guy I was hooking up with. When this happened, I mean. He said that he was sorry, but that he would be there for me. He said 24/7. I believed him."

"Did you go to school with him?"

"He's a senior. Although I guess not anymore. I mean, graduation was like last month. He's probably in the Marines now. He said he was going to enlist."

"Does he know you're here? Does he know you're carrying his baby?"

Annie looked deep into Taylor's pained eyes. Taylor needed to unburden herself. She wanted to talk about it.

Now was finally the time.

"He knew I left town. He knew my brother rented the truck. Derrik works at the gas station—or at least he used to. My brother wanted to pound him when he found out, but I made him promise he wouldn't. Maybe I should have said it was okay. Doesn't seem to have made any difference, one way or another."

"What did your mom say?"

"She's dead. I was twelve. It's just me and my dad and my brother."

"What did your dad say?"

Taylor dropped her face and stared at her hands. "He made me leave. He gave me fifteen hundred dollars and told me he didn't want any whore living under his roof."

"He didn't!" Annie replied, yet knowing that some fathers could be that cold to a child.

Taylor sniffed loudly. "Maybe not in those exact words. But that's what he meant. He sells insurance, and he said that me being knocked up and not being married would be rotten for his business. So he gave me the money and found the ad in the paper for Mr. Korzak's place and said to leave."

"Have you talked to Derrik about any of this?" Annie asked. "If he's the father, then he needs to support this baby. He needs to know."

Taylor shook her head no. "I thought about calling him. But I wouldn't know what to say. I mean, he was a senior and all that. I didn't really know him all that well. And he might be a Marine by now. I wouldn't know how to get ahold of him."

For one fleeting moment, Annie wanted to stand up and shake the young girl by the shoulders. She wanted to shake some common sense into her.

But at the same moment, she realized that perhaps everyone in Taylor's life wanted to do the same thing. Then Annie realized just what Taylor needed—love, pure and simple, and unadorned compassion. So instead of a lecture, Annie leaned in close and embraced the young girl. Wrapping Taylor tightly in her arms, she stroked her hair and said soothingly, "Everything will be all right. You'll see. Everything will be all right."

ॐ　　ॐ　　ॐ

The quiet of the morning enveloped Annie as she sipped at her coffee. Taylor was sound asleep as Annie padded down the back stairway. Petey was curled up in her office chair.

"How do you always seem to know where it is I want to sit?" she asked him as she gently picked him up and placed him on a copy of yesterday's *Tribune*. The cat blinked his eyes, stretched once, and went back to sleep, snoring loudly.

The laundromat was open but, as of yet, still empty. Annie was amazed at times like this, even in the midst of a bustling city. Quiet clouds floated by every so often, when the banging and bleating of the neighborhood disappeared for a few seconds. These brief silences she cherished, wishing each time they could be longer, knowing that soon enough a bus would cough its way up the street or a young boy with spiky hair and a loud boom box would break the magical moment.

This time the silence was shattered by a much more unlikely culprit.

A woman sidled into the laundromat, bouncing the door open with her hip. It was Miss Ehrler. She was not carrying laundry, but something large, bulky, and light, wrapped in a faded floral sheet.

Setting her coffee cup down, Annie hurried out of the office. "Let me help you with that," she called out.

"I can manage," the former high-school German teacher answered, bustling toward the office. "Just keep the door open." Annie chuckled to herself. As always, Miss Ehrler's hair was done in tight curls. And she was wearing one of the shiny rayon dresses in a floral pattern with a matching belt that she had so favored. Like Annie, Miss Ehrler had never married.

Annie did as the older woman commanded. Petey jumped out of the way as Miss Ehrler dropped her package with a *thump* on the desktop.

"There." Miss Ehrler exhaled loudly. "You're young. You can get it up the steps by yourself. Or get one of those men who come in here to help."

Annie did not respond quickly. Of all the people she might imagine would barge into her office, Miss Ehrler was not high on that list.

Miss Ehrler appeared to glare at Annie with tight gray eyes. Then her face softened into a smile. She grabbed at the sheet and unloosened it.

"It's a cradle," she declared.

Annie gasped. She was dumbfounded. "It's beautiful," was all she managed to say.

The old woman gently touched the carved headboard of the cradle. At each corner a small, grinning cherubim seemed to float in space. On the headboard was a woodland scene with flowers and trees cut into the buttery-colored wood.

"My father made it for me. . .a long time ago," Miss Ehrler said softly, her fingers resting lightly on the wood. "He was a farmer who wanted to be an artist. And he wanted me to marry."

She looked away. "Neither of those dreams came true."

Miss Ehrler sniffed and straightened. "So I displayed a few of my dolls in this cradle for years. Who can help overhearing Mrs. Alvarez and Mrs. Lang and the others talk about that poor girl upstairs? I thought to myself that this cradle needs a flesh-and-blood baby in it at least once, at least for awhile. So here I am. And here it is. You don't have a cradle yet, do you?"

Annie shook her head. "This is so beautiful," she whispered. "Taylor will love it."

"Taylor? That the girl's name?"

Annie nodded again.

"Annie, you don't listen to those who say bad things about that girl. 'And whoso shall receive one such little child in my name receiveth me.'" That's Matthew 18:5 (KJV). And I believe it with all my heart now—even though I haven't always acted like it. Especially when God didn't give me the desire of my heart: to marry and to have a child. I would have loved a whole houseful. So Annie, you do what your heart says to do, and don't listen to those busybodies."

"Thank you, Miss Ehrler. I am sure Taylor and the baby will love this. It's *beautiful,*" Annie said softly. She was amazed. Miss Ehrler's Teutonic façade had always seemed completely impenetrable. But this morning, for some reason, the lines about her eyes had smoothed. Almost as if she had just reached some conclusion that had just changed her inside—and outside.

"This wood will cry with joy when it holds a child," Miss Ehrler added. "At least that's what my father said when he gave it to me. And I've decided that unfulfilled dreams aren't all bad—not if they can be used. Like this cradle. So you take care, Annie. Don't listen to anyone who says bad things about you, the girl, or the baby. That's not what the Good Book says to do. And maybe, for the first time in my own life, I'm listening."

Miss Ehrler sniffed once more, then suddenly turned and marched with great purpose out of Annie's office. Annie stared in awe at the crusty old teacher's transformation as Miss Erhler headed toward the street.

Then, overhead, the floor creaked. Annie knew Taylor was now awake. She wondered if the girl would appreciate the true delicate beauty of this wondrous cradle. After all, she was of a generation raised knowing only unnaturally colored plastic and disposable items.

Yet both of them held each other and cried when Annie showed Taylor the gift.

§ § §

Late that afternoon, during the nap that she made Taylor take, Annie pulled a short stepladder into her bedroom. She pushed aside the row of coats and shirts and dresses and climbed the ladder, reaching behind the boxes on the top shelf. She knew exactly what she was looking for—a large, sturdy cigar box at the very back of the shelf, buried under a stack of old tax receipts and income records.

She sat on her bed with the box in her lap. Nearly a quarter hour passed before she lifted the lid. Inside was a thicket of loose photographs. Some were black and white, with scalloped edges. Some were square, thick, and colored, the tints drifting to faded reds and yellow. There were ticket stubs, five report cards, an embossed pass to the Senate floor in Washington, and the program for the musical *The Fantastiks*.

Annie knew what two pictures she wanted to see—no, that she *needed* to see.

The first was a small color photograph of her mother, seated on the front steps of a house. A young Annie, at twelve, rested next to her. Her arm was around her mother. It might have been Annie's birthday. Her mother wore a simple house-dress. Annie remembered the color as robin's-egg blue—but the photograph registered it as nearly indigo. Her mother neither smiled nor frowned. She looked tired, the lines around her eyes deep, darkened by the afternoon sunlight.

Annie stared at the picture for a long, long time. She

turned it over and read the year printed on the back. She could find no hint, no clue that would bear witness to the fact that in less than three months from this snapshot, her mother would be dead.

Annie lay the picture down gently, near the pillow of her bed.

She stared at the second picture. It was taken some time after the funeral. Her older brother must have taken it, for it showed her and her father, standing side by side on the driveway, next to the brown Ford LTD that he had purchased a week after her mother's burial.

She held it close to her eyes, staring intently. She tried again to see what was in her father's eyes that day. For years she had seen only anger there. But was it sadness instead? Or pain?

She lay the second picture down next to the picture of her mother and herself. There it was—a family in two parts, in two phases, fractured one October day into too many pieces to ever repair.

All that was left was the anger in her father's eyes, his utter and complete anger at Annie for surviving. Annie knew that every time her father looked at her, she reminded him of what he had lost.

And at that thought, at that all-too-familiar realization, Annie felt the tears come. She let them fall, silently, not waking the young mother-to-be, asleep less than twenty feet away.

Petey nosed open the door and, without being bidden,

jumped into her lap, looked up into her watery eyes, and purred and pushed his head against her chest, settling down into a soft gray circle.

"And this is why you're still here and not out on the street," Annie whispered, wiping at her eyes with the back of her hand.

Six

THE TAPPING ON THE glass startled Annie just enough. She jerked at her coffee cup and sloshed a few drops, which fell on Petey the Cat, who launched himself off the desk like a furry, angry rocket. It wasn't that the coffee was hot, but that Petey hated liquids of any kind. The one bath Annie had tried to give him after he encountered a plastic bag filled with cotton candy that she had purchased at the River North Fair had ended in unmitigated disaster for Annie, the cat, and most of her apartment.

As Petey arced into the air, Annie pulled back and splashed most of the rest of the coffee in her lap, so that she jumped back, knocked over the chair, and dropped the coffee cup. It, of course, shattered as it fell.

She turned toward the window, glaring.

It was Daniel Trevalli, from Westlake Maintenance. His smile slowly eroded. "I guess I owe you a very expensive lunch, don't I?" he called through the window.

Annie's glare disappeared quickly. "It's a good thing I own a laundromat," she replied, pulling at her khakis, soaked with coffee, cream, and artificial sweetener.

Daniel jogged around the side of the building and hurried inside and into her office. "Please, Annie Hamilton, don't hate me. I didn't mean it. I really didn't."

By this time, Annie had begun to grin. After all, they were old khakis. And Petey could not be upset enough to run away from home. She wondered, during that instant, if there was anything she might do that would be drastic enough to make him run away on a permanent basis. But the biggest reason for her grin, and the reason she would not admit, was that Daniel was there. Unexpected. And apparently asking her to lunch.

"Yes, you do owe me a lunch—if that's why you're here, that is."

All of a sudden, a chilling thought passed through her mind. *What if he was just passing by? Could I have made a bigger fool of myself? And with these wet pants—I must look demented!*

"That is the reason I came, Annie Hamilton. You, me, and lunch."

She liked it when he repeated her last name like that, as if it were an old private joke just between the two of them.

"I think I need to head upstairs," she replied softly. "Maybe find something either less wet or perhaps waterproof."

Daniel laughed. He had nice teeth, she thought, and a pleasant laugh.

"I'll wait here for you. And decide where you want to go for eats. The sky's the limit—to make it up to you for the coffee and all. And the angry cat."

She took the stairs two at a time, startling poor Taylor, who had been reclining on the couch, thumbing through a laundromat copy of a month-old *People* magazine. She sat bolt upright—not an easy or quick task for a woman only a month away from becoming a mother.

"What happened? Why are you running? Why are your pants wet?"

Annie leaped into her bedroom. "I spilled coffee. And Daniel's here. He's taking me to lunch. The lunch he promised me last spring—when you first moved in with me."

"Daniel?"

From somewhere in Annie's closet, her voice called out. "He called me. He was busy. He said he would stop in soon—and now he's here."

She stood in the doorway and held a skirt in one hand and a dress in the other.

"What should I wear?" Annie could not remember ever having said those exact words to anyone, even in her high-school days.

Taylor pushed herself into a standing position. "Not the dress."

"No?"

"Too early. I think it says you might be, like, desperate."

"I'm not desperate."

"I know," Taylor replied, even as Annie was admitting it to herself. *I'm not really desperate, but I have given this day way too much thought.*

Taylor put her hand on her chin and cocked her head to one side. "The skirt will be fine. I like that color on you. You have a top to go with it?"

Annie shrugged. "I. . .I don't know. Could you look while I iron this?"

Taylor eventually came out of Annie's closet with a striped top, a pair of shoes, and a belt. "These will look cool together. At least it won't look like you had this outfit set aside for him or anything."

Annie was startled again. *Would he think that? Do guys think like that? And since when do I worry about that? And when did I start calling them "guys"?*

She dressed quickly, since Daniel may not have unlimited time for lunch. As she reached the steps, Taylor intercepted her with a small black bag. Unzipping it, she pulled out a compact.

"I don't have time to give you a makeover," the girl said, her excitement obvious, "but you need some powder and a little lipstick."

Annie, too flustered to disagree, let Taylor spend thirty seconds on makeup.

"Purse your lips."

Annie did as directed.

"There. You look great," Taylor stated.

Annie paused. Whispering a soft "thank-you," she hurried down the steps.

Taylor loudly whispered after her, "Take him across the street so I can see him."

Annie grinned and waved her left hand behind her.

§ §   §   §

After lunch, Annie and Daniel stood on the other side of MacKenzie for nearly a half hour, talking and laughing. Annie did not dare consult her watch, not wanting to even hint that she wanted the lunch to end. But she could see the giant Rolling Rock Beer clock in the small window of the Sportsman's Tavern and Social Club five doors down.

Daniel had insisted on lunch at Spago, and if he thought the prices were high, he did a great job of hiding that from her.

Now he reached out and took her hand, then encircled it with both of his. He gave a polite squeeze—manly, but not boastful. "Annie Hamilton, I had a wonderful lunch. Thank you so much. I liked that you laughed at all my jokes."

"I couldn't help it," she said, smiling. "You were funny. And you spent way too much on lunch. I didn't expect such an expensive repast."

"An expensive repast was the least I could do for scalding your cat—and ruining your pants."

Only then did he glance at his watch. "I must scoot, Annie. I will call you. Maybe a movie or something?"

She waited a heartbeat, not wanting to appear too anxious or desperate, and replied, "That would be nice."

He let go of her hand, bobbed his head, offered a sort of half-wave and half-salute, then walked back to his truck, double-parked in the alleyway.

She waited until his truck pulled away, then waved to him as he drove north. When she turned back and began walking across the street, she glimpsed Taylor's face in the window. Taylor's grin was as big as Annie had ever seen.

Her first words to Annie as she walked up the steps were, "He's cute."

§ § §

That night, as Annie struggled to fall asleep, she kept seeing images of Daniel in her thoughts. She faced into her pillow and finally nodded off. During the darkness, a dream came to her. . .she and Daniel together, holding hands. In the background was the sound of a baby crying.

When she awoke, she knew it would not take a therapist to decipher that specific dream.

§ § §

Mrs. Alvarez slowly lowered herself with a moan to the bench out front of the laundromat.

"It's hard to get old, Annie," she said as she massaged her left knee. Annie sat next to her, holding two cups of coffee.

"Here you are," Annie said and sipped at her cup. Annie found these small moments precious: sitting with an old friend—old enough to be her mother—and watching the traffic and pedestrians on a pleasantly warm Sunday afternoon with a cooling breeze off the lake. There was a hint of salsa music coming from the Sportsman's Bar, where the clientele appeared to change according to the season. Sundays brought out a more "working man" type of crowd—landscapers, construction workers, and the like—who worked six days a week in good weather. Sunday was their day to relax and perhaps watch a soccer match on the bar's wide-screen television.

"So how is our mother-to-be doing, Annie? Not much longer now, is it?" Mrs. Alvarez asked.

"She says she can't sit up or lie down without help," Annie answered. "She looks big, but the doctor at the clinic told her everything is normal."

"First babies are big—at least in my family. My first—David—he was nearly eleven pounds."

Annie nodded but had no frame of reference to know if that was a big baby or a really, really big baby.

"She's getting nervous. From her calculations and what the doctor says, she may only have two weeks left."

"Those two weeks will be the longest two weeks of her life, Annie."

"I know. I'm doing all I can to make it easy on her," Annie said, taking another sip.

"I know you are, and you're such a sweet thing to be doing this—for a stranger and all."

"I just knew she couldn't stay at Mr. Korzak's. Not by herself."

Mrs. Alvarez nodded smugly. "I told you that. No windows. He still hasn't got it rented—even at that cheap price. No one wants to live in a place with no windows. Except Lithuanians."

Annie tried not to giggle but couldn't hold it back.

The older women turned to Annie. Her face was lined with concern. "Has the baby's father been in contact?"

Annie shook her head, not volunteering any additional information.

"I had a dream. It was a bad dream," Mrs. Alvarez said, frowning.

Mrs. Alvarez often shared her dreams with others. Mercifully, she seldom asked for freelance interpretations.

"It was about the baby," the older woman said. "That someone came into the apartment and stole it. I thought it might have been the father—but I guess he don't know anything about it. . .right?"

Annie shrugged.

Then the older woman smiled broadly. "And what's this I hear about a handsome Italian fellow chasing you around, Annie? Mrs. Lang will be really happy."

Annie could not do anything but smile and remind herself to tell Taylor not to tell Mrs. Alvarez everything—even if she asked.

"His name is Daniel, Mrs. Alvarez. And we've only gone out a few times. We had lunch a couple of times. And went once to a nice dinner at the Italian Village."

The memory of each one was vividly imprinted in Annie's mind.

"Do you like him?"

Annie nodded.

"Then don't end the chase too easily. Don't let him catch you, Annie—and you know what I mean. You don't want to end up like poor Taylor with a full belly and no husband."

Annie knew Mrs. Alvarez meant well, but she still bristled inside. "You don't have anything to worry about," she replied, all the while thinking that Mrs. Alvarez had no right to interfere—or advise. Wasn't she a grown woman who could make her own decisions? Besides, the relationship wasn't even close to anything like that!

No, Annie concluded, it was not Mrs. Alvarez's right to intrude on her privacy. But then why was it that everyone felt that they could? Was it because Annie was still single, so they didn't consider her a grown-up?

"All the young girls say that, Annie. And even though you're not exactly a young girl anymore, don't think he's the last man you'll meet. Don't make his work easy. You're a good girl, Annie. You go to church," she said. "So you listen to what the Bible and God tell you to do. You're doing a good thing for Taylor—more than most would do. So don't erase that good thing by doing a bad thing."

Annie stiffened slightly. "Mrs. Alvarez, you really don't have to worry."

The older woman drank the last of her coffee, handed

the cup back to Annie, then embraced her in a fierce, motherly hug.

"Don't let him hurt you, Annie. You be careful. Don't let him hurt you. Men can hurt you by dying too young—or by leaving you. Don't let that happen."

Annie felt another squeeze, almost painful. Although Mrs. Alvarez loved to talk and give advice, for the first time Annie wondered if there was more to the older woman's story. Or if she were simply being protective of Annie, whom she considered a daughter.

"You tell him that if he hurts you, you got friends who know people who know people. You tell him he has to treat you like a lady—or else."

Annie giggled as she imagined the conversation. All the tension disappeared from her shoulders. "I will tell him, Mrs. Alvarez. And thank you for caring about me like that."

Mrs. Alvarez stood, pushing herself up with a moan. "You don't have no mother, Annie. Somebody got to tell you things like this. Somebody needs to be honest with you. I can do that for you. What your mother would do."

This time it was Annie embracing the well-meaning old woman in a tight, almost teary hug. No one could replace her mother, even all these years later. But it was nice to know that there were people, like Mrs. Alvarez, that Annie could count on.

ⓢ   ⓢ   ⓢ

Annie insisted on taking a cab back from the clinic, since

Taylor was counting down to days rather than weeks.

"It's too late to be out in this neighborhood. I'm calling for a taxi."

Taylor meekly nodded and stood behind Annie as she whistled loudly. Few cabs drove through the projects willingly, and even though there was a steady stream of potential customers at the medical clinic, Annie knew there might be a long wait.

Better this than walking five blocks at night to the bus stop.

But they were fortunate this evening. A cab slowed at the corner and stopped, letting a single passenger exit.

"Can you take us to MacKenzie and Dickens?"

"Sure. Hop in."

Taylor laid her head on Annie's shoulder. By the time they were in front of the laundromat, the girl had fallen asleep. Annie slipped a five-dollar bill to the driver, placed Taylor's arm around her shoulder, and the two of them wearily made their way up the steps.

Earlier that evening, Taylor had asked, apologetically, if Annie might attend a birthing class with her.

"They say that it helps mothers not to use drugs during delivery, Annie. But I need to have a coach. And I don't know anyone else to ask. I know I only have a few days left—but they said there was still time. I've just put it off until now."

Of course, Annie said she would be delighted to help—and in truth, she was. But as she said yes, she found herself wondering if this might be as close to motherhood and the birth experience as she would ever get.

§   §   §

Annie expected stares from the other couples in the class. But no one said a single word about the fact that two women were in the birthing process together. There was nary an arched eyebrow of concern or haughty disapproval. Annie figured the mothers-to-be were much too nervous to make value judgments, and their husbands or partners knew better than to cause any undue consternation.

Annie thought Taylor tried her best during the class, breathing as instructed, counting, relaxing, all according to the often-employed process of pain and stress elimination. When the instructor told of the severity of the pain and how long the contractions might last and various other calamities that might befall them, Taylor would look up at Annie, searching for comfort and support. Annie tried her best to remain calm and reassuring, whispering, "You'll be fine," in all the right places.

Yet Annie saw in the girl's eyes a sense of true and total fear, as if she had simply plunged, headfirst, into a world that so greatly frightened her. Taylor was young—too young to be facing such responsibilities. She should be living the carefree life of a teenager. But she had made a decision one night that had changed the course of her life.

Annie wondered what Taylor would do after the baby arrived. She, of course, could stay with Annie, and Annie often extended that offer. But Taylor would thank her with downcast eyes, then insist that as soon as she was able, she would be getting out of Annie's hair. "You don't need a squalling baby around, Annie. I'm sure we'll be fine." Annie had tried to talk with her about other options—like adoption—but Taylor had changed the subject every time. Annie had finally sighed and given up. She had planted the seed idea, but only Taylor could make that decision. And yet Annie worried—it would be a tough life for Taylor, who was so young herself, and the baby who was soon to be born.

ら　　　ら　　　ら

That night Annie helped Taylor into bed and tucked her in, silently slipping out the door. When a soft tapping came from the front door that faced the street, Annie glanced at her watch. It was a few minutes after nine.

Could it be Daniel? Wouldn't he have called?

She hurried to the front window and peered down. Whoever it was stepped back, into the light of the street lamp, and looked up.

"Mr. Korzak?"

"Miss Annie? It late. I know. But this letter. . ."

He held up an envelope toward the window, almost as if he thought she could read at great distances.

"I'll be right down."

Mr. Korzak, a small-framed, wiry man with hair that always looked as if it needed a trim, bobbed his head in a curious half-bow. "My wife get this letter. Frightened. Postman make her sign. She frightened. Then I come home. She wants to hide letter. But I see. Then I tell her letter is not for her. For that girl downstairs. Taylor girl. Letter for her."

Annie tried to follow his broken, heavily accented English. Then he pointed at the address. "Taylor Evans."

It was a registered letter for Taylor.

"You give letter to Taylor?" Mr. Korzak asked. "If postman ask, I tell you have?"

"Yes, of course, Mr. Korzak. I will give Taylor the letter. I'm surprised that Andy didn't know Taylor was staying with me."

Mr. Korzak nodded, his mouth and eyes tense. "Not Andy. Postman I never see."

"I'll tell Andy in the morning. Tell your wife not to worry, Mr. Korzak. She's not in any trouble."

"Good, good, thank you, Annie," he said and scurried across the street. Annie could see his wife's face framed in the tiny window in the kitchen. Annie waved and Mrs. Korzak ducked away.

Back upstairs, Annie scrutinized the letter more closely. It was registered with a signature required, so whoever sent it would know it was received. But who could decipher Mrs. Korzak's badly scrawled signature? Annie considered that she might have done so on purpose, for if the letter was from the Immigration Service, they could deny ever having received it.

The return address is what surprised Annie. There was no name on the envelope, but the address read: *Blair's*

Butternut Lake Lodge, Mercer, Wisconsin.

It's not Taylor's father. She said he sold insurance. And she said that the baby's father was off somewhere with the Marines.

Annie stared at the letter. The handwriting was block letters, done with angles and edges. Not neat, but not quite sloppy.

It doesn't feel like good news. If it was from someone who cared, they waited a long time to contact her.

What was the Butternut Lake Lodge and who there would be sending a registered letter to Taylor? And why?

While Taylor slept, Annie sat there until midnight, agonizing and debating. Could she simply say she had not received it? Or was she obligated to give it to Taylor, despite the fact it was probably bad news? And if it was bad news, how would it affect Taylor, with her due date so close? *What should I do, God?* she pleaded.

Annie had prayed before, of course, but her requests had never seemed quite as urgent. Prior to this dark night, her faith had never fully been tested.

But no immediate answers came. So instead of leaving the letter on the table, as Annie routinely did with all her mail, she carried this envelope into her room and slipped it into the drawer of her nightstand.

She could not recall enduring a more fitful and restless night—even that night so long ago when she was young and in love.

That night when Steve—the man she'd dated for nearly five years and had concluded she'd eventually marry—had said good-bye and moved to California. She even remembered the color of shirt he was wearing, the scent of his aftershave, and the song that was playing on his car's radio as he drove away. That night seemed easy in comparison.

Seven

ANNIE DID NOT OPEN the drawer to her nightstand for the next three days. She stared at the drawer when she fell asleep each night, and the nicked, worn handle was the first thing she saw when she awoke.

It was as if the drawer held some malevolent, pulsing force that Annie had to keep contained, lest it contaminate her apartment, her life, and both hers and Taylor's futures.

Each morning Annie resolved to tell Taylor about the letter and present it to her, but each morning her resolve quickly waned. She told herself that the shock would be bad for a very pregnant woman—that the doctor at the clinic warned them both to avoid any extremes in the last few days. Annie was pretty sure at the time that the doctor meant extremes in diet or exercise or activities—not necessarily emotional extremes. But Annie had too much invested in this pregnancy to risk even the faintest and farthest evil that might befall the soon-to-be-born child. Somehow, amazingly, as she saw Taylor's belly grow, Annie's love for the child— still unseen—had also grown. It was a gift, even if vicarious, that Annie thought she'd never have.

So each morning, after preparing Taylor's healthy breakfast—whole-grain bread, organic peanut butter, juice, cereal with no salt or extra sugars—she would slip downstairs to the laundromat office and begin another eight hours of obsessing about the letter that lay in the drawer of her nightstand, surrounded by cough drops, earplugs, hair bands and scrunchies, two-power reading glasses from Walgreens, and a flashlight with batteries that had not been changed in nearly five years. And despite Annie's assumption that Taylor's belly could not enlarge any more, every evening Annie would slowly climb the stairs, find Taylor reclining on the sofa with the television softly droning in the background, her belly expanding even farther.

By evening Taylor would have gathered a pile of magazines on the couch beside her. "Nothing keeps my interest now," she complained. "Not even the soap operas, and I used to watch them all the time before. Now all I do is stare at my stomach and hope it doesn't get any bigger." During the day she flipped through the pages of the magazines in a languid fashion, not reading, but merely skimming the words and pictures. Every few minutes she might glance up at the television, some action having caught her eye for a moment. She claimed she simply felt like an observer and was no longer a participant in anything.

Annie knew that mothers-to-be were more emotional. Actually, she didn't know this from firsthand experience, but from the collected experiences of all the older women in the neighborhood. Some said that when they carried their children, no one would get near them for fear of a tongue-lashing. Others, like Mrs. Alvarez, claimed that carrying a child was as close to sainthood as anyone could imagine.

One evening, when watching the television together, Taylor burst into tears while watching a commercial for McDonald's—an ad featuring a little boy and his father sharing an order of fries. She sobbed on Annie's shoulder for nearly thirty minutes.

Because of episodes like that, Annie kept the letter hidden for as long as she did.

§ § §

On Sunday morning Annie awoke, stared at her nightstand for a long guilty moment, then went into the living room to find Taylor, fully dressed, sitting on the couch, hands folded in her lap—or what was left of her lap. A white bow held her blond hair in a demure ponytail.

Annie blinked her eyes awake.

"I'm ready to go to church," Taylor said cheerfully.

"All right," Annie said, "but you know you're an hour and a half early."

Taylor smiled and shrugged. "Who can sleep? And I want to walk. I don't want to take a cab like last week."

"Walk? In your condition?" Annie said, a bemused look on her face. "No, Taylor, we'll get a taxi."

The young woman shook her head with determination. "No. We'll walk. It's supposed to be a good thing. Helps the baby come. And I'm. . .like. . .I'm ready. I can't imagine being any more ready than I am." It was not the first time Taylor indicated her eagerness to be done with being pregnant.

Annie nodded, then replied softly, "Then I guess I'll get dressed. But we can stop halfway there for breakfast. . .if you get tired."

Taylor sighed like a little child. "It's only six blocks. We're not climbing Mt. Everest."

Annie hurried to get ready. By seven-fifteen, both women were walking on MacKenzie. Taylor squared her shoulders, hiked up the waist on her very generous pants, and set off, with a determined waddle, toward Webster Avenue Church.

Neither of them spoke as Taylor made her way, carefully stepping along the cracks in the sidewalks and negotiating curbs with her hands splayed away from her body like that of a tightrope walker.

Annie would reach out and take Taylor's hand, take it firmly, and help her navigate over the more treacherous terrain. The girl always hung on a second longer than she needed to hold on, like a child who is unwilling to release a mother's hand as they stand in front of kindergarten for the first time in the fall.

The six blocks, normally a walk of a few minutes, took the two more than fifteen minutes. Taylor stopped often, hands on her hips—or at least where her hips used to be—and breathed deeply.

"Let's stop at Dugan's," Annie suggested. "You can get lemonade and a bran muffin. You haven't eaten this morning, have you?"

Taylor shook her head. "Lemonade would be fine. A muffin would make me gag. Do they have. . .donuts or a Twinkie or something junky like that? I really want something bad for me this morning."

After getting her seated, Annie returned to the table with a latte for herself and a lemonade and two glazed donuts, coated with purple sprinkles, for Taylor.

"Now this is what I call a breakfast!" Taylor said with glee, taking half a donut in a single bite.

Annie wanted to cry out, *But what about the baby?* Yet she knew that a single donut would not cause irreparable harm. She sipped at her latte as Taylor dove into the second donut.

Four bites and they're gone, Annie thought as she watched.

"Can I get one more?"

As Taylor finished the third, she leaned back, sighed, and patted her very ample midsection. Annie checked her watch.

"We still have a half hour. And only a few blocks to go. Ready to start again? Or do you need a rest from eating so fast?"

Taylor pushed herself away from the table and upright.

Within a minute they were standing on the northwest corner of Oz Park, under the canopy of old elms that lined the sidewalk.

"Annie, how do you know when you've made the right decision?"

"What sort of decision?" Annie replied, trying to hide her surprise. Taylor was not given to much obvious introspection.

Taylor gestured with her left hand, tracing outlines in the cool air. "Not, like, knowing if you bought the prettiest twin sweater set or anything like that—or lipstick color or what-ever—but with *big* decisions. How do you know you made the right one?"

Annie arched her eyebrows. "I guess it sometimes takes time to know. Like buying the laundromat. I wasn't sure if it was the right choice. It took months, even a year, to realize that I did the right thing. Other times. . .you might never know."

"Never?"

"Like breaking up with somebody. It may feel right at the time, but afterwards you can spend a lot of time regretting the decision. But that's what life is like. Sometimes you know right away that it was the right choice. Sometimes it takes a long time to figure it out. And maybe you never really find out. Maybe not until you're in heaven."

"Heaven?" Taylor asked. "You do believe in God and heaven, then?"

"I do. I mean. . .we've been praying together about the baby ever since you came to share my apartment. And you've been coming to church with me all summer. What they say there—

I have slowly come to believe it. I used to go to church as a kid, with my mom, but stopped going after she died, when I was twelve. I started going again when I moved to Chicago and bought the laundromat. Somehow stepping through the doors of that church was like coming home. It made me feel less lonely. At first I wasn't sure what to believe, but as I've listened to the messages and begun to read the Bible again for myself, I've learned that God can be personal, not just some concept 'out there.' It doesn't mean life is always easy—I have a long way to go—but I do believe."

Taylor edged forward on her seat, readying herself for the long push into a standing position. "Annie, you're the best, most honest person I have ever met. Who else would invite a stranger to live with them like this? And one in my condition."

Taylor grunted as Annie helped her up. It was a struggle, but finally Taylor stood, then smoothed the fabric of her dress over her belly.

"A lot of people back home go to church all the time," Taylor said thoughtfully, "but don't live like they do. Or they go and don't pay attention—but are there because it makes sense for business reasons."

Annie knew what she meant. She knew plenty of people in that same category, including her father—the few times he *had* gone, for business reasons. But she didn't judge him, since she still often placed herself in that "I'm-going-to-church-but-I-still-make-the-wrong-choices" category. She had so much to learn—and understand—about being a Christian.

Annie steadied Taylor as they climbed the steps of Webster Avenue Church and sought cool refuge in the rear pew on the right side, nearest the rest room. As Annie glanced at the bulletin, she winced. Pastor Yount's sermon was entitled "Dangerous Secrets."

She offered a quick and silent prayer that the title was simply a red herring to distract the congregation as to the real topic.

Annie's prayer was answered quickly.

And the answer was no.

She spent the entire time thinking about the letter in her nightstand.

§   §   §

Annie did not have to do much persuading to get Taylor to acquiesce into taking a cab home. The sun felt much warmer, and the humidity was approaching an uncomfortable level.

Taylor reached out for Annie's shoulder as the two of them slowly made their way up the steps of the apartment. Twice Taylor stopped and took deep breaths, then nodded that it was safe to continue her climb.

The first thing Annie saw when she entered the flat was the small drawer on her nightstand, peeking out from behind a crack in the bedroom door. Still smarting from the sermon, Annie knew now had to be the time.

"Taylor," she said as she settled the young girl on the couch, "I have a confession to make."

"Confession? Shouldn't you do that at church?" Taylor smiled.

Annie just grinned back.

Taylor jockeyed her shoulders and hips, attempting to find a comfortable position. "Then go ahead and confess."

Annie's grin vanished. She closed her eyes for a second to steady her nerves. "You got a registered letter a few days ago. From back home. I didn't tell you about it. I thought it might be bad news. I wanted to protect you. I'm really sorry."

Taylor's expression gave no indication as to her emotion.

"It came to Mr. Korzak, and he brought it over. I'm sorry I didn't give it to you right away. Let me get it now."

Taylor waved her back. "No."

"No?" Annie was more than a bit puzzled. Taylor did not appear upset in the least.

"I mean. . .I'm sorry too, Annie. I know about the letter."

"What? I mean. . .how?"

"Mr. Korzak told me the next morning. Don't be mad at me—or him. He was being friendly, that's all."

"But you do want the letter, right?" Annie stood.

"No. I mean. . .I have a confession too. When he told me. . .I sort of snooped around and found it. I already read it. Please don't be mad at me for going into your bedroom and into your private space."

Annie's emotions whipsawed back and forth. There was guilt and relief and surprise and something akin to anger. She had spent days in turmoil—for no reason!

"Then you read it?"

Taylor nodded, her ponytail bouncing like a little girl's.

"And you put it back in the drawer."

"I tried to tape it back together. . .but I guess you didn't look at it closely."

Annie had not opened the drawer since putting the letter there.

"Well. . ." Annie found no words at hand. "I guess that since you've read it and all. . ."

Taylor stared at her hands. "Do you want to know what it said?"

Annie wanted to know—but, just as much, wanted *not* to know. "Yes. No. If you want to tell me. It's none of my business."

Taylor tried to smile. "It's nothing much. . .really. Just some news from home."

And as she said the last word, her face tensed up in a scowl. Annie stared. It was not a scowl, exactly, but. . .

Taylor's expression changed. It went beyond a scowl or a grimace into something that radiated a much bigger surprise. Her mouth tightened. Annie could almost hear the pregnant woman's jaw clench together. Taylor gasped, then grabbed at her stomach with both hands and pushed gently.

What Annie had feared in the letter was forgotten in an instant.

"Ohhhh. . ."

Annie hurried to her side.

"Taylor—what is it? What's the matter?"

Taylor's scowl was more of a wince, as if she had been

given an injection by surprise and the doctor had left the needle under the skin. "I can't say for sure. . .but this sure feels like what they told us it would feel like at the birthing classes. Ohhh. . .yes, I think this is it. I think the baby is coming."

Annie stood up. They had prepared for this for weeks and weeks. And now, at this particular moment, she had no idea what to do next.

"I think I better. . .ohhh." A thin beading of perspiration formed on Taylor's forehead. Annie still could not move.

"Maybe you could call for a cab?" Taylor whispered between gasps. "I'm not sure. . .but it felt like two separate contractions. And they were really close together. I think it's time."

Nothing in the childbirth class had really prepared Annie for "the moment" the contractions would start—or the severity of them. She bolted for the phone, jabbing at the dial. While it rang, she grabbed the satchel from Taylor's room that had been packed for a month. She jabbed at another number. Meanwhile Taylor stood and waddled to the front door.

"The cab will be here in a minute. Mrs. Alvarez is getting her son-in-law to watch the laundromat. He'll feed Petey. The doctor is on the way. I've got your bag. You have your papers in your purse, right?"

Taylor grinned as she held a palm firmly at her side. "Annie, slow down. I'll be fine."

Annie grabbed Taylor's free hand. "This is it then, right?"

Taylor offered a most beatific smile, angelic in its sweetness. "This is it. Thank you for everything, Annie."

And the two of them embraced solidly. Then Annie backed away and began to head down the steps first, holding onto Taylor and the handrail at the same time.

§   §   §

Annie had never felt the impact of potholes and bad rear springs more fully than she did this Sunday morning. Every bounce and jostle she imagined as being painful to Taylor and harmful for the baby waiting to be born. Taylor leaned into the cab seat already worn into a groove by thousands of passengers. She tilted her head back and closed her eyes.

"She not have baby in cab, right?" called out the frightened cab driver as he hurried to Weiss Memorial Hospital. "I don't help with babies. I cab driver, not doctor."

Annie had taken offense. "Listen, we're not asking you to help. All I want is for you to get us there safely and miss as many potholes as you can."

"Yes, yes, sure, I do, I do, I drive good."

Annie gripped Taylor's hand. "Everything will be fine. You'll be fine. The doctor said there's nothing to worry about. Women have babies all the time."

Taylor did not open her eyes. "Then let them have this one." She moaned loudly.

"No baby, no baby," the cabby shouted as he swerved in the street.

"There's no baby," Annie shouted back. "Just get us there." She looked out the window. "Where are we?"

"Shortcut. No baby."

Taylor squeezed her hand. "Tell him to hurry."

"Hurry! Please!" Annie shouted, now getting more nervous, if that was even possible.

"No baby, no baby!"

Taylor moaned again, and the cab took the final corner on what Annie imagined to be the two right wheels only.

The cab squealed to a stop midway between the emergency room entrance and the general public entrance.

"No baby, no baby," he called as he held out his hand for the fare. Annie stuffed a wad of bills in his hand, ran out, grabbed a wheelchair, and spun it back to the cab. Taylor eased her way into it. Annie grabbed her case.

"Emergency? Or regular?" she said to Taylor.

Taylor shrugged. "Regular, I think, will be fine."

The doors hissed open, and Annie sped Taylor toward the admitting desk.

ॐ   ॐ   ॐ

In less than ten minutes, which Annie thought was nothing short of miraculous for a public aid patient, Taylor had been examined and was on a gurney, prepped and on her way to the delivery room.

No one back in her hometown of Mercer had offered to provide support. Her father had sent back the medical form with his scrawled signature, stating that Taylor was no longer receiving any support from him. Taylor had signed the papers indicating that she had no contact with the birth father. The bureaucracy required all these cold acknowledgments to proceed with their begrudging assistance.

Taylor, covered up to her neck with a hospital sheet, appeared all of fifteen years old. Only her swollen midsection gave away her innocence.

Annie had hardly let go of her hand since the first contraction. Taylor lifted her head and looked slightly bewildered. The sedatives were taking effect.

"Annie," she said in a soft slur, "you are the best thing that has ever happened to me. If it wasn't for you. . .I don't. . ."

Her words dissolved into gentle tears.

"It's fine. Everything is fine," Annie repeated, almost as a mantra.

Taylor pushed herself up on her elbows. "You're going with me, aren't you? You're coming into the delivery room, right? They said you could go with me. They promised. You promised. I don't want to do this alone."

Annie stepped back and held out the green hospital gown she was wearing. "I got ready while they got you ready. I'm not leaving you, Taylor. I promise."

The young girl relaxed. Slowly her head fell to the gurney.

A swirl of doctors and nurses swept past. A short nurse,

built like a fireplug, stopped in front of them. She grabbed the chart from the bottom of her bed. "Taylor Evans?"

"I'm here," Taylor responded weakly, raising the hand without the IV inserted.

The nurse flipped up a page of the chart. "Contractions?"

"Every three minutes," Annie answered.

"Fully dilated?"

Taylor looked to Annie.

"That's what the doctor said," Annie replied.

The nurse glared at her. "You her. . .friend?" the nurse asked, her world-weary tone indicating that in her time at this hospital, she had seen it all. Two women heading into a birthing room was, apparently, a very normal arrangement these days.

"Yes," Annie answered, wanting to set the nurse straight, to explain the relationship, to tell her in no uncertain terms that nothing untoward or unnatural was involved, but did not, realizing immediately that this was neither the time nor the place. "Yes, I'm her friend—and her coach for today."

The nurse nicked her head an inch to the left, acknowledging the fact. "Annie Hamilton, right?"

Annie offered the same insouciant nick of the head.

"Then it's party time, Taylor. Let's get this baby born."

Inside the birthing room, the staff scurried about with instruments and supplies, getting Taylor situated just so.

When there was a momentary lull in the activity, Taylor took Annie's hand again. "Do you want to know what was in the letter?"

It took Annie a few seconds to realize what Taylor was talking about. "The letter? Oh, you mean at home? I don't. . . I mean. . .you have other things to worry about, Taylor."

Taylor took a deep breath. "It was from the baby's father. He's back home, and he wanted to know how I was doing. . . that's all—"

Taylor's words stopped abruptly. She looked into Annie's eyes with fear, squeezed her hand harder, then screamed.

It was time.

A time to be born and a time to die.

Eight

IT WAS MORE THAN Annie had ever imagined—and it was less as well. To her, the actual birthing process seemed like it lasted only a scant moment. She realized Taylor might have a different perspective, though. And even though the time of the actual event may have been brief, everyone's actions—their movements and even their words—appeared to progress in slow motion. Nurses and doctors huddled about and called out their requests to Taylor in that loudly enunciated manner parents use on children and tourists use on people who don't appear to speak English.

There was much less blood involved than Annie had thought. From watching television and movies, one might envision that gore filled the delivery room. *Why else would there be the need for multiple clean sheets?* But there was precious little blood, which was a good thing for someone who intensely disliked the sight of it.

There was some shrieking. Annie again thought that with modern pain medication, women simply entered into the delivery room and came back out with a baby, hardly mussing their hair and makeup. But while the time was brief, Taylor made her discomfort well known, squeezing Annie's hand with surprising vehemence as she moaned and pushed.

"Am I okay, Annie?" Taylor gasped.

Annie bent down close to her face and whispered back, "You're doing fine. Everything is just fine."

When the doctor called out for Taylor to push hard, her young and unlined face contorted into a grimace. Then there was a brief pellucid silence. As if the volume had been muted, Annie saw the doctor's eyes crease, as if he were smiling under his mask. Then he nodded and bent closer. In a heartbeat he pulled back with a tiny bundle of blue and red and pink and blond and fingers and toes.

Then sounds of approval cascaded over the room.

"It's a boy—a strong, healthy boy," the doctor crowed, almost as if he had been responsible for the birth. A nurse grabbed the newborn, whisked him to a side table, cleaning and weighing and measuring and checking reflexes.

Annie bent close to Taylor. Neither appeared surprised that the other was in tears.

"It's a boy, Taylor. He's so beautiful. Blond hair—just like yours."

Taylor's lips trembled, and Annie brushed a tear away from her cheek.

"You did it, Taylor. A beautiful baby boy."

And as the child was placed on her chest, wrapped in a blue hospital blanket, Taylor did what countless other mothers have done before her—checked each hand and foot, counted fingers, traced the soft sculptured line of the ear, touched the perfect cheeks, rounded the soft head with a tender stroke of the palm. Then, holding the infant close to her heart, the new mom took a deep breath. She appeared unwilling to close her eyes for even a moment, lest the child disappear.

A short time later the nurse leaned in close to Taylor. "We have to take the baby for a little while."

Taylor nodded. Annie knew the girl was exhausted. For the last few weeks she had slept fitfully and now that the test was over, her eyelids began to flutter.

"You sleep, Taylor," Annie said. "I'll go with him."

Taylor offered a weak smile. Then she closed her eyes and settled into the pillow.

"Do you want to carry him?" the nurse asked.

Annie felt a rush of nervousness. "Can I do that? I mean. . .he's so little and. . ."

The nurse smiled knowingly. "He won't break."

And with that the nurse picked the baby boy off his mother's chest and placed him in Annie's arms.

Annie had never steeled herself for the flood of emotions that coursed through her in that instant. Tears came and she began to sob—in joy, in relief, in utter and total amazement over the great gift that came from God. The baby squirmed in her arms, and she felt the strong push of his legs and the turn of his shoulders.

Such a huge miracle in such a small body.

And as he squirmed, Annie's heart suddenly expanded with a tremendous love for this helpless bundle. She had never felt such a visceral, overwhelming emotion before in her life. It was almost as if her DNA was being altered to allow a greater love to exist in her heart. As if, for the first time, she really caught a glimpse of God's unending and fierce love.

In the time it takes to blink.

"This way, Miss Hamilton."

Annie stepped into a room that was warm and humid with heat lamps. It held clear bassinets and scales. Another nurse gently took the precious bundle from her arms.

"Time for your first bath, little one."

Annie stared as the nurse unwrapped the baby and began to tenderly and carefully wash and clean the tiny body.

Halfway through, the baby boy, now nearly fifteen minutes old, began to squall with heartfelt intensity, as if just waking from a long, pleasant dream.

"This may be the only time we're glad to hear them cry," the nurse said, smiling. "Helps get their lungs going."

And with that, the baby pitched his cry even higher and louder, struggling against the ministrations of the nurse.

"He's got a good set of lungs," she said as she rubbed the sponge over the child's head.

Annie leaned back against the wall. She felt exhausted, almost as if she had physically shared Taylor's experience.

The nurse, as she cleaned, began to softly sing. "Jesus loves me this I know, for the Bible tells me so. . . ."

Annie began to sob again.

But after a few more words, Annie began to sing along—the baby's first song. A song her mother used to sing to her. A song Annie now believed with her whole heart.

§   §   §

Late that same night, Taylor held the tiny boy in her arms and stared into his face. "He's a cute baby, isn't he, Annie? I mean, all babies look sort of, like, scrunched up—but he's cute, right?"

Annie sat beside Taylor's bed. She had already determined that she couldn't leave Taylor's side that night. "Yes, he's very, very cute. Out of all the babies in the nursery, he is the cutest." Annie was not trying to make the new mother feel good. She meant it. The little one, as yet unnamed, *was* the cutest baby in there.

"What have you decided about the name?" Annie asked with some trepidation.

The two of them had spent hours and hours debating the strengths and weaknesses of various names. Taylor had a predilection for a few names—most of which Annie thought sounded as if borrowed from a soap opera cast. *Dax* and *Tad* and *Harley* and *Brock* and *Dixon* and *Shayne* were some of her favorites. Annie, with gentle nudging, tried to persuade her to think otherwise.

"Charles. You liked Charles, didn't you?"

Annie nodded. "That's a good name."

"But I think I'll call him Chance for short. That's a pretty cool name, isn't it?"

Annie thought for a moment, then nodded. The name might be on the edge of soap-opera-ish, but somehow it seemed to fit the squirming bundle Taylor held at her side. After all, with Chance's birth, Taylor now had her biggest chance—to decide how she would live after this point.

Other than Annie, Taylor had no visitors in the hospital. Mrs. Alvarez called, getting a full report, and promised to spread the word to all of Annie's friends.

"We cleaned up your apartment," Mrs. Alvarez chimed with an obvious note of pride and a minor chord of condescension.

But I had left it clean!

"And Mrs. Lang is starting on the laundromat itself. She's a terror when it comes to dirt, I tell you."

But I left that clean as well!

"And Mrs. Halliston—she's organizing meals to be made. You like Italian, don't you? And maybe some Polish?"

But I had a freezer full of dinners!

Annie tried to read the expression on Taylor's face. There was only a touch of the awe Annie obviously felt over the birth of this child and a hint of something more distant, more removed. Annie could not translate the half-smiles, the darting eyes, into a discernible emotion.

"Yes. . .Chance sounds right, somehow," Annie agreed.

"Good," Taylor said, nodding. Then her eyes darted to the door. "Isn't the nurse coming back to feed him? She said that the first night the babies stay in the nursery. So the mothers can sleep and all. Is she coming back?"

Evidently they had not discussed everything about birthing babies.

"You're not going to try breast-feeding?" Annie asked.

Taylor made a face, as if she had tasted strong, unsweetened lemonade. "Ick—no," she replied quickly. "That's just for poor people who can't afford formula and bottles and all."

Annie sighed. "No, Taylor, it isn't," she replied patiently. "Remember what they said in birthing class? That it's good for the baby. Keeps him from getting sick."

Taylor fussed in the bed. "Where is the nurse?" she said, sharper than Annie thought appropriate. "And I don't care. I'm not doing it. Bottles are just so much easier. I mean, can you imagine me at a mall, having to feed the baby? Where do you go? The ladies' room? I don't think so."

The nurse appeared. She consulted the chart, took Taylor's temperature, frowned, took the baby, and slipped back out without saying a word.

A moment later a doctor slipped back in. "A bit of temperature?" he asked as he stood next to the bed.

Taylor appeared surprised. "I do? I mean I don't feel bad. . .do I?"

The doctor smiled in that crisp, professional, yet condescending way. "Not unusual after birth for a fever to start.

The Unfolding

We just need to make sure you don't have any infections. Antibiotics for awhile. We'll check your temperature every few hours. May have to stay for another day."

Then the doctor, who appeared to be at least ten years younger than Annie, cleared his throat. "If you could excuse us? I have to do an exam."

Annie backed quickly out of the room. Five minutes later the doctor appeared in the hall.

"Miss Hamilton?"

"Yes, is something the matter? Is she sick?"

The doctor pursed his already narrow mouth and lips into a circle. "She has a fever. Too early to tell if there is anything wrong internally. Is she breast-feeding?"

"No," Annie replied. "Is that a problem?"

"No, that's good. Antibiotics may not be good for the baby. Painkillers aren't either. And based on what I can see, you know, down there, after all the other shots wear off, she'll be asking for more. And we know that's not good for a baby via mother's milk," the doctor said, his voice oddly edged with embarrassment.

Annie thought it strange that a doctor might be embarrassed about such things—but he was so terribly young.

"Well. . .what do I do? What should I do?"

He rubbed at nonexistent whiskers on his chin. "I would think that for Taylor," he said, looking at the chart for the name, "another day in the hospital is required—maybe two. We want to make sure it's not a staph infection. That can happen. Is her husband here? Could he take the baby home?

Or any other family? After the circumcision—tomorrow morning—the baby could go home."

"No family. No husband. I guess I'm what she's got."

The doctor checked his watch. "Then I guess you better prepare to take the baby home. We don't want them in the hospital any longer than necessary. Too many bugs around here. It's safer at home."

Annie felt her breath catch in her throat. "Tomorrow morning?"

The doctor was already halfway down the hall. "Eleven o'clock or so. Make sure you have ID with you. The hospital won't let you leave with a baby without a photo ID. And. . . Taylor, right? She has to sign the release forms for the baby. It's pretty routine here."

And with that, Annie was left alone in the long hall, with the muted lights of evening. The sounds of the hospital were now low. The subtle drone of the television in Taylor's room was the only recognizable thing in Annie's hearing.

§　　　§　　　§

Taylor actually appeared greatly relieved when Annie broke the news.

"That means you can get him home and, like, settled. You don't seem as nervous around him as I am. This will be cool, really."

To Annie, Taylor had gone from pregnant girl to mother, back to a seventeen-year-old girl complete with giggles and an attitude in the span of twenty-four hours.

Annie was more than surprised as she talked to the nurse.

"There are lots of aunts and uncles who aren't really related and a whole lot of mothers-in-law to common-law marriages. That means there's no official relationship—at least as far as the government is concerned. But as long as the mother signs all the proper release forms, the baby can leave with just about anyone," the nurse said.

She must have noted Annie's scattered emotions. Perhaps her face showed signs of near panic.

"Go home tonight," the nurse said soothingly. "The mother will be asleep. The baby—we can take care of the baby. It's our job. You look like you could use a rest. Go home. Get a good night's sleep. Come back tomorrow. You'll have enough time to be sleepless after the baby goes home."

Annie surprised herself by not arguing with the nurse's logic.

"And be prepared. I've seen this before—the infection and all. It can be up to a week until they get it under control. Sometimes it's overnight—but sometimes it can be a lot trickier."

Annie thanked the nurse for all her help, although since acknowledging that she would be taking the baby home alone, she had not heard more than a scattering of what anyone had said.

She would have walked home, except it was dark. There were a few neighborhoods between here and there that Annie might have traversed in daylight, but not at night. She considered the bus but knew she could not handle one more jarring experience. Instead she hailed a cab.

She stepped inside. The cab did not move. She looked up.

It was the same driver who had taken them to the hospital that morning. It seemed like days and days ago.

"Baby? You have baby there in time?"

Annie grinned with a bone-weary joy. "Yes. Yes, we did. She had a fine baby boy."

The cab driver spoke for a moment in his own rattling language. Annie knew it was an African language but did not want to ask.

"What did you say?"

"I ask God to bless baby. Baby gift from heaven. God must bless. Precious gift."

Annie nodded and felt herself slump into the seat, murmuring, "Indeed they are."

And as they pulled out into the darkened street, Annie closed her eyes. For the first time in her life that she could remember, she offered God a *conscious* prayer of thanksgiving—for the wondrous miracle he had provided that day. When her lips stopped moving, she opened her eyes, not really focusing on the neon signs and flickering headlights outside.

Annie knew that God loved her, but as she held this infant in her arms and felt his warm breath on her cheek, she realized she had not understood love at all. Never understood that all-encompassing, terrifyingly powerful love—a love that would allow sacrifice and pain in order to spare the same for others.

In that instant Annie saw a glimmer of the true import

of God's gift to her. She knew she could never take that for granted again. Nor could she ever again treat God's love with indifference.

Then she asked God to let the baby grow up to love Him as much as Annie loved this child.

ⓢ   ⓢ   ⓢ

Taylor stayed in the hospital a full week. The infection that the doctor had found was indeed pernicious and stubbornly refused to respond to a host of antibiotics.

During those first few days, Annie felt continually off-balance, as if she had been transported to a new life, a life in which she had no previous experience. The second night after the baby's birth, Annie had indeed taken him home.

Settling him in had been chaotic. Mrs. Alvarez and Mrs. Lang argued back and forth for an entire morning about which formula would be best. Mrs. Halliston claimed goat's milk would be the perfect alternative. Then all three argued about how much to dress the child—a lot (Mrs. Alvarez), very little (Mrs. Lang), and in thin layers (Mrs. Halliston).

Annie held the baby in her arms as the trio barked out experiences from their past—now decades and decades old—as if those events had occurred yesterday.

"Goat's milk—the best we found was from a Puerto Rican man on Racine Avenue. He had a few goats in his backyard—I don't think the city knew about them, of course—and his uncle was the assistant to the ward boss, so no one bothered him."

"Is he still there?" Annie had asked, thinking that perhaps goat's milk might be good.

Mrs. Alvarez snorted. "He died just after the war."

Annie responded with a blank look.

"Nineteen forty-five."

The other two women nodded, waiting only a minute before launching once again into the debate concerning the proper amount of clothing.

And through the torrent of words and hand-wringing, the newborn slept.

Annie had read some books on parenting over the past few months. She had baby-sat as a young girl. And when she was twelve, the next-door neighbor had a baby, so Annie got to see firsthand how a newborn was cared for. But none of that prepared her for the intense experience of interacting with a new baby twenty-four hours a day.

On the third day, Annie woke to the little one's stirrings. She had pulled the bassinet from Taylor's room to her own. She could not imagine letting the child sleep alone in a big empty room.

She glanced at the clock. It read 4:30. Dawn was an hour away. The city was at its quietest ebb. Annie crept over to the child. There was a faint mewing, rustling sound.

"Good morning. . .Chance," she whispered. "Do you know that it is much too early to wake up?"

The baby boy waved his right arm as if he were looking for a set of lost keys in the dark. Annie bent and gathered the slight bundle into her arms.

"Are you hungry already?" she cooed. "You ate at midnight. Is it time again?"

The child moved against her chest, then arched back. Annie felt his right hand against her cheek. Tiny fingers clutched and grabbed as if seeking purchase on her flesh. He cooed back, gurgling slightly. Annie nestled into him, breathing in the newborn scent, holding him close, feeling his heartbeat against her temple. His hand wavered in the air, then found a strand of her hair and encircled it. His tiny, perfect fingers formed a tiny, perfect fist. He called out in his own language, excited.

"Your mommy will be home soon," Annie whispered. "Then we'll be a big, happy family."

The baby flexed slightly in her arms, and Annie leaned back, awake now, and sad. She shuffled into the kitchen to prepare the formula.

Will we be a family? If I were Taylor, I would head home.

And as Annie imagined that scene—Taylor holding this child and walking away—a catch came to her throat. She would have cried had she allowed herself to hold that thought. Instead she began to measure out the water and the scoop of formula. She would lose herself in the tasks at hand and allow the future to take care of itself.

ᔕ ᔕ ᔕ

When Taylor finally came home from the hospital, she

insisted that Chance stay in Annie's room.

"At least temporarily," she said with a nervous tone. "He's, like, used to it now. Right? He's been there a whole week. And you know what to do when he cries."

Annie would never have admitted it, but she was relieved. She had grown to expect to hear the faint rustlings during the night. She would not have the baby wail until someone arose to tend to him. Annie could be at his side in a heartbeat.

"Besides," Taylor said as she sat next to Annie, who was holding the child and feeding him, "you are so good with him. I've never been around babies. I was too young to remember my younger brother as an infant. I have to tell you—babies sort of spook me. You never know what they're going to do—and you never know what they're crying about."

"You'll learn his ways soon enough," Annie said encouragingly. "You can tell what he wants by the way he cries—at least most of the time."

Taylor turned to Annie and the baby. "He is a cute baby, isn't he?"

Annie grinned. "You should see what Mrs. Alvarez and the rest do when they are with him. I almost have to step between them—there are so many hugs and kisses. Mrs. Alvarez keeps saying that this baby is the most perfect child she has ever seen. Like the baby on the Ivory Snow box, she says."

"Ivory Snow?"

"It's a detergent, Taylor. They have a picture of a baby on it."

Taylor shrugged. "I didn't do much laundry."

Annie knew that was a classic example of an understatement. She fretted in silence as to how Taylor would cope with all this additional responsibility. Two months before the birth, Annie had asked Taylor if she was considering adoption. Taylor had responded with a hard, cold, silent stare. And, after a minute, she had added that the baby was *hers*, and she was keeping it. The response had been so vehement that Annie hadn't dared bring up the subject again.

Later that evening Taylor had fed Chance for the first time—his evening bottle. The way she fidgeted, even a stranger might have surmised that the new mother was anxious and nervous. Annie saw it but refused to dwell on it.

It will take some time, maybe, but she'll come around. That motherly instinct will kick in—I'm sure of it. She'll get the hang of it soon enough.

Annie offered to take Chance and change him and get him ready for bed. Taylor eagerly agreed.

When Annie returned to the living room, Taylor was curled up at the end of the couch with a can of diet Coke and the remote control for the television.

"It's so cool that you get VH-1 and MTV on your cable. We didn't get cable at home. My father said it was foolish to spend money on something you mostly get for free. So I only got to see it when I was at Becky's house. Her father didn't care. I mean, they weren't rich or anything, but she got what she wanted."

Annie watched the news on television and an occasional

Cubs baseball game, but not much else. She folded the blue cotton blanket she held in her hand, smoothing the material into a neat square.

"Taylor," Annie said softly, so softly that Taylor didn't hear and Annie had to repeat it again, louder, over the mumbling blare of the television. "Remember. . .before the baby. You got that letter. . .from home."

Taylor glanced over to Annie. "Sure. It was from Derrik."

"Derrik," Annie repeated, already disliking the name. "Does he know? I mean. . .what did he want? I thought he was in the Marines."

Taylor flipped her hair with a toss of her head. "He was. Some sort of six-month program for the reserves or something. He was back home for awhile."

"Does he know about the baby?"

Taylor shrugged, glancing at the television. "I don't know. It didn't sound like he did. Maybe. Maybe that's why he sent a registered letter. But up in Mercer, a lot of people send registered mail. Makes the postman go to the door, rather than leave the letter out in the mailbox at the end of the road. Kids steal stuff. Maybe he thought they do that in Chicago. I'm sure he thought they do."

Annie could not imagine holding such wonderful news as a baby a secret.

"Derrik said he saw my little brother and got my address. He didn't say it, but I think he sort of knew what happened—like, with the baby and all."

"And he didn't want to know about the baby?"

Taylor appeared peeved and turned back to the television. "Like I said, maybe he didn't know. Hard to keep secrets in a small town. Maybe my dad kept a lid on things. That's what he wanted to do. That's why he threw me out— and sent me here. Keeping a lid on things."

"So you're not going to tell him? He is the father, right?" Annie said, hoping and praying that Taylor would have no more secrets come to light.

"Yes. He's the only one. I mean, I went out with Kurt for, like, months and months, but that was before Derrik. And Kurt and me—we never did anything. I mean we never, you know, went all the way. It had to be Derrik. He's the only one."

"But you are going to tell him, aren't you?" Annie asked, smoothing and resmoothing the diaper she had draped over the arm of the sofa.

Taylor stared at the ghostly images dancing on the screen—bodies writhing and twisting to a dense rumble of drums and bass. "No. Maybe. I mean. . .I don't know."

Annie tried to breathe normally, but found her breath hard to control. It was as if she could no longer draw air deeply into her lungs. She desperately wanted Taylor to stay here, to stay with her, to stay with her child in the third bedroom, to stay with Annie so she could hold that squalling, squirming little bundle every day until she could hold it no longer. But she could never say that to Taylor. She could never admit that desire to anyone. After all, it was not her child, and it was not her life. It was but a momentary interlude, a gracious wondrous moment of beauty and love and transcendence. A true chance to experience what motherhood—something she'd never have—was like.

But she could not ask for it to remain permanent. As much as everything in her cried out to do so.

Like an unfolding that Annie might build with her art, this was one moment, one event, that would unfold and unfurl and slip away.

Annie felt a tear, then willed it to stop.

"You need to tell him, Taylor. He should know. He deserves to know that he is a father."

Without looking at Annie, Taylor shook her head. And in that instant Annie saw a deliberate and demanding six-year-old child, insisting that the world conform to her manners and her ways. And yet this "child" was now a mother, and the baby was not a doll.

How is Taylor going to cope? Annie agonized inwardly. *And what about Chance?*

"No. I won't tell him. Not now," Taylor replied. "I know you'll start quoting the Bible or what Pastor Yount said last week. But I'm not telling him."

"But why?"

"You don't know Derrik. He's so beautiful, but he's, like, on the wild side. At least now he is. He likes to party. He's already got a house rented in. . .well. . .in Madison. That's right. That's where he's going to school this winter. He rented a big house in Madison—where the University of Wisconsin is—on the south side of the city, I think. I mean, do you think he's going to want some crying baby living there with him? I don't think so. Derrik knows how to party—with real bands and everything. His parents are pretty rich—and he said that he saved almost all the money he made in the Marines so he could leave for school early and get established, he said."

"But he needs to know. He's a father."

"No," Taylor responded and pointed the remote directly at the television, turning up the volume.

It was clear all conversation was at a standstill.

Annie waited only a moment before hurrying to her bedroom door and snapping it shut, shielding Chance from the cacophony that filled the living room.

§   §   §

As the weeks turned into months and Thanksgiving approached, it was Annie who took care of Chance the most. And today Chance would be two months old. Annie dealt with a few laundromat issues, then hurried out toward the bakery on Lincoln Avenue. She had been amazed how easily the laundromat ran itself since Chance's birth. During the day, when Chance napped, she took the monitor with her, popped downstairs, refilled the change machines, tended to the soap dispensers, swept the floor, and greeted her customers.

They all, of course, asked about the health of the baby and if he was sleeping through the night. Annie would offer her soft, knowing smile and tell them he was working on it.

Taylor and Chance and Annie were a familiar sight in the neighborhood. Even though Mrs. Alvarez deemed it foolish to take such a young baby for a stroll, they did it anyhow, in the warm afternoon sunshine. Taylor complained of sore feet within three blocks and waited at Dugan's while Annie and Chance headed farther south and toward the lake. Chance appeared to love being outdoors with the sun on his cheeks. He burbled and cooed, his arms waving and his tiny fists clenching and unclenching as they traveled along the sidewalks.

Today Annie was on her way to purchase a two-month birthday cake. Taylor had not once talked about leaving, nor had Annie had the nerve to broach the subject again. She wanted one such celebration for certain before this magical world disappeared.

Her apartment was slowly becoming filled with baby things: a wind-up swing, a portable crib, a changing table, activity mats, all manner of plastic rattles and toys, and a bouncer, which hung off a wide door frame. Some of the things Annie had bought on her own limited income; others had been donated by her well-meaning, even if sometimes interfering, neighbors. Despite loving order and pattern, Annie had surprised herself. She found she loved the chaotic nature of the hurricane of needs and cries and obligations that this child brought.

As she crossed MacKenzie heading east, Annie reassured herself that Taylor seemed to be getting the hang of tending to the child. She would now change diapers—a task that up until a week ago left her gagging and breathless. She woke for some early feedings, if Annie asked her to. Annie knew those quiet early morning hours, when the rest of the world seemed asleep, was a wonderful time for bonding.

Annie smiled as she recalled coming out, for the fourth day in a row at 5:00 A.M., to find Chance on the couch, sleeping next to Taylor, her hand still on the remote, the television softly hissing an almost-mute version of MTV.

Tonight Annie was going to celebrate. When she got home, she would call Mrs. Alvarez and the rest and they would have cake and vanilla ice cream and she would make everyone sing "Happy Two-Month Birthday" to little Chance, even if the women didn't want to. She carried the bakery box holding onto the string they tied around it to keep the box closed.

Not many bakeries still tie boxes with string, do they?

Annie had been out all afternoon, with a list of various appointments to be kept. In the two months since Chance's birth, she had hardly ventured outside. Today she had tackled her growing list: a doctor's visit, a trip to the dentist, a stop at the eyeglass store, plus a quick trip to the hardware store.

Once back at the laundromat, Annie nodded to Juan Patillo, who had been a resident of the neighborhood for nearly as long as Annie. Last spring he had returned from Mexico with a very beautiful bride. Even after several months, the new Mrs. Patillo still appeared to be scared—as if she were an alien on an odd and strange planet.

Two months earlier Annie would have stopped to talk and gently reassure them both.

But not today.

§ § §

Annie shouldered open the door in her office and the door to the steps. She tried to avoid the squeaks, thinking Taylor and the baby might both be asleep for a late-afternoon nap.

By the time she reached the top step, her heart was beating fast—not from the steps but from a sudden, overwhelming fear. Something had happened. She did not know why—but she knew. Annie was not a woman given to relying on her intuition. But at this moment something made the hairs on her forearm stand on end. Her skin felt paper-thin.

Then she knew what it was. The apartment was quiet. With Taylor, there was never quiet. The television, radio, or CD player—and sometimes everything at the same time—was always on.

But not today. It was still and quiet.

Annie almost tossed the cake onto the kitchen table. It slid within inches of falling to the floor. Running to the third bedroom, she threw the door open.

When she saw that the bed was made with sharp, squared corners, Annie stopped, as if paralyzed. Her fear grew. Taylor had never once made the bed in her entire stay—not once.

Next she yanked open the closet door. The closet had been piled high with Taylor's outfits and clothes. Now it was empty. And the luggage that had stood in the corner was gone.

Taylor had taken everything she owned and slipped away,

out of Annie's life. And without a good-bye. Annie's heart twisted.

Why did she leave this way? She could have told me! I would have understood.

Even more chilling came the thought, like a boulder crashing into a peaceful village, that Chance was gone from her life as well.

And as that cold reality swirled in her mind, she fell to her knees in tears and pain. She had known the loss was inevitable, but she was not ready for it. She would *never* have been ready for it. She buried her face in her hands and sobbed.

Taylor said she hated good-byes. I should have listened. She said she hated weepy, teary scenes. I should have realized she would simply disappear like this—but. . . Oh, God, help me!. . .I'll never see him again, my wonderful little baby, Chance.

Feeling faint, Annie extended her hand and slumped, like a puddle, to the floor of the deserted third bedroom. Alone in her cold apartment, with only the hissing and whirring of a fraying laundromat below for companionship, Annie cried. She cried for herself, having lost such a bright beacon of joy. She cried for her future—having to face it without ever once again holding that cherubic infant in her arms. She wept for that child, praying that Taylor would provide a good life for both of them.

As her tears continued to fall, harder than she had ever cried before, she turned to her only hope of solace. She wiped at her eyes, sniffed, then folded her hands.

Annie believed. She believed in all of it—God, His Son, God's perfect gift, salvation. All the truth that Pastor Yount preached. And yet she had known nothing about love—real love—until Chance was born.

She knew about faith. She knew that a faith in God offered protection and provision and comfort. But until now faith had simply been a word, a term to be agreed upon, nodding during a Sunday service.

Annie's faith, a Sunday sort of faith, was now being called upon to offer that protection and provision and comfort. And Annie was so very afraid.

Dear God, she pleaded heavenward, *I am lost. She all but told me she would leave like this, but I didn't believe her. God, please be with that little boy, your child. Protect him. Taylor is a nice girl, but she is so young and so nervous around him. Keep little Chance in your arms, God. Bring someone into his life when the time is right to bring him to You, Lord. Taylor might not be that person, Lord, so I am asking You, even now, to prepare Chance to be able to find You. Provide him protection, and send him love. Let him grow up with everything I didn't have, Lord. Please be gracious to that small innocent child. Please be gracious and hear my prayer. Please protect him, Lord. Keep him surrounded by loving arms.*

Annie sobbed as she prayed. . .then sobbed some more. And when the sobs became only tears, she tried to take a deep breath into her lungs. She drew in the air and held it for a moment.

And in that fraction of a heartbeat, she could still hear

the tiny, throaty cry of Chance. It was uncanny, almost eerie. She blinked away the tears, hoping the sound would not echo in her head forever, haunting her like other sounds in the past haunted her.

Then she heard it again.

And that's when she stopped crying.

She scrambled to her feet and ran, knocking Petey the Cat out of her way as she raced to her bedroom at the far opposite end of the apartment. She nearly slid past the door and grabbed at the doorknob, her hands frantically scrabbling at the latch. The door bounced open.

There, in a pool of diffuse light from the street lamp on the corner, stood the baby's bassinet.

Annie dared not breathe.

In that bassinet lay a gently awakening Chance.

She left the baby! She left Chance behind! My God—she left the baby!

And in another heartbeat, Chance began to whimper, calling out with his mewing cry, asking in his own way for his dinner.

Nine

A MERE SECOND AFTER Chance whimpered, Annie grabbed the child and held him tightly against her chest.

"You're hungry, aren't you?" she crooned.

In a teary blur, Annie made her way to the kitchen and began to measure out the right amount of powdered formula. She tried three times, but each time her hands shook so much that formula dusted the counter and the floor.

Annie's breath caught in her throat as she gazed down at Chance through the veil of her watery eyes. Chance squirmed a bit and opened his eyes to Annie's. He had stopped mewing, now content to simply stare at Annie, his dark eyes focused hard on her face. His little arm reached out and grabbed at the air by her cheek. Then the little hand, with five perfect fingers and five perfect nails and five perfect sets of fingerprints, fell open against her cheek. For a magnificent moment, his fingers softly clenched against her smooth cheek. He mewed as he grasped.

Without even being aware, Annie slipped to her knees in the middle of the kitchen, then slumped to a seated position on the floor. The strength had drained from her legs. She could not stop her tears from coming now, as the infant seemed to pat her cheek, soothing her, telling her, as if he could, that everything would be all right. She bowed her head into the crook of his neck and wept.

It may have been for a quarter hour that she silently cried with Chance in her arms—tears of fear and joy, of anxiety and wonderment, of pain and great relief.

Then she sniffed loudly and pushed herself from the floor.

"You're still hungry, my little man," Annie whispered into his small and perfect ear. The child responded by turning to the sound, both hands waving in the air.

This time her formula-making attempt was successful. She screwed the lid back on the bottle and shook it as she made her way back to the darkened living room. She adjusted the cushions and sat on the window seat, cradling Chance in her arms and on her knees, holding the bottle with her left hand. Chance took to it with passion. As he drank, she smoothed his fine, blond hair.

She watched him eat with great intensity. And she sang softly, "Jesus loves me, this I know. . . ."

As she sang, the moon, fully round and yellow, rose from beyond the lake and appeared to hold still in the sky. And the child she loved with all her heart was once again back in her arms.

§   §   §

"Annie! Get up!"

A loud voice startled Annie from her reverie. Glancing at the clock by her bedside, she sat up with surprise. *6:00* A.M.*!*

Scrambling out of bed, she ran to her door, then realized no one was there. Then, as her thoughts cleared, she realized the sound must have come from her second-floor window, slightly ajar.

Spreading the draperies a few inches, she peered out onto the street below.

It was Mrs. Alvarez, and she was standing on top of Annie's bench with her skirt gathered in her hand. Her laundry basket rested on the sidewalk.

As soon as she had Annie's attention, the old woman lowered herself carefully off the bench, then shuffled toward the screen door, holding her plastic bin full of laundry.

In a moment Annie slid to the front door and unsnapped the lock and dead bolt. She had thrown on a very loose and wrinkled gray sweatshirt and pants. She wore no slippers or socks.

"You sick, Annie?" Mrs. Alvarez said, eyeing her up and down.

Annie looked at Mrs. Alvarez's plastic bin and smiled. It was so Mrs. Alvarez. Even though it all needed washing, each item was carefully folded—whites on top, colored items in between, and darks on the bottom.

"Is there anything wrong? It isn't like you to miss opening time."

"No, I'm not sick, Mrs. Alvarez," Annie replied, smoothing her hair. "Something. . .something came up. That's all."

Mrs. Alvarez thumped her laundry onto the top of a double-load washer. Then she grabbed Annie's hand. "It's not drugs, is it?"

Mrs. Alvarez had been appointed a neighborhood watch captain three years ago in a large ceremony with Mayor Daley. It was a position she took very seriously.

"No, Mrs. Alvarez, it's not that. Really."

The old woman narrowed her eyes, increasing her grip on Annie's hand. "Is it a man? Do you have a man up there—that no-good Italian boy I've seen around?"

Annie was too sleepy to argue that such a question was none of Mrs. Alvarez's business. More so, it could never be true.

"No. There is no man up there—and that Italian boy's name is Daniel," Annie said wearily. "And he's a nice guy. He really is."

The older woman pulled Annie closer. She wizened her mouth into a tight period and drew her eyes to slits, examining Annie with great detective zeal.

Annie sighed, knowing the old neighbor would not stop

the investigation until she reached a conclusion.

"Can you keep a secret? At least for now? You promise?" Annie asked quietly.

Mrs. Alvarez offered a confidential nod. She peered around the empty laundromat, as if checking for eavesdroppers. Then she leaned into Annie, her shoulder nestling against Annie's stomach.

Instead of whispering a secret, Annie stepped away and pulled Mrs. Alvarez toward the office and the back stairway.

"You promise me on the Bible that you won't tell *anyone?* I need time to think."

"I promise, sweet one," the old woman said, obviously baffled by what the secret might be. The two of them made their way upstairs, slowly. Mrs. Alvarez took the handrail and, with each step, boosted herself along and up.

Annie led her by the hand into her bedroom. She pointed to the bassinet, obviously inhabited by a sleeping baby.

"Taylor's gone," Annie said. "She packed up everything she owned and disappeared. She left the baby, Mrs. Alvarez. She left the baby with me."

And Annie began to cry.

Mrs. Alvarez was obviously confused. She stared at the child, then Annie, then back to the sleeping baby.

"Are you sure, Annie?"

Annie nodded. "Everything Taylor owned is gone. Everything. She took everything except the Bible I gave her. She left that and all the baby's things. I think she went to find her boyfriend—the boy she said was the father of the baby."

Mrs. Alvarez muttered something in Spanish, almost as a prayer, under her breath, and genuflected. Then she put her hand on the bassinet. "She left the baby? She left this most perfect child behind? How could she do that?"

Annie had never felt so close to being overwhelmed. "I don't know, Mrs. Alvarez. I truly don't know."

"Did she say anything? Did she leave a note?"

Annie shook her head no, unable to speak.

§   §   §

Two mismatched teacups sat on the kitchen table. There was a tin of store-bought butter cookies. A box of Lipton tea bags. A bowl filled with sugar cubes. A plastic container of half-and-half.

Annie slowly turned her cup back and forth, using both hands, never once tasting the tea.

"What should I do, Mrs. Alvarez?"

For once Annie had shocked Mrs. Alvarez into silence. The woman appeared as if about to speak several times, then closed her mouth, pursed her lips, and retreated back into hard concentration.

After another moment, she tilted her head. "She left the Bible?"

Annie nodded.

"You open the Bible?"

"No. Why?"

"People leave notes in Bibles," Mrs. Alvarez said hopefully. "Maybe there's a note."

Annie ran to her room and came back in an instant, holding the Bible and a single sheet of paper in her right hand. She was walking slowly.

It only took a moment to read the message.

"She said she's leaving. She said she's too nervous and too young to be a mother. She said I should find a home for the baby."

Mrs. Alvarez snatched the note away and scanned it quickly. Then she harrumphed. "I cannot believe that a mother. . .any mother, young or not. . .would do such a thing."

Annie took the note back. "She said I should find a home for Chance." She leaned toward the bedroom, thinking she heard the baby stir.

"You got to keep him, Annie," Mrs. Alvarez finally said with great finality.

"Keep him?"

"She said to find him a home. You have a home. You love him, Annie. Anyone can see that."

"But I can't. . .I mean, I have to notify somebody," Annie said with pained hesitation. "A social worker or the child-welfare people—don't I?"

Mrs. Alvarez smacked the table with her palm so loud and hard that Annie nearly fell from her chair. "You don't tell them anything!" she hissed. "They know about the little one—they'll take him away and put him in a terrible foster home and you'll never see him again. Or the mother. They won't tell the mother a thing about where he's gone. You don't tell them a thing Annie. Mrs. Wolters—over on Burling Street? She had a daughter—same situation. Had a bellyful early, got scared, left it with friends. The 'friends' turned the baby over to somebody with the state. You know what happened, Annie?"

"No," Annie whispered.

"They found the mother and had her arrested. 'Abandonment' they called it. They put her away for three years. And all the while the baby goes to one foster home, then another—and Mrs. Wolters spent every penny she had trying to find her grandchild. It has been five years, and she still doesn't know nothing. She thinks the baby has already been adopted."

She paused. Then, with an intense glare, she insisted, "Don't do it, Annie. Don't tell them anything."

Annie's breath came in shallow draws, like the ancient wheeze of a water pump. "I should just keep him? Just like that?"

"The mother said to find him a good home. You did that, Annie. This home—your home—it's a good home."

"But what do I say to people?"

"Tell them to mind their own business, Annie. People got no right to butt into your personal affairs. You got a baby, and no one needs to know a thing. No one who knows you is going to say nothing to nobody."

"I should just keep him?"

"You should keep him, Annie. Maybe this is God's surprise—His way of giving you a baby."

Hope glimmered in Annie's heart. "I should just keep him?"

Mrs. Alvarez pulled her chair closer to Annie. The metal legs squealed on the linoleum. She wrapped her arms around Annie and squeezed. Annie's breath was cut off, so powerful was the old woman's embrace.

"You keep him, Annie. I don't gossip—you know that."

Annie smiled. She knew that statement wasn't quite true. But she also knew that Mrs. Alvarez, for all her judgmental ways sometimes, was loyal to the core and could be counted on to help out, no matter the cost.

"I know of other babies being raised by aunts or uncles," continued Mrs. Alvarez, "or whoever from the family—and they get treated just like a son or daughter. Maybe even better. Open your eyes, Annie. Maybe this is God's plan for you. Maybe this is the fulfillment of the longing of your heart—a baby."

"I should just keep him," Annie whispered, though the words sounded less like a question and more like a simple statement of fact.

Then Mrs. Alvarez began to rock Annie in her arms and whisper soft, cooing sounds, telling Annie that everything would be all right.

ဈ   ဈ   ဈ

Two days later, on a cold, overcast afternoon, the front-door buzzer sounded. Holding Chance in her arms, Annie peered around the wall and down the steps. She smiled and pressed the buzzer to unlatch the lock.

"Annie," came the loud whisper, "I didn't wake him, did I? Please say he's still asleep."

"It's fine, Mrs. Lang. Loud noises don't seem to bother him much. Please come in."

Mrs. Lang carried a large, two-handled, paper grocery bag. A long loaf of Italian bread peeked out of one corner. The older woman grabbed the handrail and pulled herself up.

"It's why I live on the first floor," she said, laughing. "I live higher than that and I never come out. Or find a building with an elevator. Take care of your knees, Annie. They go and your world shrinks."

Annie slipped down the top few steps and retrieved the shopping bag. A hint of Italian gravy swirled in the narrow hallway.

"It's stuffed manicotti," Mrs. Lang said. "I figured you haven't had a lot of time to cook."

Annie placed the bag on the counter, filled the teakettle, and set it on the stove. Mrs. Lang took the baby in her arms. Even a blind man could see both the pleasure and the wistful tone in her eyes.

"I can't stay, Annie," Mrs. Lang said, even as she was sliding the kitchen chair out with her foot. "Only for a few minutes."

She handed the sleeping baby back to Annie. Annie set Chance in a tabletop bouncer and draped a blanket over him.

"Looks cold, Annie. Better get another blanket."

Careful not to show her smile, Annie did as instructed. Mrs. Lang and Mrs. Alvarez were still relentless on matters dealing with hot and cold and appropriate dress. Annie found it easier to do as they wished—and reverse the action as soon as they left.

Annie poured the hot tea and sat at the table.

Mrs. Lang patted her forearm. "Mrs. Alvarez told me, Annie."

Annie did her best to look both surprised and relieved. It wasn't hard, for that's just how she felt.

"Don't be mad at Mrs. Alvarez. She didn't want to tell me. She said it was a secret, and I respect that. So then she told me what happened. . .with the mother and all," Mrs. Lang said, her words hushed and secretive.

Annie knew the entire neighborhood would all tell each other under vows of strict secrecy. But she also knew that such a secret could not remain a secret for very long.

"You're doing the right thing, Annie. My husband, God rest his soul, had a cousin who worked for Social Services. That man was the laziest man I ever met. He didn't care about nobody's problems but his own—and most of them problems was where to have lunch on the cheap. Anyhow, my husband's cousin—he told tales of kids getting lost in the system, and even the caseworkers didn't know where they were. Babies going to a foster home at an address that don't even exist. Children being sent crosstown on a bus and never showing up and no one caring about it. Stories that would keep you up at night. It's all terrible, Annie. So you do the right thing. You have to. You keep the baby, Annie."

Then Mrs. Lang peered around the room, as if someone else might be looking. "The mother—she told me things, Annie."

"What sort of things?"

Mrs. Lang opened her palms up to the ceiling. "Like she didn't want to be a mother. Like she was so scared by the baby. You can tell who should be a mother and who shouldn't in the first five minutes. And that girl should not have been a mother."

Annie sighed. "She is just so young."

"And she thought you would be a good mother. That's what she said to me. 'Isn't Annie just the best with the baby?' she said. She really wanted you to have Chance."

"She said that? Really?" Annie wanted to believe the old woman more than anything in the world.

Mrs. Lang gulped her tea. "You're doing the right thing. You give this baby up and who knows what terrible person will get him. You keep him, Annie."

She stood and hugged Annie around the shoulders. "That's what we all think, Annie."

Annie felt the squeeze again and wondered if all old women were as strong as Mrs. Lang and Mrs. Alvarez.

"And enjoy the meal. The gravy is made with homemade sausage. Call me if you need help. I can baby-sit anytime. You call me. I like 'em when they're babies."

Annie hugged her in return. "Thanks for the manicotti. It smells delicious."

§   §   §

Annie sat alone in the kitchen. She could hear the gentle hum of a couple of dryers downstairs and the gurgling rumble of one of the oversized washers. She managed to keep a close eye on the laundromat—and headed downstairs almost once an hour—just to make sure nothing was malfunctioning.

"The place could run itself," Danny had told her once as they'd sat together in a small restaurant on Webster Place. Annie no longer counted their dates as second or third or fourth. "You got everything nice and tidy, and nothing's broken. Take an afternoon for yourself now and again."

He had said that before the baby arrived home from the hospital. Now she felt even more tethered. There would be no way to "take an afternoon" for herself now.

But as she sat in the near silence, she smiled.

It didn't matter that she couldn't just take off. It didn't matter that life had offered her such an immense and complete change. It didn't matter that she hardly slept more than four hours at a stretch.

All that mattered now was a blond-haired baby, sleeping in the front bedroom, clutching at a blue knitted blanket, cooing in his sleep.

Families were created in odd ways. Annie realized afresh that not every family was built with a mother and father and child. It seemed that since Chance had come into her life and created this new family, Annie kept seeing or reading about or being told by one of her older women friends of another family that was like hers—brought together by circumstance, rather than blood. Most of these new unions may have danced in the grayness of the law, but they were families nonetheless.

Ten

A MONTH HAD PASSED since Taylor had left.

By now the bassinet had been pulled to within an arm's length of Annie's bed—actually closer than an arm's length. Annie would edge toward the side of her bed, so her face was inches from the slats of the bassinet, and watch the fluttering rise and fall of the baby's chest. At times the baby's blanket would all but obscure the breathing, and Annie would slip her hand through the slats, touching the infant's cheek or chest to set her mind at ease.

Once she saw the chest rise and fall, she would take a deep breath herself and rest easy—if only for a short duration. Then the worries would begin again. She told herself, in the midst of a dark, moonless night, that all new mothers had the same sort of fears.

But I'm not really a new mother. She pushed that reality away from her thoughts.

Then other questions came. *But then what am I? And what am I doing with this wee, mewing miracle?*

As the child neared his three-month birthday, Annie's panic had begun to fade. No longer did she wake with a dull, hulking dread, bleary and indistinct, gripping her heart and her thoughts with the sucking, strangling grip of an octopus. When she had set one fear to rest, another would take its place and slowly insinuate its way into her thoughts until it was all she could think about. Annie found the care of a newborn to be a relentless task, carried out in the dark early morning hours, when there seemed to be no one else awake.

But gradually, over the weeks, she adjusted to Chance, and he adjusted to her.

Since Taylor's disappearance, Annie had not ventured farther than the Treasure Island store on Fullerton. She hadn't gone to church—how would she manage to get *herself* ready, as well as the baby, in time? A few of the church people she had seen each week all summer phoned, asking after her. Annie chatted cheerfully, never telling them that Taylor had gone.

"How's the baby?" they would ask.

"He's fine," she would reply.

"And how's the new mom?" they would ask.

"She's fine," she would reply. "Every day it gets a little easier."

Twinges of guilt tweaked at her heart when she lied like that.

But it's not really lying, she reasoned. *I am sort of a new mom—and it is getting better every day.*

Even though she found a way to make it sound normal and standard and acceptable, she knew it wasn't. A baby lay in a woman's arms. There was no blood between them. There was only love.

It's just like an adoption, Annie reasoned. *I know there are a lot of agencies that let the birth mother select the parents-to-be. This was just like that. Taylor picked the parent and it was me. That happens all the time.*

Annie was now aware of dozens of other families that had been "built," instead of born. Children living with aunts and uncles, not parents. A child's friend, perhaps alienated and forced out of the family home, living with a friend's family, almost as siblings. Grandmothers raising grandchildren. An aunt in name only taking on the children of another woman. In a big city like Chicago, such things happened all the time. Maybe not always legal, but people did what they had to do. If a smart lawyer came in, most of these "families" would be torn apart and children tossed into foster homes. That would be the legal system's only recourse. It would be cold and hard and dispassionate. And Annie would not let that happen to Chance.

But even as she voiced that argument in her thoughts, she knew this was not like an adoption at all. It was an abandonment and a rescue—not an adoption.

So many times over the last few weeks, Annie had picked up the phone and dialed all but the last number of the church. Over the summer and her interactions with Pastor Yount, she had grown to respect him. He would give her sound advice, she thought. He would pat her on the hand and tell her everything would be all right.

But she never completed any of those calls because she also knew the more likely scenario: He might pat her hand, all right, but with the other, he would have to call the authorities. He was a man of God, committed to the truth. He could not do otherwise. He would have to call someone.

What if I tell him that all of my questions are part of a private discussion between a pastor and a member of the church? Annie argued with herself. *Then he would be breaking a sacred vow if he tells the police. Or do all ministers consider talking confidentially to be a sacred vow?*

A simpler solution, she discovered, was to not tell him at all. To leave him out of this moral dilemma. *He has enough problems to deal with*, she thought, *without having to add my situation to his litany of problems.*

So instead of asking Pastor Yount, Annie prayed. Ever since Chance's birth, Annie had rediscovered prayer and her relationship with God. Now she prayed a lot. She prayed as she fed the baby. . .in the chilled, silent time when he awoke, fussing, at 3:00 A.M. She prayed as she rocked him over her shoulder after breakfast. She prayed as she sat in her office in the laundromat, one ear cocked to the baby monitor, crisping with static, as Chance took his nap. She prayed as she lay on her bed, still wearing the clothes she fell asleep in, one arm outstretched to the bassinet, her fingers extended, barely grazing his chest as it rapidly rose and fell with his tiny baby breath.

In all this prayer, in this constant communication with her Creator, she found peace. . .but few answers. Heaven seemed silent, so she had only her own thoughts—and worries—to fall back on. One day, calling the authorities seemed to be the answer. The next day, keeping the child secret felt like heaven's leading.

She heard and reheard the words of the delivery doctor at Weiss Memorial who said that lots of babies go home with people who are not their parents—only friends and relatives. Families are made up by more than blood, he had said. Or at least Annie thought he had said that.

Mrs. Alvarez stopped by every day. So did Mrs. Lang. So did other neighbors, mostly older women, long past those sweet and hectic baby years. Annie would gratefully let them hold Chance. She would smile wearily as she watched their wrinkled faces glow with the loving intensity that only a baby can elicit. As they grinned and pulled Chance close to their faces, creases would mark the corners of their eyes. Smile creases. Sorrow creases.

Chance seemed to enjoy their interest. He would wiggle and coo and wave his arms, searching for a cheek or a nose or an ear and would gurgle with delight when he found one. When the old women would laugh, the sound was spirited and young—the kind of laugh that was unafraid of the task ahead.

No new mother had this laugh, Annie decided. At least no first-time new mother. It came with experience. That joyous, heartfelt tone had been burnished by hundreds of nights of waking and fitful sleep, polished by hundreds of bottles tested against the skin above the wrist, and had the glow, the soft patina, of hundreds of spooned breakfasts and dinners.

Annie hoped that one day she would have that laugh.

Each day, as Chance took a nap, she'd hurry downstairs to her office to catch up on paperwork. But then she'd spend most of her time wondering and fretting about the safety of the baby, listening for clues over the monitor. Once upstairs, she would wonder about the laundromat, worrying that a customer had lost his change in a machine and, frustrated, had gone elsewhere, vowing never to return.

Annie felt as if she were in a curious limbo—her mind seldom seeming to occupy the same space as her body. Each followed the other, changing places, fidgeting and nagging, waiting for the other half.

Yet when she was holding Chance to her chest and when he stared back into her eyes, she experienced a joy so total, so overwhelming, that she could not have imagined it only scant months earlier. And she'd certainly never experienced it in her entire life, up to now. It was as if every atom in her being, every conscious thought and nerve in her body, was attuned to another being—a baby. Like a thousand gears meshing perfectly, it was then that Annie felt at peace with God, her world, herself, this child. . .and the future.

Such moments would slip past all too quickly, but Annie

now understood the magnitude of the gift of a child. It all made perfect sense—in those brief, heart-stopping moments.

Then like an old, comfortable robe—familiar, expected, and draped over the shoulders—the worries and anxieties would slowly elbow that peace away and take over Annie's thoughts.

§   §   §

Annie pulled off the old page of the calendar. November fluttered into the trash, and she stared at the expanse of numbers on the new page.

"Christmas is only twenty-five days away, Chance." Annie hummed as she stirred the bowl of oatmeal. Chance had eaten, with great relish, his strained organic peas and a mashed banana. Now he was captivated by his right hand. He appeared to be grasping at invisibles in the air, clasping and unclasping, gurgling with soft contentment.

Annie wanted the oatmeal for herself. She was steeling herself for her trip outside. She had checked the weather channel several times already. Crisp, but not yet cold. A slight breeze off the lake. Sunshine.

It would be safe to take the baby with her—properly bundled up, of course. She had decided she was visiting the church today. It would mark her first trip to Webster Avenue Church since the baby had been born and her life turned upside-down.

Linda Marstle, the efficient church secretary, had phoned

the day before to chat. She had said that Annie had been missed, and she'd love to see her. Then she asked Annie about the Christmas pageant this year. Last year Annie had been in charge of costumes, and everyone said they had been the best ever. Annie had loved being involved since it helped her get to know people at the church and also allowed her to use her artistic talents. . .an area in which she'd discovered she really shone.

But this year she had other priorities. "I am sort of busy," Annie said, hoping Linda would take the hint. Yet even as she said the words, she realized that Linda was not a person who understood subtleties. Even a firm "no" was not always enough to deter her from a goal. Being simply busy was a very flaccid excuse, Annie realized.

"Busy? Is the baby still with you?" Linda asked. "How's the new mother getting along?"

"The baby is fine—but you know how much work they are," she replied.

"How old is he now?"

"He'll be almost three and a half months old at Christmas."

"How's Taylor? She getting on all right?"

Annie bit her tongue. *How do I answer?* "I guess. . .I guess she's doing fine."

"It takes awhile for a new mom to get comfortable."

"I guess it does," Annie said, her cheeks burning with shame.

"So you'll help with the costumes then?"

"I guess I can," Annie mumbled, realizing she couldn't

get out of this predicament without telling the whole truth. So she inhaled deeply, then asked, "Is the pastor in today?"

"He'll be in this afternoon." Suddenly there was a corporate edge to Linda's voice. Annie knew the secretary had to guard his time.

"I hate to bother him"—Annie hesitated—"but do you think I could see him for a few minutes? Maybe *two* minutes?"

She heard Linda flip a page on the big appointment book.

"He's free. I'll make a note that you want to drop in to see him."

"Thanks."

And as Annie hung up, her heart began to pound.

What am I going to tell him?

ᔕ   ᔕ   ᔕ

Pastor Yount's office smelled of old books and newsprint. Dark oak bookcases blanketed three walls. Each was overflowing with books. From a step back, one could easily see the droop in each shelf as it groaned under the weight. In the corners were piles of magazines and newspapers, most marked with a fanning of yellow sticky notes. It appeared to Annie that most of the stacks had not changed position since her last and only other visit to this office, just prior to the previous year's Christmas pageant.

To Annie's recollection, the pastor wasn't a man who was easily surprised. Yet when Annie stepped in, pushing a carriage with the sleeping Chance inside, he appeared to be taken aback—if only for a second.

"Baby-sitting? That's so nice of you, Annie. New mothers need a break now and then, don't they? How is. . ."

"Taylor."

"That's right. How is Taylor doing? I haven't seen her around for awhile. . .and I haven't seen you either, Annie." He grinned knowingly. "Funny how I can spot the few people who are gone every week. My wife says it's a gift. I think it's more of a curse. Someone is out for a week, and when I see them back, I always find myself asking where they've been. Puts people on the spot, doesn't it, Annie? I don't mean to pry—at least not all that often. It's just what I notice."

He widened his smile, as if trying to tell Annie that her attendance was voluntary. She knew he, as a man of God and the shepherd of a church, probably felt otherwise, but returned his smile, though less enthusiastically.

"So how is Taylor?" he asked.

The pastor was standing, leaning against the edge of his desk. When Annie looked up, her eyes begin to tear. She wiped at them with the back of her palm and straightened in her seat.

"Pastor, I don't know. She's gone."

He tilted his head to the side. "Gone?"

Annie nodded and scrutinized her nails. It had been weeks and weeks since she had tended to them. She bent her fingers under, forming a gentle fist.

"Gone. She left more than two months ago. She left a note saying she didn't want to be a mother and that she wanted me to find a good home for the baby."

"She's gone? She left her child? Where did she go?"

Annie sighed. "She didn't go home. I talked to her father. They haven't seen her. He said he didn't care where she was. I think she went to be with her boyfriend. She said he was the baby's father."

The words were still fresh in Annie's mind. Nervous as she had ever been, Annie had called Taylor's father. Annie was certain he would want to know what had happened. She was wrong. His clipped, gruff responses reminded Annie of conversations with her own father so many years before. He didn't care at all. It wasn't hard to understand why Taylor had run. Annie would not judge her harshly.

"Where is he?"

"She said he was a student at the University of Wisconsin in Madison. I called the admissions office. They said they had no record of him."

Pastor Yount folded his arms over his chest and chewed at his lower lip. "And you've kept the baby with you since she left?"

Annie nodded. As the baby stirred in the carriage, she reached over and began to softly rock it back and forth. The stirring stopped.

"Have you called anyone else?"

"Like whom?"

"I don't know, exactly. Like the police? Wouldn't they try and track her down?"

Annie shrugged. "But she left willingly. She *purposefully*

left the baby with me."

The pastor sighed. It was obvious to Annie that he had already reached a decision, and her heart began to beat faster.

"Annie, you need to alert Social Services. Or the Illinois Department of Children and Family Services. You have to notify the authorities. It's only right."

Annie nodded. Somehow she had known that would be his answer.

"And you've taken care of him all by yourself since Taylor left?"

"I have. I am."

"Does anyone else know you have the baby?"

Annie inclined her head toward the carriage. "You do. And a few of the older ladies in the neighborhood."

"And didn't they tell you that you should tell the state?"

Annie repeated their stories and their advice—all of them saying the same thing: *Keep the baby, and don't tell anyone official.* After all, they told her, you have his birth certificate. That's all you need, they said. A school or a doctor's office never asks for a parent's identification—just as long as an adult has identification for the child.

Pastor Yount nodded as he listened but otherwise did not move. He kept his arms crossed over his chest.

"I love this baby," Annie concluded. "He's been abandoned once—by his mother. I can't abandon him again. He'll wind up a ward of the state—or in some horrible foster home. I won't let that happen to him."

Pastor Yount remained silent.

After a long, long silence, Annie pleaded, "You won't tell the police, will you? This is a private conversation, isn't it—like between a priest and a parishioner?"

"Do you want it to be like that, Annie?" the pastor asked.

She looked away and nodded gently.

"Then I won't tell anyone, Annie. But you know what the right thing is, don't you? You know what you should do, don't you? I won't tell anyone about this—as long as you tell me you know what you should do."

She did not glance up at him. "I know what I have to do," she said softly, yet with a metallic firmness.

"That's not what I asked, Annie. Do you understand what the right thing is? Have you prayed about this? What does God say?"

She waited a full minute to answer. "I know what the right thing is for this baby. And that's all I have been doing since Taylor left—praying for this baby and what I should do. I can't let him go. I can't. I love him too much. He means more to me than life, Pastor Yount. I can't give him up to a stranger. I've been caring for him since the day he was born." She sniffed loudly, her head still down. She knew that, by now, her eyes had to be red and swollen from her intense emotion.

"You haven't answered the question, Annie," he said more firmly. "I know this is hard, but that doesn't mean you simply do what you feel like doing. God allows trials in our life to test us, Annie. He's testing you right now. He's asking if you know what the right thing to do is. He wants to know your answer, Annie. Hard or not, He wants us to do the right thing. Do you really know what the right thing is?"

Now she glanced up at him, her eyes aflame and angry. She started to speak, then stopped. Finally she said, "Yes, I know what the right thing is."

"Good," he answered, sounding relieved.

"And I know that what I'm going to do is the right thing for Chance," Annie said and stood up. She gripped the handle of the carriage. "Thanks for your time," she added quickly.

The pastor opened the back door to his study, and she slipped out into the darkened hall without saying another word. The only sounds surrounding her as she exited the building were the squeaking rusty wheel of the carriage and her own loud snifflings.

Eleven

SINCE HER VISIT TO Pastor
Yount's office, Annie had tried very hard not to think about
his advice. For the past two weeks she had been angry at him.
Then, in the last several days—in less emotional moments—
she realized he had said the only thing he could. . .the only
thing that was technically legal. She was sure that he knew she
loved the baby. And she also knew she had put the pastor in a
most difficult situation—a very thorny moral dilemma. So no
longer did she hold his words against him. But those words
had not changed her resolve to keep the baby. They had only
made her more cautious about what she said to people about
Chance.

Now as Chance drifted off to sleep at last, Annie
snugged the blanket close to his chin. The baby's lips pursed;

his jaws moved and fell still. The clock radio on her night-stand glowed 2:07 A.M.

When is he going to sleep through the night? she wondered. When he awoke hungry like he had just done, Annie would find herself awake for hours afterward. She had never been a sound sleeper.

Now she padded out into the living room, wrapping her thick chenille robe around her. She switched on the television, hit the mute button, and spent a few minutes traveling through the channels. Finding nothing worthy of her interest, she clicked it off. Then she picked up the journal and pen that lay on the coffee table and began to write.

Tuesday, December 19

Winter is coming. There is a chill in the air. The weather forecasters are predicting snow flurries tomorrow. It can't be Christmas without a little snow.

Chance is getting so big—he's no longer a newborn. I know I will come to miss these late-night feedings with him. . .when the sky is dark and the city is quiet. When the whole world shrinks to just the small patch of land that he and I occupy. He lays in my arms, trusting and still, taking his formula with closed eyes. Occasionally he drifts off, and I have to nudge him awake to finish his meal. He almost seems perturbed at the interruption.

Mrs. Alvarez said this morning that she has never seen a healthier, happier, and more beautiful baby. I try not to take pride in that, knowing I had nothing to do with his creation—but I cannot help myself. I agree with her. She holds him and rocks him and sings to him in Spanish. Her voice is like an angel. I never would have imagined that. Chance quiets immediately when she sings to him. How I miss my mother at times like this. Maybe Chance will see Mrs. Alvarez—and all the others—as communal grandmothers, to be shared and enjoyed.

Every day I marvel at this little creation. What I did—and will do again with my art (at least I hope I will have time in the future) is all but a pale imitation to the creative powers of God. A whole new life, an entire new being, was created out of nothing—and imbued with such a powerful life force. Chance demands to be fed and cared for—he demands to be given a chance to deal with life.

Since talking to Pastor Yount, I seem to be embold-ened. Taylor gave him to me, and I will raise him. I am his mother. I take him out for walks almost every day. I love it when we are out and people stop and smile and chuck their fingers under his chin. They ask how old he is and if he is sleeping through the night. And I soak it all in.

It has amazed me how much a small child is a natural conduit for people's care and concern. Total strangers commiserate with me over the fog of sleep deprivation. Before Chance came into my life, I never realized what a different world parents inhabit. What I once heard and rolled my eyes over I've found to be true—that the world is divided into two groups. Those with children and those without. It's a club that many join unwillingly or passively—but once joined, there can be no turning back. Life is changed.

When I hold Chance and he takes my finger in his little hand and squeezes it, I feel so fulfilled. It is like a pump filled with love—he squeezes and my love overflows. I never thought such a depth of feelings could exist in my heart.

And I thought of myself as a loving person before this.

But I was not. That love was just a reflection in my own mirror.

This love—the love I have for Chance—is real and deep and powerful.

Annie lay down the pen and stretched. It was nearly three in the morning. She debated. *Should I remain awake or try and catch a few hours of sleep before Chance wakes up?* He always woke at 6:00. He had a built-in alarm clock, she theorized.

She lay back on the couch and closed her eyes, hoping sleep would pounce upon her. It did not. She sat back up. Sleep would be impossible for the remainder of the night. So she arose and slipped downstairs to fetch the mail.

Collecting the mail had been one of her quirky, yet

comforting rituals. She loved the mystery and surprise of it all—even if the mail was mostly advertising and bills. Since Chance was born, however, mail occasionally collected underneath the mail slot for two days in a row—once three days. The mystery of the mail seemed inconsequential when dealing with the mysteries of late-night feedings and sleeping for more than three hours at a stretch.

A larger-than-usual stack of catalogs and mailers and cards waited for Annie, piled haphazardly under the mail slot in the front door.

It is the Christmas season, after all.

She bent down and gathered the stack in her arms. As she slowly made her way up the steps, she pushed and prodded the letters and cards into a neater bundle. Then she flipped through them as one would flip through a Rolodex.

But one envelope stopped her cold—stopped her flipping and her climbing.

She ran her finger along the top of the envelope and touched the return address. It was an address she had not seen in years, nor thought of for years more.

The return address bore the slashed, thick handwriting strokes of her father.

She closed her eyes to calm her nerves and finished the last couple of steps into her apartment.

ⓢ   ⓢ   ⓢ

Her father's note consisted of only three sentences. He had

asked if she would meet him at the Palmer House in the Loop area of Chicago. The date named was December 21—only two days away. She knew Jack Hamilton—her father—always stayed at the Palmer House when in town on business. It was a marvelously elegant and ornate hotel, a circa 1875 jewel among more modern facilities.

Leaving the laundromat for an afternoon was easy. Since Chance had been born, Annie found out that the place really did run itself. Of course, living upstairs helped. A half-dozen times a day, she would run down the stairs and do a quick inspection. She would greet customers, check the change and soap machines, and tend to any chores that required her intervention.

Leaving Chance for an entire afternoon was much more problematic. Other than the one afternoon when Taylor had taken off, Annie had not left Chance's side for more than a few minutes since his birth. Mrs. Alvarez was out of town this week—in Elgin, visiting her daughter. Mrs. Lang had picked up the flu several days earlier and had begged off any baby-sitting duties. Others in the neighborhood "grandmother circle" had casually volunteered over the past couple of months, but Annie knew that some were too old, too unsteady, or too nervous to entrust with a baby for more than a few minutes.

Mrs. Alvarez cheerfully offered her daughter's services. "She can do it, Annie. She now has two of her own. She won't even notice the addition."

Annie fretted over the decision because she didn't know Rosa that well, but finally relented. *Everything will be all right,* she convinced herself. *If Rosa is anything like her mother. . . And, after all, with two of her own, she ought to know what she's doing. . . .*

But as the day grew closer, Annie's heart was still pricked with a niggling uncomfortability. . .and perhaps a little fear.

§   §   §

December 21 broke with a gray, cold bluster, and shards of snow flitted in off the lake. Annie bundled up well and tucked Chance in as many blankets as she could fit in his carrier.

The bag she packed for Chance was as big as most going-on-vacation-for-three-weeks sort of luggage. Although her visit with her father would be short—probably an hour at most—she had included in Chance's bag enough food for two days, just in case. She added four outfits, another heavy blanket, a dozen diapers, and slipped in as many toys as the bag could hold, in addition to a full kit of medicines and ointments and powders.

Hefting the baby into his carrier, she thumped the heavy bag against the small of her back. Then, once out of the laundromat, she stepped into the wind. At the end of the two-block walk to Rosa's, her shoulders had tightened in protest and her right arm had stiffened, even though she switched arms every half block.

Rosa came to the door, near panic on her face. "I can't take Chance," she blurted out. "I mean, I want to, but my baby has been throwing up all morning and now he has a fever. My husband is coming home so we can take him to the emergency room. It's probably just the flu—but then I'd have to take Chance with us. I'm afraid he'd catch it from the baby. I don't know what to do, Annie. I know you were counting on me. I called around and couldn't find anyone home. I even called my husband's sister, and she said she would help, but she's way over in Humboldt Park."

Annie did not know what to say in response.

"I guess you get a cab to her house. I'm so sorry, Annie."

"No. It's not your fault," Annie said, trying her best to be calm while her thoughts swirled. "Your baby's sick. You need to take care of him."

"What are you going to do, Annie?"

Annie's decision was swift. "I guess I'll just take him with me. He can ride in a cab, right?"

"I am so sorry, Annie," Rosa repeated. A phone began to ring.

"You get the phone," Annie said. "I'll be fine. It's not that big of a problem."

She considered taking a bus downtown. The bus stop was three blocks over. There was a bus shelter, but the wind was off the lake and it would be chilly. Buses, she knew, ran less than regular schedules on cold and rainy days—at least it seemed that way to anyone who rode buses often. She would not dream of standing outside for more than a few minutes with Chance exposed to the elements.

So, against her thriftier instincts, she hustled one block over to Lincoln and hailed the first cab she saw. She did not call out a destination until she was sure she could get the baby's carrier attached to the seat belt. Once she clicked it into place, she looked up.

The driver—a Bosnian, Serb, or Slav—smiled back at her. "Baby safe? Belt fit? Good. Make sure belt fit."

Annie nodded. "The Palmer House, please."

The cab lurched off into traffic and rushed toward the Loop.

⑨   ⑨   ⑨

A ten-minute cab ride later, Annie stood on the busy street corner of State and Monroe, with streams of Christmas shoppers and office workers hurrying back from late lunches. She held Chance's carrier with both hands in front of her, the hard plastic resting against her knees.

She eyed the wide steps heading toward the second-floor lobby of the Palmer House.

The uniformed doorman, with top hat and a long coat with a black fur collar and gold epaulets on the shoulders, watched her for a few minutes. Then he made his way near. "Can I help you, Ma'am?" In his eyes was genuine concern.

"No. . .I mean—" Annie glanced toward the formal doors again, then down to Chance. "I am supposed to meet someone inside. And now, all of a sudden, it doesn't seem like that good of an idea."

The doorman nodded, as if he understood every implication and fear in her words. "A relative?" he asked, his eyebrows arched, his words telling her it would be all right if she did not answer.

She nodded. "My father. I haven't seen him in years."

This meeting, a chance meeting between two strangers, now assumed a level of immediate intimacy. It often happened that way to Annie. Within minutes, people would confess their deepest fears to her. Now she was confessing hers to someone else. It was a most liberating experience.

"He doesn't know about your baby?"

Annie's expression widened. She had not even considered the impact Chance would have on this meeting. After all, he wasn't her baby, not really. She tried to find an answer. "No. . .I guess he doesn't know."

The doorman leaned closer and offered her a weary smile that revealed both compassion and understanding. "Go see him. It's Christmas. He needs to see his grandchild. Don't deny him that. God says we need to forgive."

Annie had seldom felt more like crying than she did at that moment. Too many memories came rushing back in a twisting storm. Images of the three of them together, images of her mother, images of a casket, draped in black bunting. . . and a flood of anger and bitterness.

She swallowed. "You're right. I should forgive him."

But at the same moment, she knew it would not be easy. However, for the first time since their last tumultuous meeting, she was willing to try. For herself. . .and for Chance. Adjusting the carrier in her hands, she marched toward the massive decorative doors with new resolve. The doorman hurried to swing them open for her.

And slowly she mounted the many marble steps to the top.

§　　§　　§

Annie often arrived at places and events early. It did not matter what the affair was. She believed that punctuality was a sign of respect and proper breeding. And to Annie, an on-time entrance was five minutes before the appointed time. Such a buffer allowed her to relax and take in the surroundings.

On this day and with this meeting, she knew she would find no glimmer of relaxation.

Amidst the Victorian glitter and gilding of the vast lobby, Annie felt small and insignificant. She found a soft velvet chair, out of the way, in an alcove by a corner, and sat down. She placed the baby, in his carrier, at her feet. She tucked the blanket about his head. He had yet to awake, despite being jostled during the cab ride and chilled by the cold air outside. His eyes remained blissfully shut.

Annie tried to ease herself back into the fancily trimmed silk pillows of the chair. As she watched the steady stream of people making their way in and out of the historic hotel, she realized how woefully out of place she was, in the sea of expensive fur coats and cashmere and scarves that alone cost more than Annie made in a week. She caught glimpses of diamonds and gold and carefully done hair and precise makeup. She heard the elegant clicking of Italian heels on polished marble. Pervading the cavernous space were exotic scents of exclusive colognes and perfumes, the mixture sweet and cloying.

She found herself pulling her plain wool coat closer to her neck, as if to hide. Examining her boots, she noticed they were scuffed; rings of dried salt marked the ankles. She tried to pull them under the glamorous twisted fringe of the chair skirt, out of sight.

Then her breath caught in her throat.

She saw him—from across the lobby. She saw him slowly scan the room, his eyes piercing every corner of the great, open space. Then he stopped. He had seen her. She saw his almost imperceptible nod as he began to walk, with solemn purpose, toward her.

He looked older, much older than Annie remembered. He still had those piercing dark eyes and that jutting, powerful chin. But the flesh had begun to sag. Small rolls of skin formed at his collar. His hair, once thick and dark, had thinned some and was streaked with gray. As he neared her, he seemed to grow taller; his shadow nearly encompassed her.

For a moment, panic threatened her. She wanted to grab Chance and bolt from the room like a slow antelope fleeing before a hungry lion. Her hands clutched at her coat. Her breath came faster. Her heart thumped irregularly.

She decided to stand. When she did, she saw the slight alteration of his stride, as if he had not expected her to move but remain still until he drew closer.

It was as if the attacking lion was surprised by the flight of the prey.

Smile!

She responded to her panicked thoughts by plastering her most sincere, fake smile on her face, as if she were greeting a tax auditor or an unwelcome salesman.

Jack Hamilton was no closer than twenty strides away when she heard him boom out her name. "Annie."

It was the voice she remembered—loud, clear, full of command, demanding attention. Her back stiffened in a visceral response.

"Dad," she replied, waiting until he drew closer to offer her much smaller, quieter words. "It has been a long time."

He did not smile but tilted his head in reply.

"You look good," she said. "You've lost weight."

At that he smiled. "I go to the club five days a week. A personal trainer at fifty dollars an hour helps. I should pay that to someone who steals my food before I eat it. Be ahead of the game."

She remembered the big house in Inverness, its air punctuated by both angry shouts and long periods of leaden silence. She remembered, while her mother was still alive, a time when Christmas was marked with red bows and tinsel, a tree in the corner by the fireplace, an abundance of gifts, and the scent of eggnog and cinnamon.

She tried to recall when the smiles had left her parents and they no longer began to care about maintaining even a cheerful façade. She blamed her father, with his focus on material things, on the stuff of life, on money. She never considered her mother as willing of a participant as her father.

"Fifty bucks an hour," her father repeated for emphasis.

His words snapped Annie back to reality.

She heard his words. What would she say to that? What *could* she say to that? That she understood about spending fifty dollars an hour to have someone watch you climb endless steps on the Stairmaster? When her own income was limited to start with and further taxed by a baby's needs?

"And you're looking. . .well," he said. It was obvious to Annie that he did not mean it. She felt his eyes travel over her face and body, seeing, evaluating. She wanted to pull her coat even more closely around herself but knew how desperate the gesture would appear.

"Thanks," she replied. "You're here on business? Late in the season, isn't it?"

She assumed he still worked for Mathers and Joyce, an engineering firm that specialized in large-scale road and transportation projects.

"Yeah. I'm making my rounds distributing Christmas cheer to clients. Hard to send bottles of Chivas through the mail."

Annie nodded, wishing there was some other way to acknowledge his statement without appearing to agree with him. When he didn't speak, she felt her face flush. With her thoughts in a whirl, she had no idea of what to say next.

"You still at that. . .that laundromat place?"

"I am," she said, a hint of a smile on her face. "I enjoy it. It's profitable."

"Profitable." Her father snorted in derision. "Well. . .that's good, Annie. Always wanted to see my daughter running some nickel-and-dime laundromat."

Nothing has changed, she thought. There was no mellowing over the years, no growing acceptance of her choices or of the fact that Annie was now responsible for her own life. Even though her finances were tight, Annie wouldn't dream of trading her "small life" (as her father would see it) for her father's cold wealth.

At that minute her father glanced down, down to the bundle that lay at her feet.

"That's a baby," he said matter-of-factly.

"It is," she replied.

And for the first time in nearly two decades, he looked directly into her face. "A *baby?* Is it yours? Or are you babysitting on the side?"

She pursed her lips, preparing to answer her father. "It's. . ."

Then she stopped. A sudden weariness crushed her heart. How would she explain all this to him? How would she explain that she had merely befriended a young, frightened woman? How would she explain that a stranger had abandoned her child into Annie's care? How do you explain a *de facto,* unofficial, unsanctioned adoption? Especially to a father you haven't seen in over twenty years? A father who never understood you anyway? Who was never around when you were growing up?

She slowly exhaled the breath she didn't know she had been holding. There was no way to neatly and cleanly explain it, she realized. No simple words to make it understandable and normal and acceptable.

And this was because it *wasn't* standard and normal and acceptable. In fact, what Chance represented was what Annie's life was all about—the odd, the unusual, the non-standard. A life she was finally accepting as God's gift to her.

She looked up at her father. He had grayed, she thought, and there was a deep creasing about his eyes that had not been there before. His voice was even deeper and darker and filled with gravel.

"His name is Charles. . .Chance. And he's mine."

She gave her father credit. He did not appear surprised. He did not flinch. His expression did not change.

"And you're not married, I take it. I would have heard if you had been, right?"

She squared her shoulders. Chance began to stir.

"No. I'm not married."

A look crossed her father's face—a look that summed up years of disappointment. The muscles in his jaw tensed, and a vein in his forehead pulsed.

"Annie, this is the last straw, " Jack Hamilton hissed. "You have embarrassed me for the last time. You buy a god-forsaken laundromat. It was like you wanted to be poor just to throw it back at me. I found your mother in a two-bit, Podunk town in the middle of nowhere, Wisconsin. I worked like a dog. I bought her a big house. She had a nice car. I even bought her a mink, for Pete's sake. And did she thank me? No. Just like you. You had a good life. You had everything you wanted. I busted my hump for you. And what did you do? Chuck it all and leave with your hippie friends on some moronic quest. What were you looking for? Truth? Knowledge? Come on, Annie, you just left to get back at me. You think it was all my fault, don't you? You're just like your mother—no brains at all. And now you come here with a bastard child and expect me to say, 'Why, hello, that's my pride and joy?' Well, it's *not* going to happen. If you want to sleep around with all your hippie or punk or whatever you call your friends, then be my guest."

His anger had roiled to the surface in an instant, just as Annie's had done all those years ago. Maybe she was more like her father than she'd thought.

But the years had mellowed her, made her more mature and wise. And Chance in her life had given her a new focus that now became a steely resolve. This time she would not slink away in tears.

Her father consulted his Rolex watch. "I will never understand why you wanted to hurt me this way. It doesn't make sense, Annie. You are just like your mother."

From the reaches of Annie's distant memory came a fleeting image of a young girl lying at the top of a darkened stairway, listening to the slurred shouts and accusations bellowed and shrieked from the kitchen below. Today Annie heard the same sounds. . .and felt the same sense. For the first time she realized how her mother must have felt all those years she was married to Jack Hamilton and why she always saw sadness on her mother's face.

Then she remembered the horror of her mother's death. It was not as if she had ever stopped remembering that day.

She had let herself in after school. The house was quiet. She called for her mother. Her car was in the driveway, so Annie knew she was there.

It had taken Annie nearly twenty minutes to find her mother. She had used one of her husband's handguns in the walk-in closet of her bedroom. Her clothes, her shoes, her mink—all were splattered with crimson.

The police had searched for a note and found none. But one policeman had remarked that every hanger and cubbyhole of the closet had been so filled with clothing and shoes that there was no more available room. Now every article had been tainted with her blood and would have to be disposed.

"What a waste," the policeman had said. They were words Annie had never forgotten.

Annie shook off the feelings just in time to hear her father's next words.

"I had hoped you would have come to your senses by now," he said, his voice dripping with venom. "That you would want to rejoin my life in Inverness. I would even have offered you a place to stay again at the house. I would have forgiven you for all your hateful words all those years ago. But I can see you haven't changed—and you don't want to change. You're still throwing your failed life into my face— as if somehow *I* am responsible for your failures. Well, I'm not. You made your own bed, now you can lie in it. I'm not giving any bastard child any of my money."

Annie waited a full minute before she softly replied, "I'm not asking for any money. I just thought. . .I just thought you might have wanted to see me. Especially since you made the contact. And I thought that maybe you'd want to see your grandson. But I guess I was wrong."

She bent down and pulled the carrier to her waist. Chance opened his eyes and stared about, the vastness of the room and the noise waking him quickly.

"Well, I don't want to see him," her father stated flatly.

She nodded, as if expecting that very response. Then, eying her father straightforwardedly, she said calmly, "Then have a good life, Daddy."

With those few words, she walked away, out of the room, with head held high. She didn't turn back once. She didn't even sneak a glance over her shoulder at the top of the stairs. She didn't scream at him for his insensitivity or stomp her feet in a petulant rage. No, this time she decided she would exit differently. Gracefully. So calmly, evenly, with slow measure, she descended the steps of the Palmer House, opened the heavy door, and stepped into the frigid winter air.

The doorman from before was nowhere to be seen. For that one small thing, Annie was grateful to God. If he had been there, she would have been reminded of his encouragement and most likely would have burst into tears because of it.

Instead she waited until her cab passed Oak Street before letting the tears flow. She did not stop crying until they reached MacKenzie.

Once again her father had betrayed her. And this time it had cut even more deeply—something she had not thought possible. Why? Because this time his betrayal had also affected

Chance, the love of her life, the desire of her heart. The person she couldn't imagine living without. The person she cared about more deeply than anything else on this earth. . .except for God, who had brought this treasure into her life.

But this time she was a woman, not the confused and angry teenager who had screamed at her father before running away. The pain was still there, still fresh, still throbbing. Her mother had taken them both to church. Her father went along, smiling at first, but Annie and her mother knew that his attendance was for show and not for spiritual reasons.

Even now Annie wasn't sure if her mother had found faith somehow. . .before she ended her life. Her parents, Annie's grandparents, seemed to speak in spiritual terms, so Annie assumed her mother had been raised in a house with faith. Annie remembered her mother teaching her the song "Jesus Loves Me," with both of them singing it as if they meant every word as true.

With Chance now in her life, Annie had rediscovered her relationship with God. And so she felt a sliver of pity, rather than pure anger, toward her father. Her mother had abandoned Annie to escape her own personal pain. And her father had abandoned her because he could not deal with something that did not have a price tag attached.

People leave for reasons that make no sense, Annie thought. As she hefted the baby carrier out and up the steps, she said, as both a prayer and a promise, "I will never leave you, Chance. I will never abandon you. You will always be in my life, so help me God."

Twelve

A FULL YEAR PASSED. It was a time filled with such busyness and tumult—but more joy than Annie could have imagined possible. And now the Christmas season had circled around again. For the past three days, friends had stopped and delivered Christmas greetings. That was not unusual. But this year they brought gifts. That was unusual.

"Christmas is no good without children, Annie. The baby is old enough to understand. Last year he didn't know anything about Christmas," Mrs. Alvarez said with a broad smile, carrying three large boxes, wrapped in paper that Annie guessed was nearly a decade old and had been used and reused.

Annie chuckled inwardly. *She's a thrifty woman.*

She loved to watch fifteen-month-old Chance, who appeared both bewildered and excited by the pyramid of boxes and ribbons and balloons stacked in a great heap on the dining-room table. He continually crawled and clawed and maneuvered himself to the base of the table. Balloons fascinated him, but Annie was vigilant to keep them out of his reach. She had heard the horror stories of children choking on bits of rubber.

"Chance," Annie said, lifting him to her hip, "these are all for you."

Chance bent from the waist, earnestly attempting to snag a red balloon with a Mickey Mouse printed on it.

"Miggy! Miggy!" he cried and flexed his fingers and arms, as if hoping the extra quarter-inch of extension would gain him the object of his desire.

Annie pulled his hand back and kissed it. "Not today! You'll get a balloon when you're. . .fifteen," she said, laughing, and twirled him in a grand circle about the room. His frustrations vanished, and he began to clap his hands together, as if spinning was the high point of human endeavor.

She ended the spin by collapsing in a giggling pile on the sofa. She had glanced back before she fell, making sure no toys were hidden in the quilts and baby blankets. Chance clapped harder and grabbed at Annie's hair. He tried to pull her closer to him, cuddling into her neck. Draping herself around him, she embraced him, breathing in his baby scent. Life would seldom have a chance to be better than it was at this moment.

She cradled Chance against her legs, now propped on the sofa in an inverted vee. Chance stared at her, then out the window. A light dusting of snow—mostly lake-effect snow, as the wind trickled off Lake Michigan, heading west—was falling.

"Snow, snow!" he cried and pointed.

"Yes, that's snow. If it snows enough, I'll get a sled and we can go sledding over in Lincoln Park." There were no hills to speak off in Lincoln Park, and Annie did not know if sledding was even allowed, nor did she have a sled yet. But she knew that Chance would love to sit, bundled up, on an old Flexible Flyer sled, while she pulled him along in the white, powdery snow. She would do all that to listen to him laugh and gurgle and talk as he experienced something new.

Annie glanced at her watch. It was twenty minutes past ten in the morning.

"Nap time, Chance."

She marveled at his ability to fall asleep so quickly and so soundly. By the time she was out of his bedroom, his eyes were shut and his breathing already slow and rhythmic. Carefully she eased the door shut, holding the latch so it would not click loudly. She knew he wouldn't wake if it did click, but it was habit on her part.

Then she evaluated her living room. What had been so neat and orderly and "decided" a little over a year ago was now a mishmash of toys and baby gear and clothes and diaper bags and blankets and shoes and all sorts of things.

"It goes with the territory," Mrs. Lang had said as she

found Annie fretting one day. "And don't worry. Chance doesn't care if you're neat. And if you lose friends because you haven't picked up a couple of socks, then they weren't such good friends to begin with."

Annie sighed and fell back into the sofa. She wondered if she should head downstairs to check on the laundromat. She had been down earlier that day and everything seemed fine. All the machines were in order, the coin changer was filled, the soap dispensers had product, and there was only a two-inch stack of bills and letters in her office. All seemed well. Customers had nodded to her. Some had offered small waves. Those she knew well would stop and chat and ask about the baby.

She would smile and answer, "He's not a baby anymore. Fifteen months! Can you believe it? I blinked my eyes, and he's already starting to walk and talk." Then she would pull a handful of snapshots from her office.

"Such a handsome little boy," they would say. And, "He'll break a few hearts when he gets older. . . . He's always laughing or smiling, isn't he? He must get that from you."

Annie basked in their compliments.

Over the past ten or so months, she had attempted to contact Taylor twice more. She had called the number she had for Taylor's father. It must have been her brother who answered the phone. He said they had not heard from Taylor in a long time and had no idea where she might be. Annie thought he might not be telling the truth and wondered why. So she sent a registered letter to both Wisconsin addresses—

to Taylor's father and the father of the baby. Both were returned with "Moved/No Forwarding Address Known" stamped on the envelope.

Now that more than a year had passed since Taylor had left, Annie was finding it harder and harder to recall when Taylor was there, sharing the apartment, belly growing bigger and bigger. Although the details of Chance's birth had been crystal-clear at the time—and the most poignant memory of her life—the threads of that memory had begun to fray over the past year. Now the once-detailed images were becoming more like an impressionist painting—hazy, fuzzy at the edges—but still powerful.

Even so, it didn't mean that the memories were any less precious.

But time had dimmed the urgency and panic of those first few months. Annie no longer lurched awake in the middle of the night, worrying if she was doing a good job. Little Chance seemed to thrive. He ate well. He slept well. He was growing like a weed through a crack in the sidewalk. He was happy and joyful.

Annie had relaxed. She began to smile more often.

The first few months had been akin to torture, both physically and emotionally. After all, Annie had lived every waking moment with the reality that she had possession of another's woman's baby! And she had no legal right to possess the child. She knew that. Legal or not, moral or not, Annie felt that pressure every day. And every day she had prayed that Chance would be able to stay with her. That she could continue to mother this child she so loved. That Social Services, should they ever find out, would understand that all these months of caring for this baby had made him hers—more than a blood-tie ever could.

Annie never truly relaxed—totally and completely. She knew that if anyone called Social Services, the possible and probable outcome would be that Chance would be taken from her and placed in foster care—or even adopted by a more traditional family. But she was just as certain that those who knew her would not consider making the call because she gave Chance more love and devotion than any foster family might. She was just as certain that if there had ever been a hint of abuse or neglect, phones would be ringing immediately.

Having Chance in her arms was something akin to. . . to. . . The only way Annie could describe it was to compare it to one day of her life each year when she was a child. She had never rushed down to the tree on Christmas morning. Instead she would wait until her parents were awake. She would insist on breakfast first. She would actually dawdle as she opened presents—for she knew that once the last gift was unwrapped, Christmas was forever over.

It was the only happy time she could ever remember in her family, for it was the one day her parents seemed to get along. The one day her father stayed home and acted relaxed and happy. The one day they actually sat side-by-side on the couch and watched Annie open her gifts. Then too quickly that magical day was over, and life returned to its unhappy norm.

She hated that empty, lonely feeling of a Christmas gone by. Of a family fractured by unhappiness and yelling.

As she grew older, she would save one present for weeks afterward—never unwrapping it—all to hold onto the joy and wonderment of Christmas for a bit longer.

Yes, having Chance in her arms was something akin to that emotion.

At first, after Taylor left, she feared that if she fully embraced him—if she ever truly opened her heart to him—she would lose that wonderment, that precious gift. . .and it would disappear like a faint chimera. So she had held it at arm's length, at least emotionally, the first few months, always worried that Taylor might appear and snatch the child from her arms. But every day the fear diminished, like a heartbeat, one small step at a time, one single cell at a time. It was a most gradual process.

But during the night, when all else was quiet—that was when the anxiety would flourish. The fear would uncoil and race about, tearing her fragile peace to crystalline shards. She would squeeze her eyes closed until the muscles hurt, attempting to force the thought—even the possibility—from her mind.

Such a terrible thing will never happen, she would tell herself. *It could never happen. Taylor is gone—for good. She will never come back to such a responsibility. She was too young and just wanted to party.*

In the still and the dark, Annie would hold herself rigid and wait until the terrifying specter passed and sleep would free her from those fears once again.

She could not pray about it. She could not ask God to remove that fear. Perhaps it was because the possibility of losing Chance was the one thing that paralyzed her. Finally it seemed that someone truly belonged to her, but for how long?

She prayed incessantly about Chance and that he grow up healthy and wise and joyful. She prayed for herself—for some wisdom to deal with the insanely complicated process of raising a child. She prayed for patience and guidance in her finances (her limited monthly budget began to stretch and stress with the addition of another person). She prayed for so many things. She prayed for Taylor, on occasion, that she would find happiness—and the path to God. That she would remember the times the two of them had prayed together, had gone to church together, and had talked about God.

But she felt like it would not be Christian of her to pray that Taylor might never return, might never once ask how her child was growing. Annie could not pray for that complete and terrifying silence.

Just then the ringing of a bell and a knocking grabbed at her thoughts and yanked her back into consciousness. At first Annie had no idea of where she was or what time it was. Such was the result of fewer hours of sleep and a thousand times the responsibility.

She patted at her face, smoothed at her hair, and stood up with a wobble. Someone was tapping loudly at the door—the door that faced the street.

It would not be her coterie of neighborly widows. They

would not stand in the cold. Instead they would have come inside and gone in through her office and tapped at that door—or simply come up the steps. Each considered herself as a *de facto* grandmother, instead of merely a friend.

Annie looked down at herself. She was presentable—khaki skirt, blue blouse—wrinkled, but as yet unmarked by drool or baby food. She glanced at her watch. It was several minutes before noon. She had slept for no more than an hour.

She hurried down the steps, pulling at her hair, attempting to smooth it behind her ears, trying to corral it into some tamer fashion.

It was not a very successful effort.

὚   ὚   ὚

"Daniel. What a nice surprise."

Snow continued to dance and swirl happily. A dusting of it gathered on his shoulders and blue knit stocking hat.

"I haven't seen you in awhile. I fix your machines too good, I guess."

Annie smiled warmly but did not laugh. She had not seen Daniel in a few months. He had called, not often, but he had called. Once Chance entered Annie's life, she had found a social life much more difficult to manage. Finding a baby-sitter she could trust was not an easy task. Most of her older women friends would fall asleep at eight in the evening, and Annie was uncomfortable with that fact. There were young girls in the neighborhood who offered baby-sitting services.

But Annie couldn't bring herself to trust her most prized possession in the whole world to a young girl who was insanely enamored with some tattooed and pierced boy band. Annie had read enough of the magazines scattered about in her laundromat to understand the truths about the current dating scene. Babies intimidated most men. Babies meant commitment and a long-term relationship. Babies most certainly intimidated single men dating single mothers—at least that's what most articles claimed.

Even though Daniel's calls were infrequent and the dates they managed to arrange even more infrequent than that, Annie looked forward to hearing from him.

They had done dinner a few times, all local places within five minutes of the laundromat. They had shared a movie or two. On three occasions he had joined Annie and Chance as they strolled about the neighborhood. Annie wasn't certain, but she imagined that Daniel felt embarrassed being seen pushing a baby carriage. He never said so directly, but Annie was good at extrapolating such motives.

"You must. Perhaps I should take a hammer to some of the old ones."

"Now, Annie Hamilton, I know you wouldn't do that. You care too much."

"You're probably right," she said. She stepped back into the cramped foyer area at the base of the stairs. "Would you like to come in? I have a pot of coffee on. It's almost fresh."

He laughed.

The laugh was forced and just a bit too loud, she thought.

"No, Annie Hamilton. I can't. I would like to, but I'm just passing through and wanted to stop in and drop something off. I'm on my way to a job in Skokie, and you know how those people up there can be."

He dusted the snow off a square box and extended it toward her. "It's for Chance. I wanted to tell you that I think he should be a baseball player—you know, like in 'Tinker to Evans to Chance.' "

Annie smiled. "Yes. . .but he'd be called Chance Chance, then."

Daniel laughed again. This time it was genuine, she thought. She missed hearing his laugh.

He looked down at his feet. "It's a Cubs hat, Annie. And a little baseball glove and ball. The lady at the Wrigley Field gift shop said it was good up to age three. I'm not a good judge of sizes. . .especially with little kids."

Annie gazed into Daniel's eyes—but only for a moment. He immediately averted his eyes and focused on something past her shoulder.

"I'm sure it will fit him," she said. "He'll love it. I think he recognizes the Cubs logo from seeing it on the billboard across the street. I'm not sure if he knows what baseball is. . .yet."

Daniel smiled broadly and nodded. He lifted his sleeve and glanced at his watch. "I have to run. That account in Skokie is waiting."

"Thank you so much for the present. I am sure he will love it. Maybe after the holidays you can come by and show him how to use it."

"Well, now, Annie Hamilton, maybe I will do just that. When things settle down. I mean, no one calls us between Christmas and New Year's. Clothes still get dirty, don't they? But it's like magic. Nothing breaks that week. So maybe I will call you—and show the little one how to throw a slider."

Annie smiled, trying to remain gracious. "Chance would love that." But even as she said the words, she knew with certainty that Daniel would not call her between Christmas and New Year's. She knew from the way he said it and the way his hands moved and the way he avoided finding her eyes with his.

And suddenly she knew why. . . .

When she was a little girl, her mother had offered to buy her a new dollhouse. Nothing fancy or elaborate—but a wonderful dollhouse, nonetheless. A fully built model rested on the top shelf of the toy store, complete with shutters and furniture.

"You can have that one," her mother had said. "Or we can buy the one that needs to be put together."

Annie did not hesitate.

"I want to put it together," she had said with ten-year-old finality. "I want to decide where the walls go and the wallpaper and the colors. Please, Mom. I don't want the one that's already built."

Daniel had the same pleading look in his eyes and the same tone in his voice as she had had as a ten year old. Could he love a child like Chance? Annie was sure he could. She knew his heart was kind. But she also realized another truth.

Daniel was a builder. He liked building things. She knew, even from the first time they met, that he would prefer to build his own—starting from the beginning and not accepting another's work. He would prefer being the real father, not just a *de facto* father.

"I'll talk to you later," Daniel said as he backed into the swirling cascade of snow. "I'll call if it's not too busy."

She waved as he hurried down the street and toward his truck. In less than a block, she could hardly see him.

"Thanks," she called out after him, knowing her voice was muffled by the white lacings of snow. "I'll send you a picture of Chance with the hat and glove."

She waited at the bottom of the steps for several minutes, until the cold frosted into her bones. Then she shut the door slowly and held the latch, as she would in Chance's bedroom, so the noise of it shutting would go unheard.

ᔕ　　ᔕ　　ᔕ

Annie pulled Chance's jacket off and hung it on the back of a kitchen chair. No longer did she have the luxury or the time to always put coats and boots in the proper, prescribed places. Chance giggled and headed after Petey the Cat, who ambled away from the crawling infant.

Petey had taken to roosting as high as he could manage the past few months, sleeping on top of desks and bookcases. He appeared to have no love toward Chance—but thankfully, no real animosity either. Occasionally Chance would capture the animal, or at least part of the tomcat, grabbing a leg or tail. Petey, so far, would patiently endure his good-natured mauling, then scamper to higher ground when released.

Annie kicked off her own shoes and tossed her winter coat on top of Chance's. She ruefully looked around the messy apartment, then at her watch. She had fifteen minutes. In a blur she raced about, grabbing loose clothing and tossing it into the spare room, grabbing bottles and plates and stuffing them into the dishwasher. She did not have time to dust or vacuum, but she was almost satisfied with her final inspection.

Not perfect, but much better than it was.

The doorbell sounded as she grabbed her coat and Chance's and hung them on the pegs in the hallway. She knew who was ringing the bell. Joan Corbin and Sandra Altman, nursery coordinators at Webster Avenue Church, had asked if they could stop by after the service. She hurried down the steps. Through the glass Annie could see that each woman was holding a large wrapped box.

"We come bearing gifts," Joan sang as Annie opened the door.

"Welcome," Annie replied. "Please come in. Would you like some coffee? Or some lunch?"

As they made their way upstairs, both said coffee would be nice but turned down any offer of food. The two women stared at the mound of gifts stacked on the kitchen table.

Sandra, an older woman with her gray hair tightly wound into a bun, cleared her throat. "Well. . .Annie. . .you know the church every year distributes toys to homes. . .without a spouse, one way or the other. . .and since you and Chance are by yourself. . ."

Annie could sense that the older woman was definitely ill at ease. Annie guessed that most of her church friends—those who knew the particulars of her situation—realized that Annie loved this little boy with a passion. But they probably also thought she and he might be better off if she allowed the child to be adopted by a "normal," more traditional family.

Joan set her box on the corner of the table. Joan was Annie's age—never married and planning to stay that way. Over the past year, Annie had become a regular attender at Webster Avenue Church. For Chance's sake and her own, she wanted to be involved—to have a church community. After a year, it was beginning to feel like family. By now, Annie considered Joan a good friend.

"Listen, Annie," Joan said bluntly but kindly, "the church wants to make sure every kid who comes to the church has a few presents at Christmas. But from the looks of the table here, someone has beaten us to it! Just tell us who it was, and we'll set them straight."

Annie's laugh was warm and considerate. "Chance has a lot of grandmothers—or kind ladies who consider themselves his grandmothers. They all want the same thing—to see Chance's smile when he opens their gift. But please, sit down. I'll get coffee. Chance is chasing the cat around. See if either of them need protecting."

As Annie hurried the coffee, she heard laughter from the front room. First it was Chance, then both ladies, then all three. It was a most comforting sound.

"He almost had the cat," Joan said. "For fifteen months, he's pretty quick."

"Either that, or the cat's pretty slow," Sandra added.

"A bit of both, I think," Annie replied. "Here's our coffee. Please, come join me."

Sandra stirred her coffee, looked down for a moment, then straight at Annie. "So tell me, are you doing okay? Chance is a wonderful, happy little boy. But we know that being a single mom is hard. You haven't been around as much this last year. Are you all right?"

Annie sipped at her coffee. "Yes," she said softly. It had been a long time since she had actually talked to a woman she considered as a contemporary. Chance's grandmother team was wonderful and kind, but they treated Annie as sort of a wayward daughter. Not the sort of daughter who did immoral things, but the sort of girl who always seemed to take the harder road, the more difficult path. It wasn't until this moment that she felt the loss of normal, nonadvisory companionship. She drew in a deep breath. "I'm not going to lie to anyone—sometimes this is all very hard. I do get lonely sometimes. I don't like not having any time to do my art. . . ."

"Your unfoldings? You're not working on them?" Joan asked. Joan was one of the few Annie had trusted enough to tell about her art. After seeing some of Annie's previous works, Joan always said Annie was wasting her time at the laundromat and that she should concentrate on her artwork.

Annie shook her head. "Not recently. I want to, but Chance is a full-time job. I thought I would resent it if any-one said I couldn't do my art anymore. But he giggles and smiles up at me and it really doesn't matter. It's more impor-tant to raise him than to worry about a shadowbox."

Joan's gaze didn't change, but Sandra, who had five chil-dren of her own, nodded in silent agreement.

"We know it's hard, Annie," Joan said. "But we do want to tell you that we think Chance is a wonderful little boy. Everyone in the nursery at church just loves him. He's always laughing."

Unbidden compliments were a balm to Annie. She loved hearing that others thought Chance was as nice as she thought he was. "Thank you. It *is* difficult sometimes. And sometimes the hardest part is the looks I get. . .when I tell people it's just Chance and me. Pity or anger or judgment. . . I'm never sure which one it will be. Even though Pastor Yount knows how Chance came into my life, I still don't think he's very comfort-able with the situation. He's never said anything mean about it. He's been so sweet to me, and he gives a big hug to Chance every time he sees him. And Chance loves it because Pastor Yount always has a sucker or two in his pocket. But I see some-thing else in his eyes. Like he wishes I would get married and buy a minivan or something. It's not disapproval. . .but he's not thrilled with everything either."

Sandra snorted. "Don't worry about Pastor Yount. It's his job to disapprove."

Joan began to giggle. "You sure that's in his job description?"

Sandra shook her head. "I know he means well. And he's a good man, really. But he's my age. It's hard to change. And he's from a small town in Iowa. I bet every one he knew back there came from the standard mom-and-dad-and-three-kids family. It's hard for him to really approve of anything different. And let's face it, Annie. Your life is so much different than anything he knew. You're single. You run your own business. You're raising Chance by yourself. And he's probably worried about you too—all the legal implications of you raising Chance."

Annie bowed her head. "Am I doing the wrong thing?"

The room was silent.

When Annie glanced up at the other women, there was a trace of tears in her eyes. "I know you know. I know you know all about Chance and how he came here. About Taylor, and that she ran away. I mean, it's no secret in church. And Pastor Yount encouraged me, when Taylor first left, to 'do the right thing'—to call Social Services. But I just couldn't. I couldn't give him up."

Joan looked away.

It was the older Sandra who answered the question. "I don't know about legalities, Annie. Neither of us do. But you love the boy, right? He's like flesh and blood to you?"

"More. It's like I was chosen," Annie said passionately. She so desperately wanted both of these women to understand, to endorse her actions. "If I believe that God has a plan for my life, then isn't this part of the plan as well? Wasn't I put here to provide a home for Chance?"

"You love him, Annie," Sandra said boldly. "That's very easy to see. Like I said, I don't know legalities, but I can see—everyone can see—that you love this little boy and are doing a great job with him."

"Thank you," Annie replied softly.

"Now go find your camera," Sandra added with a smile. "I want Chance to open our presents before we leave."

Annie sniffed once. She hoped the camera was where she thought she might have left it.

And, for once, it was.

❧   ❧   ❧

Annie turned into the slight breeze off the lake. The temperatures hovered in the mid-twenties—cold, but not frigid. She had bundled Chance up in a coat, a sweater, and two shirts—and the result was a bundle so thick he could scarcely move. He fit snugly in the backpack Annie had purchased for five dollars at a neighborhood garage sale. It placed his growing weight over her hips and made him almost easy to carry.

Owing to the snow, a walk with a stroller was nearly out of the question. Annie could not carry Chance any great distance. But placed on her back, the two could go for blocks and blocks. Annie had learned to carry a small mirror with her so she could glance over her shoulder at his face and watch his smiles as they made their way toward the park and the lake.

She walked north along Lincoln Avenue, staring in the gay and festive shop windows. Christmas, now only days away, brought out a joyous urgency that Annie had always loved. She would take Chance down to see the famous Christmas windows at Marshall Fields on State Street, but she would wait until after the holiday, when the crowds would be smaller and she could lose herself watching the colorful puppets and the happy marionettes dance to familiar Christmas music. She would buy a bag of warm and buttery Garrett's caramel corn and nibble as they walked. She would take him by the new ice rink on State Street and let him watch the skaters glide across the glassy surface. She would do all the things she had wished she had been able to do as a child. Things her father had never had time to take her to; things her mother had always been too tired to do. Chance would go to the zoo and to museums and to plays, and he would be a Cub Scout and go camping. Chance would, Annie insisted, have wondrous opportunities opened to him. She would never use the words *impractical* or *dreamer* and break his little spirit, as her father had done to her and her mother.

The sun skirted in and out of clouds. For an instant the whiteness would dazzle and blind; the next instant gray coldness tinted the air. Annie looked to the west. A thick bank of snow clouds appeared to be gathering. She carried an extra hat for both of them if the snow began.

If it gets really bad, I'll flag down a taxi or take a bus.

About six blocks from her apartment was the Lincoln Park Zoo. It was a jewel of a zoo—a wondrous assortment of animals and exhibits—free to all and open every day of the year. In the winter the sidewalks were virtually deserted and the animals paced and stared and played without much of an audience.

From the underground viewing area, Annie and Chance watched the seals in the frigid water. They would swim lazily by, upside down, then slow, as if to stare at the odd, two-headed visitor. Chance would push himself up and down as they swam past, nearly pulling Annie off balance.

"Time to go, Chance. We still have to see the gorillas."

Chance loved the monkeys and chimps and gorillas. Separated only by a thickness of glass, Chance would strain to draw his face close. Several young gorillas sat close by the glass and stared out at the sparse crowds. Chance called and bounced and tried to clap his hands together.

"Time to head home, little one," Annie said as she zippered up her coat and headed into the freshening breeze. The temperature had dropped a couple of degrees, so Annie hurried along the city blocks. Chance's face was nearly covered. Annie used the mirror to check behind her, and, halfway home, he was sound asleep.

She managed to walk the six blocks, climb the stairs, pull him out of the carrier, undress him down to his teeny long johns, and tuck him into the crib without him once waking up.

As he slept, Annie poured herself a cup of tea and sat by her big window, watching the snowflakes swirl and dance. Her legs and back were tired from the long walk, but she felt at peace and weary in a good way.

The Unfolding

Annie knew that Chance was teaching her more about theology than any hundred sermons she might hear on any hundred Sundays. Without doubt she now understood, to the core of her being, what adoption meant—and how God rejoices when one lost sheep returns. Feeling Chance's arms around her, Annie had a glimmer of God's unconditional love. And hearing his giggling laughter, she understood perhaps a small part of what joy awaits in heaven. When she read about joy and contentment and love and sacrifice in the Bible, she now knew what the words really meant.

She sipped at the warm drink. Petey the Cat climbed up onto the window seat and slowly settled into her lap and began to purr loudly.

From somewhere nearby, Annie heard the faint sounds of an Italian opera being played at full volume. She smiled and scratched at the cat's neck.

Life could not get much better than it was at that moment.

Thirteen

WINTER HAD FINALLY PASSED, and once again the leafy canopy over MacKenzie Street was in the first stages of greening. The street had lost most of the elm trees to disease, but a dozen or so remained, spreading and arcing over the sidewalk.

Annie yearned to throw open her windows and pack away her sweaters and blankets. Chance even appeared to get caught up in the desire for spring. When they went for walks in the stroller, he struggled and turned, and often, as they turned the first corner, he had his jacket unzipped or his sweater pulled up, baring his tummy to the not-quite chilly air.

The middle of April brought forth a week of unusually warm weather. Early flowers began to erupt from garden borders along wrought-iron fences and window boxes. There was a clean, crisp scent in the air.

Annie resolved once again to find some large planters to place in front of the laundromat. She wheeled past a garden center on North Avenue and noted sizes and prices and how much dirt she would need to buy.

"They say nature is free—but it doesn't seem like it here, does it, Chance?"

Chance pointed with great animation at a glasslike blue ball up on a cement pedestal. Annie smiled. As a child she had always wanted one of them for her front yard as well, but her parents had never once considered it.

"It would break in about two minutes, knowing how rough you play," her father had said harshly, splintering even that childish dream. . .as he had so many others.

"Yes—big blue ball, Chance." Annie laughed. She wheeled over next to it and let him see himself and touch the cool, smooth, metallic surface. But Chance was not content to merely touch it. He wanted to grab it and carry it and throw it. How much Chance was like her. Perhaps Annie's wanting to grab life with gusto is what had so thoroughly angered her dad about her. Her father had always lived life in a well-structured box—a box that Annie and her mother had never fit into for long. And because of that, he seemed continually disappointed in both of them.

Now Annie was the parent, and she struggled with Chance's desires every day—wanting to expose him to a myriad of sensations but constantly telling him "no" when he wanted to fully experience those same sensations. Had her father and mother experienced those same struggles with her and merely responded to them differently?

"Maybe I'll get one next year," she told him. "I think you might be a little too young."

Then again, where would I put it? I can't spend two hundred dollars on a garden ornament.

Chance began to wail as she backed away. He really wanted to hold the shiny blue ball.

"I know, Chance. Life is unfair. We see lots of things that look pretty and shiny, but that we can't have. It's just a part of life."

Her comments did little to quell his frustration. She hurried around the corner.

Maybe out of sight, out of mind.

But Chance's wails continued for another block with no sign of letup. She sighed to herself and wheeled into a small store.

"Hello, Annie." It was a friendly voice.

"Hello, Mr. Manos. Do you have a balloon you might spare?"

She had slipped into Stan and Leo's Authentic Chicago Deli, now owned by Peter Manos. Peter was a short man with close-cropped black hair. He was all but hidden by the display of meats and cheeses in the cooler.

"Sure thing, Annie."

"Chance saw one of those blue shiny balls at Merkets Garden Center. He wanted to take it with him. I'm hoping a balloon will distract him."

"Annie," Peter asked as he filled the blue balloon from a helium tank, "what are those things, anyhow? Just decoration?"

Annie laughed and shrugged. "I think so. That's all I ever see them used as. Maybe they're supposed to scare away crows."

Peter bent down to the stroller and handed Chance the string. The kind storeowner looped one end around the boy's wrist. "There you go, big boy. Have a nice balloon. And don't cry anymore. It bothers your pretty mother."

Annie knew Peter described every woman who walked into his deli as pretty. She was certain not one of them argued with his assessment.

As Annie walked toward home, she had to bob her head left and right as the balloon seemed intent on floating directly in front of her eyes. She smiled to herself. *Just a few months ago, I would have scorned the idea of giving Chance a balloon. First of all, they're not safe. And I never wanted to be one of those parents who simply took the easy way to placate a child.*

She waited for the light at Halsted Street.

But that was before I had a little boy. How things had changed in her life with the birth of this child, the child of her heart.

The balloon bounced up and down in the air and Chance giggled.

"Bawoon, bawoon, Mommy. Preddy bwue bawoon."

She smiled and crossed the street. And for some reason a chill grabbed at the base of her neck and spread its icy fingers down her spine. She shuddered, without wanting to, as if a dark, secret cloud had slipped in front of her son.

ᔕ   ᔕ   ᔕ

It was late in the afternoon. Chance had gone down for his afternoon nap. He was still napping twice a day. Annie figured that this day he was good for at least a couple of hours, since his morning nap had been shortened by the city's testing of the air raid/emergency sirens, located at the end of the block. After the sirens' wail had died down, a chorus of dog howls and barks had followed. A moment or two later Chance had joined in. It had made an already nervous morning more so.

Annie had been tense for several days—ever since their foray to the garden center—and could not, or would not, recognize the source. She sat in her office, filing paperwork, paying bills, and tidying up the office.

At first she imagined that her mind and her eyes were simply playing tricks on her due to too little sleep, too many worries about Chance. He had come down with what she imagined was a cold, and she had already worried his condition into full-blown asthma with seasonal allergies to boot. So the sight that flicked by had to be merely some sort of apparition.

She closed her eyes tightly, willing the image to disappear. She almost bowed her head in the effort. Then, slowly, she opened her eyes.

In that brief look she felt her heart stop—then begin to

pound with an erratic fury. . .as if it were a great fish, leaping and gasping on the shore, struggling furiously to return to the water and home and life and hope.

She blinked. The sight did not change. What she had seen from the corner of her eye was, in fact, reality.

A terrifying reality.

Standing on the corner, across the street, hands folded across her stomach, as if waiting for a bus or a friend, was Taylor Evans.

She seemed taller, more angular than Annie remembered. Her blond hair was even lighter, as if she had spent time in the sun. She was thinner. The last time Annie laid eyes on her, the girl was still rounded from giving birth. Now Annie was sure she could have seen her ribs, had they been exposed. Her jaw was harder, more pronounced. Her eyes were heavily outlined with makeup.

She looks like she stepped out of an Abercrombie and Fitch catalog.

Then Annie's heart thumped again.

What is she doing here?

Annie peered over her shoulder and up the stairs, almost without realizing why. Chance was up there, sound asleep, oblivious to the dangers of the outside world.

What is she doing here?

Annie stood up, her hands making weak circles, as if seeking out an action that might diffuse the situation. But immediately she realized there was nothing—absolutely nothing—that she could do.

She considered locking the office door and bolting straight upstairs.

But then what?

She considered calling. . .

Who? And why?

Her hand fell on her chest. She could feel the pulsing of her heart. She struggled to swallow. . .to take an even breath. . . to not cry or wail.

Taylor, from across the street, knew none of this, Annie was sure. She saw Annie staring and offered a shy, half-wave/half-nod, almost exactly like the greeting the first time the two women met, now nearly two years ago.

She's coming over here. Oh, no! She's crossing the street. Annie's thoughts leaped immediately into a prayer. *Oh, God, help me! She is coming here. Oh, God. . . .* Then her mind blanked out all words.

Annie forced herself—willed herself—to remain lucid and to give the appearance of calm. It was the hardest thing she had ever done in her entire life.

Taylor stepped into the laundromat slowly, as if the ground might contain a trapdoor or a land mine. Each step was deliberate and slow and cautious. It appeared as if a lifetime passed before Taylor tapped on the office door before sticking her head inside the small room.

"Hi," was all she said.

Annie tried to swallow again, but her throat was tight—noose tight. She nodded and tried to respond with an even "Hi." She wasn't sure if the word was audible or not.

Taylor slipped inside the office, her back flat against the wall. The heels of her platform shoes touched the molding around the floor.

"How are you?" she asked, her voice forced and lilting.

Annie took a breath. "Fine."

Taylor nodded. "And how's Chance? Or are you calling him Charles?"

Annie shook her head. "It's Chance. And he's doing well. He's napping right now. A big morning."

Taylor nodded in reply, as if it were two mothers comparing notes.

Annie wanted to scream or yell or jump out of her skin. Instead she exhaled sharply and asked, "Is school over? Are you on break?"

Taylor giggled awkwardly and looked away. She ran her fingers along the wood trim of the office window. "No. . .I mean, yeah, school's over, that's for sure. Yeah. . .and I guess I am on break. Sort of break, anyhow."

"How's Madison?"

Taylor's head jerked up. "Madison?"

"You went to Madison to be with your boyfriend, didn't you?"

She grinned in an odd way. "Oh, yeah. Madison. That's right. Madison is cool. I like Madison."

"You look thin."

Taylor's smile was almost genuine. "Oh, yeah. Thanks. I don't eat as well as I did when I was with you."

Annie crossed her arms over her chest. Outside she

could hear the bells of an ice cream truck a block over. Chance loved ice cream. She prayed he would not wake up.

Annie looked hard at Taylor, who was wearing a thin, old suede jacket the color of butter. But she was carrying a new Prada purse, the kind of bag Annie had only seen in magazines and fancy store catalogs. *Why the disparity?* Annie wondered.

"Taylor, why are you here?"

Taylor appeared surprised—but not by the question. Anyone would have expected the question to arise over her appearance. But perhaps the surprise was due to how soon the question was spoken out loud. Annie herself had imagined a conversation lasting at least a dozen minutes before the question arose.

"Why I'm here. . ."

Annie did not retreat. "Yes. Why did you come back to Chicago? You said you were gone forever. You wrote those very words in the note you left me."

Taylor averted her eyes again, staring into the open room of the laundromat.

Two Hispanic men sat in the yellow and red plastic chairs by the window reading the Spanish newspaper, waiting for their coveralls to dry. A truck from North Side Beer Distributors parked on the opposite side of the street; and the driver, a compact, burly man, jumped out, clipboard in hand, and headed into the Sportsman Tavern.

When Taylor turned back this time, her face had hardened. With a tense jaw and narrowed eyes, she leaned forward. "I want him back."

"You want who back, Taylor?"

"You know who. I came back to take Chance with me."

Annie hesitated. It was a question she anticipated answering a thousand times—but until this moment, that reality seemed a thousand years away. She paused and considered any one of a hundred different, rehearsed replies. None of them now felt right.

Instead she simply said, "No."

"No?"

"No. You can't have him. You gave him up. You abandoned him. You don't get him back. You left. I stayed. No. You don't get a second chance."

Taylor waited, as if expecting that response. "Listen, Annie. What I did was stupid. I was young and scared. I didn't know any better. I didn't. I didn't have anyone to talk to. Motherhood just looked so hard. I didn't think I could keep him. No one said I should keep him. It's not my fault I ran away."

To Annie, it felt as if each word had been carefully rehearsed. As if someone had worked hard behind the scenes to give Taylor this script. This was certainly not the Taylor she'd known and befriended for all those months. The Taylor who had never once wanted to talk with Annie about other options, such as adoption. The Taylor who had simply assumed, from the very beginning, that she would become a teen parent. Then, after the birth, who had merely wanted to be again the teenager. Who, when the responsibility of a young baby became too much, abandoned Chance and took off, leaving him in Annie's care.

"I mean it, Annie. I didn't know anyone here. I was young. Underage. And scared. What else would anyone expect me to do? Derrik said I had no choice."

Annie's arms remained folded. Her fists were clenched. "No."

"Derrik says I should get him back. He says it will be cool to have a little one around. He says his parents will help us with money and all. They might even let us have one of the cabins on the other side of the lake. It's real pretty up there and, like, it's real private for parties and stuff."

"No."

Taylor wrinkled her brow. It was obvious she was frustrated with Annie's repeated answer. "You can't just keep saying no, Annie. I mean, he is my son and all that. You've just been like a foster parent to him. You know, I bet you could get reimbursed for all the money you spent—like from the state or something. Derrik says they pay pretty well."

"No, Taylor. You're not getting him back. You abandoned him."

Taylor looked like she was about to stamp her foot. "No, I didn't. I was young and scared, and you made it sound so hard to be a mother. As if you had to be perfect. But now I know better, and I want him back. And Derrik says we'll go to court if we have to. And you'll lose. They don't take babies away from their mothers. Not in Chicago."

"No. Go to court, Taylor. But you're not showing up a year and a half later and asking for your baby back. It doesn't work like that. Go to court. They'll see who the mother is. They'll see who did all the work of raising him. Go to court. But you're not getting him back."

Taylor scowled in reply. It seemed whatever responses she might have planned were now lost in a jumble of anger. She jutted out her bottom lip in a pout. "Then I *will* go to court. I want him back. Derrik—he's the *father*—he wants him back. And his parents will help us. We can support him. I mean, I won't have to work like you do. We want him back. And we will go to court, Annie. Derrik says it's real easy to take someone to court. So we will, Annie. We will."

And with that, Taylor stomped out of the office and the laundromat, ignoring possible trapdoors or land mines.

It was only when she disappeared out of sight that Annie unclenched her fists. Inside both palms were four crescents of blood, her nails having pierced the skin.

Annie wobbled for a minute, then let herself fall back into her chair.

And she began to sob.

§　　§　　§

A short while later—Annie was never sure how long—she heard the smallest of cries from upstairs. Wiping her tears away with the back of her hand, Annie bounded up the stairs.

Chance was standing in his crib, holding on to the rail, and bouncing at the knees. He was crying, but not passionately.

"Mommy!" he cried when she came into the room.

She picked him up and held him to her chest, holding him tighter and longer than normal.

"Mommy, Mommy," he said loudly into her ear. "Winnie da Pooh on. Winnie."

Annie leaned him back. "He is? Do you want to watch him?"

He nodded vigorously and smiled.

"And do you want chocolate milk too?"

"Yes! Yes!"

"In your Mickey Mouse sippy cup?"

He held his hands above his head like a victorious prize-fighter and shouted, "Yes, Mommy, yes!"

In a split-second he was seated on the floor, by his favorite pillow. Petey the Cat kept watch over him, hoping against hope that Chance would drop his milk. That the cup would break and the feline could have a taste as well. Such an event had never once happened, but Annie was sure that Petey, despite his outwardly disgruntled state, was an eternal optimist at heart. The television hummed and Annie, in a stupor, wandered into the kitchen.

She tried to make a cup of instant coffee, but the simple logistics were too overwhelming. So instead she fell into a chair and cradled her head in her hands. She could stop no thought; she could control no image in her mind. Tears threatened again, and she willed them to stop.

Chance had seen Annie cry at the end of a sad movie once. And, at the sight of her tears, Chance too had begun to wail and was inconsolable for half an hour. She knew it would upset him again, so she sniffed loudly and kept her eyes closed and dry.

She thought of calling her father but quickly rejected the idea. Since that Christmas almost a year and a half ago, they had spoken only once, on his birthday, when she had phoned him. She tried her best to be forgiving and understanding. She knew it was the right thing to do. She knew what it was to be forgiven, and she wanted her father to know it too. It proved less successful than Annie had hoped. Her father had been so abrupt that the conversation had been over in less than three minutes. It was clear he did not want a relationship of any kind with her. She could never ask him for money, nor did she think he would offer any to her.

She thought of calling Pastor Yount, then stopped. The pastor was kind at heart and would be able to provide sympathy, but he would not do anything to stop what Annie slowly began to feel as inevitable—the loss of Chance. And even as she thought of it, it felt as though she had stepped into quicksand and was slowly sinking into the mire, an inch at a time. There was no way to extricate herself from the ooze.

And as that thought erupted in her mind's eye, she felt the tears come again. This time she could not stop them. They splashed silent on the table for a number of minutes.

"More chocolo milk, please."

She stood and wiped the tears away, trying not to let Chance see her face as she took the cup from his hand.

I could sell the laundromat and run, she thought as she poured the milk.

But a sale would take months. She didn't have enough money to attempt to take Chance and vanish.

She would not run. She knew that. Even though every fiber in her body wanted to do just that—to clutch Chance to her chest and run until no one could find them—she knew she would not.

Why? Because it would be a violation of the very truth that she believed in—that her mother had believed in. A violation of the faith she had come to believe in again personally, after the gift of Chance—the gift that had kept her spirit alive since his birth.

No. She would have to stay. And she would have to trust God to show her what to do next. She'd have to trust Him with the outcome. Trust Him with the person she loved the most.

But what do I do? Do I know any attorneys? Who would know an attorney? Most people around here only use them for immigration matters or wills.

She placed the cup in Chance's hand. He smiled but did not take his eyes away from the dancing and laughing puppets on the screen.

"Tanks," he said and immediately began to slurp at the milk.

Do I ask my friends to pray?

She and Mrs. Alvarez had spoken of prayer just the other day.

"I don't go to the same church as you, Annie," the older woman had said, laughing. "I don't think the hours are the same. But don't you think God would listen to me if I talked about you?"

Knowing the outspoken, quirky, but good-hearted Mrs. Alvarez, Annie had laughed then too. But now she realized that God, over the past year, had slowly become personal to her. He wasn't just some God "out there" whom she called upon merely for religious or social occasions. No, He was a God who wanted a relationship—who wanted people to talk with Him, share their thoughts with Him.

So, God, she prayed. *What do I pray about? And what words do I use?*

The heavens seemed silent, but familiar words began to fall easily from her lips.

"Our Father. . .who art in heaven. . ."

And through her silent sobs, she prayed, asking that Chance would never see her cry again.

Fourteen

ANNIE WAS LOST AND scared. She considered a hundred different options, then rejected each within moments. There was no "best" thing to do. There wasn't even a worst thing.

She considered calling Pastor Yount, then discarded the idea. Then she considered it again. He was the only person who knew the particulars of the situation and would be honest with her. He would be able to help her, she concluded. If she collapsed in tears, he was used to that, and he would hold her hand and make sure that the right thing was done.

Finally she made the call, and he agreed to help in any way possible.

"So you're Mr. Manos's son-in-law?" Pastor Yount asked

the next day as he escorted the young man and Annie into his office.

Nickolas Manos nodded and slid a business card from the breast pocket of his sportcoat. Annie noted that it was badly in need of a cleaning and pressing—but she held her tongue.

Beggars can't be choosers, she told herself. *And he comes highly recommended. Pete Manos says he has represented dozens of restaurant owners in the neighborhood. And he says he never once lost a court fight with the Department of Sanitation. And he let his daughter marry the man.*

"I am. I know the last name is the same. And I didn't take my wife's last name—it was my name first. Manos is a pretty common name in Greece. Like Smith or Johnson."

Pastor Yount chuckled. "I was wondering. And I bet you get asked that a lot."

Nickolas settled into one of the office chairs by the pastor's desk and picked a piece of lint off his trousers. He was a thin, careful man, almost wiry. Annie was sure he had a gold chain around his neck, hidden by his seldom-worn tie.

He could spend all afternoon doing that, and it wouldn't make much of a difference. Annie, always the laundromat owner, couldn't stop her thoughts.

"You know Annie asked if the three of us could meet," Pastor Yount began. "I know that might be a bit unusual."

Nickolas shrugged. "Father, I'm a lawyer whose clients are in the restaurant business. Most of my meetings are in kitchens, where I try not to let my briefcase fall into the deep fat fryer. This ain't a bad change."

Pastor Yount folded his hands together. "Annie thought it would be good to have a third party in this meeting. So she wouldn't forget to ask an important question."

Nickolas, for a moment, forgot the lint on his trousers and smoothed his hand through his dark, oily hair. "That's a good idea, Annie. I tell you, most of my time is spent explaining things I already explained. And each extra word costs the clients money, you know."

"I'm glad you offered Annie your help," the pastor said graciously.

When Nickolas smiled, Annie saw the glint of a silver filling.

"It's a favor to my father-in-law. I like to help out too. When I can, you know?"

Annie was doing her best to remain calm. Her world had threatened to spin out of control since Taylor's return. In the following week, Annie could hardly eat or sleep.

"And Annie told you what had happened?"

"Yep. She has the kid for a year and a half and *slam!* All of a sudden the real mother comes asking for him. No official papers at all in this one—not even a handshake. Everybody knows it ain't Annie's kid, but no one says a word—or tells anyone about it."

The pastor cleared his throat in a self-conscious way. "You mean the authorities?"

"Yeah. Like the DCFS people. Or Social Services. No one tells no one nothing."

"That is right, Annie?" the pastor clarified.

Annie could only nod to the pastor's question.

"Now I ain't a high-priced Michigan Avenue attorney," Nickolas admitted.

And I couldn't afford it if you were, Annie thought.

With the extra doctor's bills and clothes and equipment for Chance, Annie's budget had been strained as hard as the strained peas in the boy's lunch. Annie cursed the fact that she had never set much money aside for a rainy day. She had never anticipated Chance. She discovered that you can shower a child with love—but it takes money to support him. The amount of money the laundromat generated would not increase dramatically in the future. Annie found that the standard of living it allowed her was adequate, but she seldom went to the doctor, she seldom grew out of an outfit, she seldom grew too large for a crib. Babies do.

With Chance, she had enough—but not near enough for a polished and practiced attorney. She had cried with relief, right in the deli, when Pete Manos told her that his son-in-law, who had heard about Annie's plight, had offered to represent her at half his normal billing rate.

"But even though I ain't Michigan Avenue, I know as much as they do, Annie," Nickolas continued. "I hate to be so cold 'cause I know you love this little boy and all, but you ain't got a snowball's chance in—well, you know."

Annie swallowed, stunned and silent.

Pastor Yount leaned forward, scowling at the attorney. "But Annie is a wonderful mother. Everybody says that. I can't believe that doesn't count for something."

Nickolas shrugged, his palms facing the ceiling. "It counts that Annie is a good person. I ain't heartless. I see that. My father-in-law says she's the salt of the earth. But being a nice person and a good mom ain't going to change the facts. I'm sorry, but it don't look good. And as your lawyer, I need to be honest with you about that."

Annie was numb. She was more than numb. These were the words she had known, deep in her soul, that someone would utter someday. She had known that since the day Taylor left and she had kept Chance. She had known. . .and yet had refused to hear them.

Pastor Yount eyed Annie. He must have seen the tears in her eyes, for he renewed his argument. "But isn't there *something* that can be done? Doesn't she have any rights in this? Taylor left a letter. Annie's raised the boy for a year and a half."

Nickolas shook his head. "That's awful nice of her—but the boy weren't hers to raise. When the mother left, according to what law books I read—it's somebody's responsibility to let somebody know. Annie should have told somebody."

Nickolas turned to Annie. She had not yet said a word.

"You knew the baby weren't yours, right?"

Annie nodded.

"And you knew you should tell someone. You even told your pastor here not to tell anyone. That right, Annie?"

"Yes," she answered in a small, wavering voice.

"And you know that somebody should decide if the baby goes to a foster home and all that, right?"

Annie replied, "Yes."

Nickolas turned back to the pastor. "Hey, I could stretch things a little. But some smart lawyer—even some dumb lawyer from the district attorney's office—would send you a summons in about five minutes." The attorney narrowed his eyes at the pastor. "And you wouldn't be able to lie under oath, would you?"

The pastor leaned back as if struck. "Could I say it was a privileged conversation?"

Nickolas shrugged. "You could. But it wouldn't work. Everybody on the jury—and the judge—would know you were lying out of your socks. And from what my father-in-law says, half the old ladies in the neighborhood knew everything about this as well. You think it's hard to make a grandmother confess? It ain't. Any lawyer could have those old biddies singing like a canary. Everybody would be saying they knew all about everything and didn't do a thing. It would all fall on Annie's head. Then they could throw the book at her."

"Annie could get in trouble?" The pastor appeared surprised.

Annie's eyes widened, but only a little.

Nickolas snorted. "Get in trouble? Pastor, Annie is already in trouble. She knew right from wrong and she done the wrong thing. Trouble is already here, my friend. Now I'm hoping we can get her out of that trouble."

Done the wrong thing. The words seemed to echo, over and over again, in Annie's mind. How often she had asked herself—and others—if she had done the right thing. Now she knew the truth, and it was cold. . .hard. But it had everything to do with a little boy she had loved ever since his entrance into the world.

A tense silence permeated the room. Pastor Yount inhaled deeply, as if building up courage. "And the boy? Is there any chance she can keep him?"

Nickolas peered at the pastor, then at Annie.

Annie could feel the cascade of tears down her cheeks.

"I ain't pulling any punches, Annie. I don't give hope when there ain't any. You could refuse to let social services in and hold the boy behind locked doors, but they could bust 'em down. And how would that look? Then you could get charged with obstructing justice."

"What about restraining orders? Don't they always get restraining orders?" The pastor offered a lopsided smile, as if it were a legal trick that only he was aware of.

"Nah," Nickolas replied. "I mean, I could file for one, but based on what I know, you'd be laughed out of court. I mean, them big corporations get them all the time—but most of the time, the cases ain't all that clear-cut. This one is. It ain't her baby. No DNA tests needed. She admits it. So does everyone else. There ain't nothing to restrain."

The attorney paused, as if unwilling to continue. "I ain't lying. You can't keep him, Annie. You go to court, and you'll lose the case in about two minutes. It's a done deal."

Silence returned.

"I'm sorry, Annie. I really am," the attorney said, his voice nicked with tenderness.

In that moment, Annie knew why Pete Manos trusted Nickolas enough to allow him to marry his daughter. Nickolas might be a little rough around the edges, but it was clear he was straightforward. And that he had a good heart.

Everyone always said Annie had a good heart too. Otherwise, why would she have taken in Taylor? And, later, her child?

But no amount of "good heart" could save this situation—or Chance—it seemed.

Annie burst into tears.

ᔕ   ᔕ   ᔕ

Annie was in tears for a long time that day. She cried as Nickolas left; she cried as Pastor Yount went out to find coffee; she cried when he came back and offered her the handkerchief from his sportcoat pocket.

Finally she took a series of deep breaths and sniffed loudly. She wiped the sodden handkerchief across her eyes. "I'm okay, Pastor, I really am. I just. . .I don't know. . .I thought it would. . ."

Pastor Yount took her hands in his. "I know, Annie. We all did."

She blinked up at him, touched by his compassion. She knew then she had misjudged him in the past.

"Will you need help?" he asked softly.

"Help?" she asked.

"With packing?"

She sniffed again. "Packing? I. . .I don't. . ."

"Mr. Manos. . .the documents you gave him? The material that the sheriff delivered?" he prodded gently.

"Yes," Annie replied, her voice cracking.

"There was a court order. That's what they served you yesterday. That summons from Cook County?"

She could hardly manage to speak. "Packing?"

"The summons says you need to have Chance ready tonight. Representatives from DCFS are coming. He'll be placed in a foster home—a good foster home—until the court can decide what's in the child's best interests."

"Pack?"

"You have to pack his bag, Annie. Clothes. Some toys. They'll be there, he said, around six."

"Pack?"

Annie appeared to have lost all power of cogent speech.

"You have to get him ready, Annie." At these words, the pastor began to choke up as well. "You need to be ready to say good-bye."

And with that, Annie began to sob again—at first softly, heartfelt, then with total abandon.

§   §   §

Mrs. Alvarez, who was watching Chance while Annie met with the pastor, brought Chance upstairs. If asked, the older woman would have said that this was her darkest day, even darker than the day she buried both her parents.

"I heard, Annie. Pete Manos is a nice man, but he talks too much. He told me what his son-in-law said."

Annie could only nod. Chance smiled and giggled as she held him. Then she put him down and he scurried off toward the television.

"Clifford!" he shouted and settled against the couch to watch.

"If there was something I could do, Annie, you know I would," the older lady said softly as she took Annie's hand and squeezed it.

"You've done so much already," Annie whispered.

"If there is anything. . ."

Annie looked at her old friend, the person who had "been there" for her consistently since she'd moved into the apartment over the laundromat. Then she looked over at Chance. "There is one thing," she whispered.

"Anything, my sweet one."

"Pack his bag." In spite of her efforts not to cry in front of Chance, Annie began to sob quietly again. "I thought about it all the way home, and I know I can't do it. I can't pick up his little shirts and shorts and fold them and put them in a bag, knowing that I'll never see him again. Everything I would touch would remind me too much of him. I can't do it, Mrs. Alvarez."

Mrs. Alvarez's arms wrapped tightly around Annie. "I can do it, Annie. I picked out clothes for my mother and father before their funeral. I can do this. I can do this for you. . .and for him. Go sit with him now. Hold him—and remember every second of this. Hold him, Annie. I'll go pack for you."

Mrs. Alvarez made her way into the bedroom. She came out a moment later, holding a dark green bag. "This okay?"

Annie shook her head yes, then walked to Chance and sat down beside him. The glow of the television filled the room with a dancing blue light. Annie slipped her hand around the toddler's shoulders and gently snuggled him toward her. He gurgled as she did and let himself be molded against her. She felt his warmth. She felt his heart beating. She listened to him breathe. She stroked his fine blond hair, smoothing it back.

Pretty soon he'll need a haircut. It will be his first. I wonder if he'll cry?

Annie closed her eyes, knowing that she would not be near him when his first haircut occurred. She would not know if he cried or fussed or sat there, in the big chair, like a little soldier. She would not have a lock of his hair to save forever in a white envelope.

She gasped.

He'll be gone by tonight. The thought struck her like a physical blow.

She held him close to her, and he rested his hand across her stomach.

Clifford and his friends continued on their adventures, oblivious to the sound of a woman's heart breaking and shattering.

Mrs. Alvarez came out of the room. The green bag was

full. She carried a small plush rabbit, holding a carrot. It was one of his favorites.

Annie could not speak—just stared at the rabbit.

The bell from the front door sounded.

"It's time," Mrs. Alvarez said softly.

Annie picked Chance up and squeezed him. "Clifford is over now, Chance. And now you have to go for a ride."

Chance pushed away from her embrace. "You come?"

Annie shook her head. "Not this time, Chance. I can't go with you right now."

Then she tried to smile and tapped at his chest, just above his heart. "Remember, no matter what happens and no matter where you are, remember that Mommy loves you very, very much."

"Mommy loves me here?" Chance asked, tapping at his tummy. It was a game that never failed to amuse him.

Annie smiled. "Yes, Mommy loves there too."

Before Chance could spend the next ten minutes pointing to every part of his body, Annie stopped him. "And remember that Jesus loves you too. He will always love you. Remember what I told you about Jesus."

"I 'member," Chance said. He bowed his head and folded his hands, just as Annie had taught him. "Jesus. I pray."

"That's right, Chance," she said as she made her way toward the steps. Mrs. Alvarez followed, tears streaming down her face.

At the bottom of the steps, Annie peered out. A hubbub of people gathered around her door. To her left were two television cameras. Across the street, a trio of television trucks were lined up, their antennas tilted into the evening air.

"Miss Hamilton," a voice cried out. "Are you giving up this baby against your will?"

"Did you know the birth mother was coming back?"

"Are you going to sue the birth mother over her abandonment?"

From Annie's right, Nickolas Manos sidled up. "I'm Miss Hamilton's attorney, and she can't answer any of your questions right now. This is a very hard, very emotional time for her. Can't you see that?"

He sounded angry and perturbed, even though Annie was certain Nickolas was the one who had called the reporters in the first place. Parked by the curb was a dark four-door sedan. Small white letters on the door read, "For use by Department of Children and Family Services."

A large black man in an ill-fitting white shirt stood holding a file folder. A very thin woman with dark hair cut in a short, almost severe style stood next to him.

It was the woman who spoke first—and loudly, above the cacophony. "Annie Hamilton?"

"Yes," Annie replied.

"Is that Charles Evans? The son of Taylor Evans?"

"It is. I call him Chance, though. Everyone calls him Chance. He's such a good boy."

Chance stared all around him. He had never seen such a mélange of lights and people and microphones and sharply angled people.

"I am Betty Tyrone from the Illinois Department of Children and Family Services. We have a court order to take Charles Evans and to place him in a state-approved foster home until his mother can have her case on parental rights heard in a Cook County courtroom."

Annie increased her grip on Chance.

"Do you understand?"

Annie wanted to snap back that she was not a simpleton—just a woman whose whole life was being grabbed out of her arms by some nameless, shapeless, and, apparently, unthinking bureaucracy.

Instead she replied, "I understand."

The woman nodded back to the large black man, who tossed the file folder into the front seat. He stepped close to Annie and held out his arms.

Chance began to wail, as if suddenly realizing what was about to happen. Panicked, he grabbed at Annie, holding onto her blouse and her arm and her hair. He began to thrash and cry out.

"Chance," Annie called to him. "It's okay. Just remember what I taught you. Remember what I said."

Chance stopped his thrashing. " 'Member you always wuv me?"

Annie nodded. "More than anything in the world."

"And Jesus wuvs me?"

"Always and forever."

"Okay, Mom, I 'member them. But I not go. I stay with you."

She squeezed him one last time. "You can't, Sweetest. You have to go now."

Two cameras jostled beside her. As Annie glanced sideways, she saw the broad smiles of the reporters. They were capturing heart-wrenching footage.

She kissed Chance once on the cheek and once on the forehead. Then she placed him as gently as she could into the meaty arms of the large government man.

Her hands folded over her heart to keep it from bursting out of her chest.

"Mommy! Mommy!" Chance cried as the two of them slipped into the backseat. She saw his green bag disappear into the car's darkened interior.

Then Mrs. Alvarez pushed through the crowd, holding the plush bunny with the carrot. "This is his favorite toy. You make sure he has it," she shouted at the man in the backseat.

"I'll do that, Ma'am. You don't worry about this bunny no more, Ma'am. I'll see that he has it," he said, and his voice told Annie that he was a man of his word.

The car lurched from the curb.

Annie heard Chance shout again. "Mommy! Mommy! I wuv you!"

Then he was gone.

The television cameras followed the car as it sped down the block. When it slipped from view, they all arced backward, training their lenses on Annie, who was trying to memorize everything about her son before he was truly gone.

"So, Miss Hamilton, what does it feel like to have given

him up? How are you feeling right now?"

Annie stared at the woman who was wearing much too much makeup and hairspray. Annie would have preferred to have struck her in some way or to have passed just a fraction of the pain Annie was enduring into her heart.

Instead she pivoted away from the reporters and ran upstairs.

But in her apartment the rooms were quiet and still and dark, save the blue glow of the television as the Teletubbies now danced and sang and laughed into a room devoid of all childish laughter. To Annie it felt as if all the air had been sucked out of the space, leaving it cold and lifeless.

Annie began to walk slowly from room to room—touching the crib, running her finger over a stuffed animal, picking up one of his dozens of nubby blankets. She held it to her chest.

Petey the Cat came out of his closet, blinking his eyes. He stretched and sat on his haunches and looked around, sniffing. He stared up at Annie and cried softly, as if asking her where that small person had disappeared to.

"He's gone, Petey. The little boy is gone forever."

The cat cried once more, and Annie breathed out a sob. She carried Chance's blanket with her to the couch and collapsed there, staring out at the black and cloudless sky. . .her heart too numb to even petition the heavens.

Fifteen

ON ANY OTHER DAY any number of customers at the laundromat would have come up to Annie, smiling, and told her they saw her on television last night. She had even made the news on both Spanish newscasts, at six and at ten. Her customers would have done so—if the reason Annie had been televised was even remotely happy.

But anyone who watched the short segment saw the heartbreak in Annie's eyes and the pleading cries of Chance as he called out for his mother. The audio alone was enough to send a shudder down any parent's spine.

Annie shuffled downstairs the following morning—not because she wanted to work but because she needed to escape from upstairs. She needed to escape the ghosts and echoes that filled the rooms. Chance had inhabited every corner of her apartment, leaving a trail of toys and clothes and, in some cases, stains.

Each spot was now a painful memory to Annie, and she could neither bear to look at his things nor pick them up and pack them away. She knew she could not summon the energy even to walk across the street, though she wanted so much to escape. Instead of running, she managed to brew a cup of instant coffee and slump down at her desk in the office and stare outside at the leaden sky.

Sometime around noon Annie heard a soft tap on the glass. It was Hermes Diegos.

"I saw, Miss Annie," he said, grief in his large liquid-brown eyes. "I saw last night. I saw it and I saw how sad you were."

"Thanks," she replied wearily.

"Will the boy go to his birth mother now?"

Annie could only shrug.

"Miss Annie, I do not know how bad you feel. I never lost a child. But I pray for you. I pray all night for you as I work. God takes care of you. He will. I pray that He will."

Annie put her hand to her trembling lips. She didn't want to cry again. She hoped she could hold it back. "Thank you," she replied as he slowly went back to his washer.

God may provide. . .but why did He give me Chance if all He was going to do was take him away? It's not fair, God. It's not fair, and You have no right to call Yourself loving and kind. Taking away a baby like this—it's not loving. It isn't.

She sighed and closed her eyes. She had spent nearly all night arguing with God, explaining to Him how He had made the mistake, taking Him to task for poor planning and horrible execution as the sky grew black, then light again.

And she kept repeating the harsh, accusing words even now. . .even if it felt like He was no longer listening. In the midst of her pain, she wanted to trust God to help her, but it was so hard.

God. . .please help. You promised You would help. Please keep Your promise.

A few minutes later, she heard another tapping at the window—this time faster, more pronounced, with the metallic click of a ring striking the plate glass.

"Miss Hamilton," Nickolas Manos called out. "You are famous! I think every station carried you last night. They all are calling me for interviews. Even the national networks called me. Me! Nickolas Manos."

Annie shut her eyes. Now she knew for sure that Nickolas had called the reporters. So it had been a way to make a reputation for him, she thought. Annie blinked away the pain of betrayal. How could Nickolas care so little about the pain she was feeling? She wanted to stand up, to strike him for his callousness. But she was simply too soul-weary.

"I'm not going to speak to any of them," she said quietly, with a controlled edge to her voice.

Nickolas was about to speak when her eyes flashed, diamond cold and cutting. Annie's eyes made it perfectly clear that there would be no interviews—not today, not *ever*.

The attorney sighed loudly in resignation. "Your call, Annie. But I tell you, there might be a way."

She turned to face him. He had baited her—baited her with a lure she could not refuse.

Maybe she was wrong. Maybe Nickolas Manos was a smarter attorney than she thought. He was a most skilled manipulator of people.

"A way? A way to do what?"

Nickolas pulled a battered vinyl chair into the office and spun it backward to sit down. "Listen: Everyone saw you last night. I bet every mother in Chicago was crying along with you. They all hated them for what they did to you."

"So?"

"You know, judges watch the news too. You go talk to these reporters. The public is on your side. It's the only chance we have. It's why I phoned those reporters in the first place. Had a brainstorm in the middle of the night. You tell them how bad of a girl this Taylor was. A tramp, you tell them. You tell them she slept around—even while she was living here. You tell them how terrible she was—and would be as a mother. That she had written you a letter, putting you in charge of the baby. And maybe. . .I ain't saying that whoever gets to be judge of this case would disregard legal stuff and testimony and all, but he'll hear what you say, Annie. He'll hear how the public views it too. Annie, this could be our chance. *Your* chance, Annie. You could have him back! I feel it! It could work."

Annie rubbed her hand over her eyes. Her heart and her mind had diverged—but only for a moment. She knew what her answer had to be. It was the only answer.

"No, Mr. Manos."

"No? No to what? You want me to tell them? I can do that. But it's better coming from you. I ain't lying, Annie. They'll eat it up like a cat with milk!"

"No, Mr. Manos," she insisted. "I can't do that. I can't do that to Chance—or to Taylor. It would be lying. I just can't. I have to tell the truth."

Nickolas adjusted the sleeves of his shirt, pulling them out from under his sportcoat. "Annie, you're making a mistake. If you did this, it could make a difference. You might be able to get the boy back."

Annie's heart jumped at the very words. She felt like a fish trying to strike at a shiny lure for the second time.

I could get him back!

But she shook her head. "It would all be a lie. I can't do it."

"You sure about that?" Obviously Mr. Manos was disappointed. Did he really care about her getting Chance back? Annie wondered. Or did he just want to get in front of the cameras again? Or was it a little of both?

"I'm sure. And you can't say anything either. I won't lie about Taylor. And you can't lie about her either on my behalf."

He shrugged. "It was worth a shot, Annie. That's what they pay me for—to be a lawyer. Sometimes the things that might just work—nobody wants to try. It's okay by me, Annie. I still like you. You're a good person. My father-in-law was right. Quality, he says, always comes through. But if you change your mind, I can make a few calls."

"If I did do what you asked," Annie began. "If I told them Taylor was a bad person, could she lose parental rights?"

Nickolas held up his palms. "I ain't a judge, but it could happen. Yeah, it could."

"And if she didn't get custody, would the courts give Chance back to me?"

Nickolas stared hard at Annie. She saw him thinking, calculating. Then his gaze softened, as if in resignation. "Probably not. Like I said, I ain't a judge, but I bet they would let him stay in foster care before they gave him back to you. If you were rich or if you were married—then the story might be different."

Annie knew the condition of her bank account. And the only man she could have remotely considered, at least recently, for the position of married partner had not called her in months. She thought there had been promise with Daniel, but she must have thought wrong. Just as she had thought wrong that Chance would be in her life forever.

"I'm neither of those, Mr. Manos. I guess I wish I was both right now."

Nickolas shrugged. "Annie, making Taylor look bad might have helped—but I couldn't say for positive and absolute it would."

The attorney stood, brushed off his lapels, and nodded to Annie.

"Mr. Manos, thank you for trying your best to help, but I don't want to say anything bad about Taylor. She is Chance's mother, after all. I don't want him to hear lies about his mother, and I know he would find out about it someday. And I can't take the chance that he might spend the rest of his life in foster homes. Better with his mother, despite her faults, rather than with strangers. I have to trust God to take care of him." Annie heard the words coming out of her mouth, and she hoped they were true. She'd been so upset with God in the past day that she hadn't been able to pray.

Mr. Manos smoothed his lapels again. "The district attorney just set a court date for this—two weeks from today. They said it's going to be a bench hearing, with just the judge doing the deciding. You'll be around?"

"I'll be around. Do I have to go?"

"Be better if you did. You probably won't be convicted for holding onto the kid and not saying anything. But who knows what the DA will do? They may want to make an example out of you. Better if you were there to explain how it all went down."

Annie sighed. She couldn't remember ever being this bone-weary. Not even on the nights when it seemed that Chance, as a tiny baby, hardly slept.

"I can be there."

The attorney turned to leave. Then he hesitated. "You going to be okay, Annie? You want me to. . .I don't know. . . to get something for you? Call somebody?"

"No, but thanks. I think I'll be fine." Annie knew she did not lie well.

Nickolas tapped his forehead in an odd salute, then slipped out.

Annie was left, sitting in her office, with only the quiet hum of a pair of dryers to break the oppressive silence that now hung heavy in her life.

§   §   §

After talking with Nickolas Manos and Pastor Yount, Annie decided to go to court alone. If she brought an attorney with her, she was sure the judge would think she really needed one.

Nickolas Manos warned her not to expect to see the boy there. "Judges don't like kids in the courtroom. Even if they're part of the trial. Makes 'em think too much about what they're doing, if you ask me."

"Will Taylor be there?"

Mr. Manos nodded. "Probably just her, the boyfriend, and the DA. Or maybe people from the public defender's office. But I know there's probably not going to be a single reporter there. It's been two weeks since they took the boy. We're not hot news anymore. And since you don't want to stir up the press anymore, I'm not calling them. Besides, I get too many clients as it is. I don't need more publicity."

§   §   §

Two weeks later, Annie, dressed in her best conservative outfit, walked into court. She could not bring herself to look directly at Taylor or her boyfriend. From the corner of her eye, she saw that Taylor had trimmed her hair. She looked older, more adult now. Her boyfriend apparently chose not to impress the judge with his clothing; he wore a blue denim jacket that needed laundering. His hair was long in back and short in front, a style not in fashion in decades except with a certain roughneck culture. He slouched behind the table, whereas Taylor and their attorney sat bolt upright, hands folded in front.

Annie had seen trials on television, but this was nothing like what she expected. The judge and attorney droned through what felt like hours of preliminary reports and findings by social services and court-appointed psychologists.

It was nearly lunch when the bailiff called out Annie's name. Her eyes caught Taylor's for just an instant. Surprisingly, Taylor looked scared and confused.

For two weeks Annie had rehearsed her story. So when the judge asked to recount the events, Annie did so in a simple, unemotional way.

"Did you think Taylor was a good mother?"

Annie hesitated. She wanted to bite her lip. She wanted to look away. Instead she glanced at Taylor for a heartbeat, then at the judge. "Your Honor, Taylor was young and very scared when she came to Chicago. She didn't know a soul. I saw her with the baby."

Taylor closed her eyes, as if waiting to be struck.

"She did a fine job with him, Your Honor. She was scared, but she did fine."

"So, in your opinion," the judge queried, "she'll be a good mother?"

Annie forced herself to nod. "I think she will. She ran because she thought she was in trouble. Her father threw her out. She had no family. I think the fear overwhelmed her."

Annie was aware that the judge watched her closely as she

spoke. She hoped her words and demeanor were convincing, because it was true. Annie believed that Taylor wasn't a bad person—just young and unsure of herself.

"I think she'll be a great mother," Annie concluded. "I really do." And with this last statement, Annie tried to smile at Taylor. Once again surprise—and now relief and perhaps disbelief?—registered on Taylor's face.

"What I did, Your Honor, wasn't right. I know that now. I love the child, but I won't fight for custody. The boy's mother should have her child." Annie's throat tightened when she said "the boy." She knew that if she uttered his name, she would begin to cry. And once she started crying, she would not be able to stop.

I have to keep this clinical.

There were a few more questions, then Annie was excused. The judge called the case closed and said he would issue a ruling by the end of the week. Annie waited in the courtroom, staring straight ahead, as Taylor and her boyfriend shuffled past. Neither of them said anything to her as they went by.

Annie sat for fifteen minutes before moving.

Just as she realized she needed to leave and began to stand, the judge entered the courtroom with a brown paper bag. By the grease stain on the paper, Annie knew it was his lunch. He seemed surprised to see her still in the courtroom.

"Excuse me," she said. "I didn't know. . .I mean. . .I was just leaving."

The judge, no longer in his black robes, was now much less intimidating. "That's fine, Miss Hamilton. I don't always come back to an empty courtroom to eat lunch. But it's the quietest place. No phones or pagers allowed."

She stepped behind the swinging gate, then turned to face him. He was unwrapping what looked to be a pepper-and-egg sandwich on Italian bread.

"Your Honor?" Her voice was no more than a whisper.

"Yes, Miss Hamilton?"

"Will I ever see Chance again?"

"Chance?"

"The little boy. Taylor's child. His name is Charles, but we all call him Chance."

"That's a cute nickname—like the ballplayer, right?"

Annie nodded. Her next words were soft, but filled with a yearning and a pleading. "Will I?"

"That's really up to the birth mother—or the foster parents, depending on how I rule. The D.A. says we should refuse any visitation requests in light of what you did. I don't think he'll recommend that they prosecute you for your silence, though."

"Could he do that?"

"The D.A. can do anything he wants. But I don't think he would, in this case. By all accounts you did a wonderful job with him, and you tried to find his mother. I wouldn't take it to trial, but then it's been a long time since I worried about making a reputation for myself. Many D.A.s do."

Annie nodded as if she understood what he meant but did not. "So the answer is?" she pleaded.

"Will you be able to see him again?"

Annie held on to a sliver of hope.

"No. I don't believe you will, Miss Hamilton. Unless the birth mother gets custody and wants to share him with you. But I don't think that's going to happen, do you?"

Annie shook her head no.

I will not cry.

"I'm sorry, Miss Hamilton. It's obvious to me that you loved the little boy a great deal. None of these decisions are easy. This one isn't either."

Annie sniffed.

"I'm sorry, Miss Hamilton," the judge said softly.

And Annie was sure he truly meant it.

"Thank you," she said in a tiny voice and slipped out of the courtroom. In a minute she was out the door and on the sidewalk, her eyes fogged with misery.

She took a step toward home, then stopped. She could not go home. *Too many memories of Chance there,* she thought wildly. She turned to the right. Down the boulevard, to the east, lay Lake Michigan. She sighed. Then she started walking east, toward the cold, inviting blue water, toward the deep of the lake, to an end to her pain.

At last she understood what her mother had done. . .and the depths of pain she must have felt. For it was the kind of soul-numbing pain Annie felt now.

§　　§　　§

Before this very moment, when Annie knew she had lost

Chance, she had never considered ending her life. Even when her mother had committed suicide, Annie had merely grown pensive and quiet. In the pain of her breakup with Steve, her college boyfriend, she had grown angry and resolute. After the final battle with her father when they had parted ways, for good, she had grown melancholy and sad.

In each of these episodes from her past, there was deep hurt. She recalled the horror of seeing her mother's lifeless body. She recalled the pain of watching her boyfriend drive off to California without her. And she remembered, in a flash, the hateful words her father had shouted at her—the same words he had shouted at her mother the day before she committed suicide. But in each of these, the pain had somehow slipped into a small compartment in her heart. They had remained folded and tucked away. . .locked in a box that safely held the hurt and agony at bay.

But this pain was different. She felt it in her heart and on her skin and in her bones and in her very flesh. It was not a tiny slice, but a slashing, tearing gash into her consciousness and awareness.

Losing Chance was the Mount Everest of pain, she thought. There could be no more horrible pain inflicted upon her than was inflicted upon her by the soft, simple words of the judge.

You will never see him again.

Never.

Never.

As this pain resonated within her being like the echo of

a gunshot or explosion, she began to see clearly. She began to see that there was an answer after all. She possessed the ability to free herself from the pain. She could deliver herself. She could provide her own salvation. The promised relief was so overwhelming that she could not have held herself back from seeking it, even if she had wanted to.

As she walked east through Lincoln Park, she imagined the steely, furious waves crashing against the stone breakwater. Single plumes of cold water arced into the air and fell into a bitter mix of waves as the wind drove the water to the shore.

She walked closer, drawn to the dark anger.

To the emptiness.

To the promise of peace that the emptiness offered.

She stepped farther, her feet on the icy ridge, just inches from the edge, just inches from the swallowing lake.

She took a deep breath, feeling the wet coldness in her lungs.

She closed her eyes and waited. The lure of an endless peace was so very tempting—especially in the dark, in the cold, in the solitude.

God, this pain is unbearable. The pain was so deep, she could not even say the words aloud. *I love You. . .as best as I can. . .but when will this pain end?*

She opened her eyes and saw only icy depths.

ဪ   ဪ   ဪ

Perhaps it was God, perhaps it was just a trick of geography, but by the time she had covered the blocks to the lake, her thoughts had calmed to some degree. Her breathing was still labored and her face streaked with sweat. *Such a release cannot take place,* she reasoned, *with one so ill composed.*

Instead of simply hurling herself into the harbor or, better yet, running along the causeway into the deeper, choppier waters of the lake, she sat at the edge of the lake. Reaching into her purse, she pulled out a dainty handkerchief—one of her mother's. She had never known why she had carried it all these years. But now it brought comfort. She tried to dry her face with it and, halfway through, began to laugh at the absurdity of it all. The laughter was followed by tears—and those were followed by a numbing return to a chilled reality.

There would be no more Chance for her. She was again alone.

She took a breath and stood.

Another sob threatened as she looked at the swirling, turbulent water one last time. Then she turned and began to trudge toward home. Putting one foot in front of the other, she would walk north along the lake a short way, then west. She would return to her home—her cold and lonely home.

ⓢ ⓢ ⓢ

It was nearing dusk as Annie finally made her way toward Lincoln Park. She had walked slowly all afternoon, north past Lincoln Park Harbor and nearly up to Belmont Harbor, both nearly full of boats for the summer season, then back to

North Avenue Beach. Occasionally she stared out at the lake, into the blue waters, and wondered what it might have felt like to pull them up over her head, to be covered, to be smothered, with a liquid blanket of silence.

How would it feel to breathe in a great lungful of water?

Would it burn?

Would I cry out?

What did her mother feel before she pulled the trigger? What was so painful that she could no longer bear it?

Each time Annie considered such thoughts, an image of Mrs. Alvarez would enter her thoughts. She saw the old woman standing in the middle of her apartment, weeping.

Then a laugh, bitter and hard, formed in her throat.

And who would take care of Petey?

The zoo lay to her right, a short distance to the north. She turned along the path and walked up a hillock. The park was one of Annie's favorite places—close to the lake and the city, with a lagoon dividing it.

She crossed down to the still green water of the Lincoln Park lagoon. At the edge of the sidewalk, a small white object caught her eye. It was nearly buried under a pile of leaves. She reached down and picked it up, cradling it gently.

It was a baby shoe, the right foot. It was clean, the sole showing virtually no sign of wear. She examined the label. It had been made in Italy. The only blemish was a spot of mud, square on the toe. Otherwise it could have been placed in the window of an upscale children's shop. One side of the shoelace had a little plush carrot at the end. The other one was bare.

Annie looked around. There was no family nearby. No one carrying a baby. No one within eyesight who might have dropped the shoe.

Annie held the shoe and almost felt the warmth resonate from it. Suddenly she knew what she must do. Back home she would construct a shadowbox. The shoe would be the centerpiece. Unfolding from the lost shoe would be tendrils of a childhood denied—a toy here, a candy wrapper on that side, a pencil and a box of crayons there.

Annie closed her eyes and saw just how this would come together, everything falling into place in an instant.

Then she saw it again.

It was a page of the Bible that she had once torn out and thrown in anger. That page would need to be found and placed in a hidden corner of the box.

She sighed. She would no longer think of ending the pain, but enduring. She remembered what Pastor Yount had said in a sermon—in patient endurance she would be led to godliness. She would be led back to trusting in God and His purposes, and her faith would grow through perseverance.

But even that elevated thought didn't curb her pain.

Annie closed her eyes again as the hurt tightened hard about her heart.

Sixteen

ANNIE WAS NOT AWARE of having fallen asleep. She was not aware of waking. She was not aware of the passage of time. But slowly she became aware of a hushing of footsteps. Mrs. Alvarez, trailed by Mrs. Lang, had climbed up the office steps and entered her apartment, unbidden. They were marked in silhouette by the street light from the alley shining through the rear window.

"Annie," Mrs. Alvarez called out softly. "Annie, are you there?"

Annie mumbled a reply. The two women stopped a dozen feet from her.

Any woman past sixty—and both women were well past sixty—had experience, lots of experience, in hospitals and funeral homes. First it was older relatives and parents and friends of parents. Then it was friends and siblings. These two had ample training as to what to say in sympathy, what slight words of comfort might be offered.

Yet both women appeared muted into silence.

Annie was sure that the two of them had discussed what to ask, what to say, before beginning their climb up the stairs. But instead of expressing outrage or worry or anger or sympathy, they just stood there, in the dark, their hands folded in front of them as if in supplication. Annie was grateful for the immediate silence. It's what she preferred, since there were no words to cover the pain she felt.

Mrs. Alvarez took a half step forward. "Annie, is there anything I can get for you?"

Normally Annie knew the older woman would have added, "Is there anything I can do?" But everyone in the apartment knew there was nothing that could be done. They had all watched Chance being taken, in accordance with state law and regulations. They had seen the agency officials brandishing official folders and court rulings and thick packets of paper in blue binders.

And, through Mr. Manos, who had phoned the judge, then his father-in-law, the two older women had heard what the judge had said, what the court had ruled. There was nothing one old woman—or two old women—could do in the face of that sort of official onslaught.

"Perhaps I could make soup?" Mrs. Lang called out, as if tossing a life preserver to a drowning person, who might also be hungry.

Annie pushed herself upright and wiped her face. It was sticky; she must have been sobbing as she slept.

"No. . .nothing. Nothing right now. But. . .thank you for asking."

Mrs. Alvarez began to take a step forward, but hesitated. Then she broke, hurrying to Annie's side. Over six decades of caring for hurts and administering hugs had ingrained in this grandmotherly woman the importance of touch. It was obvious she knew no right words to say; so, instead, she held Annie in her arms, as tightly as she could, and let Annie wail into the darkness.

Mrs. Lang watched for a moment, then headed to the kitchen. She would make her soup after all. "A body needs food. Doesn't matter what the heart says," she muttered as she snapped on the light and began to quietly gather what she needed.

Both women said no more than ten words that evening. The soup was covered and left, simmering, on the stove. Each woman hugged Annie, long and hard, one final time before leaving. The steps creaked and groaned as they made their way to the street.

"I'll light a candle for you, Annie," Mrs. Alvarez called out softly. "And for Chance."

Annie offered a weak wave and shut the door. Leaning against it, she slid the dead bolt closed. As if she were in a dream—a wavering, gray dream—she walked to the kitchen. Taking out a bowl, she ladled out a serving of Mrs. Lang's soup and sat down at the table.

It took her nearly an hour to eat half a bowl. Then, like a person swimming against the tide, she made her way to the couch and collapsed in its cradling softness for the second time that day.

§　　§　　§

The phone jangled Annie awake. The sun was up, more than up, and she knew it was late. Finally, worn out with grief, she must have fallen asleep. . .and slept through till the next morning.

"Annie, is that you?"

She mumbled that it was. But it took a minute to recognize the man's voice on the phone. It was Mr. Manos.

"Are you awake? I'm in the neighborhood, and we need to talk."

From all the background noise, it sounded like he was calling from his father-in-law's restaurant. Woefully examining her wrinkled clothes, Annie sighed. Less than five minutes later, she heard someone bounding up the stairs. Opening the door, she saw that it was Mr. Manos. He held two cardboard coffee cups.

"You want one, Annie?" he asked, offering a cup to her. "I got an extra just in case.

Annie reached for one and took a sip. The hot coffee tasted good.

"Listen, Annie," he said, "can I borrow your phone? I need to make an important call."

Annie pointed to her phone, and Nickolas attacked the buttons like a bird of prey. He turned from her as he talked. Paying little attention to what he was saying, she sipped at the coffee.

"That was the D.A.'s office, Annie. I have a friend who has a friend. They suggested I call today."

Annie simply waited. She had no energy to inquire why.

"They said he's going after you, Annie."

Annie blinked, but nothing about her blank expression changed.

"You don't get it, do you, Annie? The D.A.—you know, the district attorney—said he's going to file a complaint against you. He's up for reelection next month, and I think he's grandstanding."

Annie still had not moved. "File a case?" she asked without passion or apparent concern. "For what? I lost, didn't I?"

Mr. Manos took a long swallow. "Yeah, well, yeah, you lost. But that ain't why he's filing. This is a media thing now. He's going after you for child endangerment. . .maybe even kidnapping, is what my friend's friend said. Kidnapping, Annie. That's deep stuff. Real trouble."

"But I didn't endanger Chance," she said softly. "I didn't kidnap him. I took care of him—just as any mother would."

Mr. Manos stood up and wiped his palms on his trousers. Annie noted two dark stains on his thigh.

Grease stains. He needs to use a spot cleaner. She shook her head at her own absurd thoughts in such a time of crisis.

"It don't matter what you say, Annie. They can charge you

with both and make it stick. . .maybe. This is big stuff, Annie."

"Aren't you an attorney? Aren't you *my* attorney?" Annie said slowly.

Mr. Manos's face reddened. "Sure, Annie. I am. Sure. But I ain't never had a kidnapping before. That's a big job. I mean. . .I think that's a federal crime. If the feds get involved. . .well, Annie, I don't know. Holy smoke—the feds. I ain't happy about having to fight the feds."

Annie placed her coffee cup on the side table, then adjusted it a quarter turn so the design faced the room. She folded her hands in her lap. "I guess I have to trust you, Mr. Manos."

Nickolas wiped the sheen of sweat off his upper lip with the sleeve of his sports coat. "Okay, Annie," he said weakly, "if that's what you want to do."

She could find no further words to say and nodded again.

God, she prayed, *it seems Mr. Manos is out of his league here. . .and so am I. We really need Your help.*

But as she mouthed these few words, she wondered. . .was God really listening?

And the numbness returned again.

ᔕ ᔕ ᔕ

It was afternoon before Annie moved again. She heard the faint hum and rattle of the washers and dryers. Evidently her regular customers had come in and gone about their business without needing her oversight.

She shut her eyes and tried to prevent the image of Chance from arising. If she glanced about the apartment, she would see too many reminders, too much evidence that he had been part of her life for so long. She just wanted to sit, eyes shut, and will all evidences of him away. She wished everything would vanish. Then as that thought flashed to her mind, she snapped her eyes open.

No! If it all disappears. . .then he will disappear!

Gazing around the room, she saw a blanket draped over the back of a chair, a pull toy under the table, and another dozen relics of Chance. She wanted them gone—and she wanted them enshrined. She wanted them out of her life— and she wanted them never to leave her heart.

Night had edged into the city by the time Annie managed to stand and slip on a pair of sneakers. She ran down her front stairway and onto the street. A small group of peo- ple—all regular customers—gathered inside the laundromat.

She crossed MacKenzie and again headed toward the lake. Since Chance had been taken from her, Annie had been inex- plicably drawn to the starkness of the water. She had stared at the waves for hours, watched the sun set from behind and light the crest of each wave with red. She watched as the moon rose and crackled the surface of the lake with gold or silver or gray.

Tonight she walked to the very edge of the lake and sat on the concrete slab that edged the city from the water. She let her legs dangle, only inches from the top crest of the night's waves.

Now she was in real trouble. If the district attorney chose

to pursue a case, she had no resources to fight. She would need to contact the public defender's office for help. She wondered if she would have to sell the laundromat before they came to her defense.

Then briefly she wondered again if she should contact her father. He had more than ample money to come to her aid. But it took only a split-second for her to decide no.

It would cost me more than selling the laundromat. He would exact more of a price emotionally than I could possibly repay.

And she knew that should he even agree to help her, he would hold this "favor" over her head forever. He would again gain purchase over her—the kind of grip she had fled from in her teen years.

Perhaps she could defend herself. She saw many people do exactly the same in televised court cases during afternoon television. But that was make-believe. She did not think she might fare as well against a polished and well-schooled attorney.

She stared at the eastern horizon until it grew black. She sighed as the pain bubbled up again. She had lost Chance; she was as broken as she could imagine a person being. The tiny, brilliant light of Chance was now lost—and her life appeared to be as dark and black as the eastern half of the lake.

She felt the familiar tightness in her throat.

I have nothing, God. I have nothing left.

She watched as the dark sky began to reveal the brilliance of the evening stars.

My heart has been broken, God, and I have nowhere to go. Chance is gone, and my life is empty again. What else do You want, God? What else can I give You?

You have taken my mother from me and let me find her life- less body. You let my only true love leave me. I have lost my father's love. And now I have lost the only bright spot in my life. You have taken my little boy. What more do You want? What more can I give You?

The tears flowed freely in the darkness by the shore. After a long moment, she continued to pray.

What else do You want, God? Me? You want my life too? Haven't I given that to You? I have loved You and believed in You—but right now I'm not sure of either of those two truths. I don't feel Your presence, Lord, but I'll give You my life. . .if that's what You want.

She paused and looked at her hands.

Lord. . .I don't know what to offer You. You can have me—if that's what You want. But, God, can You. . .will You. . .protect me if I give myself totally to You?

If You can, then You can have me—heart and soul and body. Protect me, Lord, she cried in her heart.

God, I am so alone and so lost. Please lead me and protect me.

🌀   🌀   🌀

Annie returned home that night well after midnight. The laundromat was dark. Her last customer must have switched off the lights. She locked the front door and slipped up the steps, then opened a can of tuna for Petey. He sniffed at it once and walked away.

Since Chance's departure, Petey had become sullen, even for a cat, and more finicky about his food than ever before. He spent most of his day staring out the front window, blinking at the sidewalk below. Every day Annie would see him, pet him gently, and tell him that Chance was never coming home again. Then she would sob and leave him at his post.

Now when he sniffed off perfectly good food, Annie sighed and walked away as well. She knew how he was feeling, and harsh words would do neither of them any good.

She slept on the couch again, in sweats. It was too much trouble to find her own bedroom, and there were too many ghosts of a baby crying in the dark. It was easier to sleep with the faint, gray hiss of the television serenading her.

§　　　§　　　§

The phone startled her awake again.

"Annie? You awake?"

By now she recognized not only the voice, but the greeting.

"Hello, Mr. Manos. More bad news?"

"No. I'm at my father-in-law's. You want coffee and a Danish?"

Annie's stomach roiled. "I don't think I could. . ."

"You'll want it after I tell you the news. Be there in five."

He was at the door in four minutes. He was carrying two coffees and two warm Danish rolls, no doubt liberated from his father-in-law's restaurant. He popped the top off his coffee and took a huge bite out of his roll, all the while maintaining a wide smile.

Annie sipped at her cup. She really liked the coffee from the deli. Somehow she could never quite duplicate the flavor.

"You're a lucky girl," Mr. Manos said through a mouthful of Danish.

Annie arched her eyes.

"They're not going to do nothing to you," he added triumphantly.

"Who?" Annie asked, almost forgetting what he had told her the day before.

"The D.A., of course. He saw the clip. I had the friend of my friend show him the clip from the news—with you and Chance."

She nodded and waited.

"He said—my friend said—that after the D.A. saw the clip, he wouldn't touch the case with a twenty-foot pole. He's up for reelection this year, and he said his opponent would make a television commercial out of that in a minute."

"So. . .I don't have to be worried about going to jail?"

Mr. Manos nodded. "He ain't going to do squat, Annie. He ain't going to do nothing. And I ain't even charging you for the phone calls." He practically beamed.

Even if he wasn't charging for the phone calls, Annie was pretty sure he was charging her for his time.

"You beat him, Annie. You're free and clear and have nothing to worry about."

ॐ   ॐ   ॐ

It was much later that same day when she realized that it may have been God's handiwork that protected her.

After all, I did ask Him to protect me from all of this.

Perhaps God *was* on her side, shielding her. But even that did little to lift the gloom from Annie's heart.

ॐ   ॐ   ॐ

Sundays used to be Annie's most favorite day. The pace of the city slowed, perceptively, and traffic and noise and clatter ebbed to the edges of hearing.

For the past year and a half, Annie had loved being in church. She had loved the music, the cool calmness of the prayers, and the soothing, dulcet words of the pastor. She had been thrilled that Chance seemed to thrive in the nursery, hardly crying in her absence. She had often helped out in the nursery, and now that Chance was gone, she tried to return, thinking it might be balm for her wounds.

She could not have been more wrong.

A few weeks after Chance was taken, she had sat in a rocking chair, holding a squalling newborn. She had managed to quiet his cries, but when his parents returned to claim him, a wave of horrible emotions had cascaded over her—similar to the ones she had felt the day Chance left her side. She had fought back tears as they signed the register book and had tried to smile as she handed them the baby and the Winnie-the-Pooh diaper bag. Then she had hurried out of the building, nearly running home, to collapse and weep alone, far from prying eyes. She knew, from that moment, that she would never be able to hold an infant in her arms again. It was too powerful a reminder of what she had lost.

Sundays used to be a day when customers were few, and Annie was free to work on her art—her shadowboxes. In a frenzy, she had completed her last work—with the child's delicate shoe. But since that time, she had felt all but incapable of doing another. She puttered about, moving objects back and forth. But she could not concentrate. She could not find a story worth telling.

There were no more unfoldings to be found inside her.

Instead she often found herself lying on the couch on Sunday afternoons, staring at some old movie flickering on the television. She would set the sound just at the edge of hearing—to distract, not inform. Even after hours in front of the set, she would not be able to recall a single image.

Her friends at church, including Joan and Sandra, phoned on occasion. With them she acted as normal as she could. They avoided asking about Chance, and she couldn't blame them. But not speaking about those months of her life seemed a betrayal too—as if they had not truly existed.

She wanted her friends to ask how she was doing, if she'd heard from or about Chance, and yet she knew if they had, she would be reduced to tears once more.

§   §   §

The months had crawled by, painfully slow, for Annie.

Now it was the season of holiday cheer, and Annie felt anything but cheerful. Once again she had been recruited to sew costumes for the church pageant. Because it was a task she had done for the past two years, she agreed to help again. But she insisted that she could only sew from home. She said she was too busy with the laundromat to attend rehearsals or do fittings at the church.

The real reason was that she knew Chance would have participated in this year's pageant. She imagined sewing a shepherd's outfit for him. . .or perhaps he might have been one of the wise men or an angel. She imagined the joy she would have felt as he took his first tentative steps onto the platform. She could hear, without hearing, the singsong repetition of a child's Christmas carol, called out in his sweet and innocent voice.

Annie knew she shouldn't, but she wanted to wallow in those images. She wanted to hear him just one more time.

So she sewed late at night, when all was still, when the wind from the lake rattled at her windows. She obeyed what she thought was God's instruction and attempted to place one foot in front of the other, attempted to move forward. She breathed in and she breathed out, trying to face her new reality. And yet the days dragged on in an endless mire of gray.

She woke to empty; she went to bed empty.

And she wondered when it all would cease.

Seventeen

ANNIE TORE OFF THE top page on her page-a-day Church Bulletin Bloopers calendar. Then she tore another and another, not reading a single one, not paying attention to the Scripture on each page. Before she reached the correct date, she had torn nearly two dozen pages off.

Since that moment when she gave Chance away, her days had grown tedious. Marking each new day had become a chore. Instead she moved through time as if she were a disinterested visitor, noting little, paying scant attention to events. Her emotional involvement had fallen to an even, flat line.

She no longer despaired. She no longer collapsed into tears at the sound of a child's voice. She no longer walked about her empty rooms, clutching at a small blanket, pain washing over her heart like a storm. But neither did she feel buoyed by her art, or her friends, or Petey seeking out comfort in her lap.

If there were no involvement, there could be no pain, she thought and drew farther and farther away from anything she thought might hurt to lose someday.

She gathered up the loose pages from the calendar and tossed them into the trash can next to her office.

Only a few weeks until Christmas. She stared blankly at the page. *I can't remember a time when I felt less like celebrating than I do today*.

Mrs. Alvarez still came by, as did Mrs. Lang and the others. The first few days after Chance's departure, they talked boldly about how unfair the system was and what they might do to get Chance back.

After the first hearing, even before Annie had returned home, they had heard. They had heard what she said and what the judge had told her.

That night their voices were softer, quieter. Annie knew they knew she had done the right thing—the right thing for Chance, perhaps. They knew there was no alternative.

"Maybe Taylor will be a better mother than we think," Mrs. Alvarez had said. "Even a bad mother is better than no mother at all."

"Foster homes are terrible," Mrs. Lang declared. "I'm sorry you didn't fight for him, Annie—I know how much you love him. But if what you did was a sacrifice to keep him out of foster homes, then God will honor what you did."

Miss Ehrler came over and simply held onto Annie. Both

women sobbed quietly. Annie offered to return her baby crib, but the old woman refused.

"No. I'll never have a child who needs it. Maybe you will, Annie. . .someday, maybe you will."

But Chance—her chance at motherhood—was gone. And the joy of spring and the languid pleasures of summer passed with Annie barely able to pay attention to the passing.

How slowly each day had passed, until each month of autumn had neatly concluded itself.

And now it was nearly Christmas.

§　　§　　§

A stack of Christmas cards lay on Annie's desk in the office. She flipped through them, checking return addresses. Some were from distant family members, whose annual Christmas card was their only point of contact. There had not been a card from her father. She did not truly expect one. She had looked each day, with all hope firmly suppressed, for a card with Taylor's name on the upper corner. So far none had arrived.

At times Annie told herself she would throw the card away if one came, so great was the pain she imagined it bringing. What would happen if it were a photo card and there was Chance staring back at her, nestled close to a Christmas tree or a department-store Santa?

On other days, she yearned, ached for some sort of word. Was he healthy? Did he ask about her? Was he happy and smiling and growing?

The complete silence was a tidal wave that had drowned Annie's glimmer of hope for a return to normal. For the faintest of dreams that Chance may someday rejoin her.

She stopped. The address on one card caught her eye.

It was from the Westlake Maintenance Company. She laid the others aside and slit the envelope open. The card was like a thousand other business Christmas cards. Nothing religious, for not wanting to offend anyone, the card expressed the company's fervent hope that the recipient enjoy the holiday season. It sent "Warm Winter Wishes" and "Hope for a Prosperous New Year." A snow scene graced the front, with a touch of silver sparkles on the card. When she opened it, she noted that the company name, printed on the bottom in silver ink, was surrounded with ten or so other names, only two of which Annie thought she recognized—the receptionist's and Daniel's. She stared at it, then laid it aside and leaned back in her chair.

Daniel had called—twice since Chance had been gone. The first time was to stumble through an expression of sympathy. Annie did not remember much of the conversation, but the truth was that she remembered so little from those first few weeks. Then he had called once more. She was surprised when he asked her to dinner and a movie.

He had picked a small Italian place on Belmont, with candles in empty wine bottles and red-checkered tablecloths. She had found her side of any conversation suddenly difficult to maintain. If Daniel found it difficult to keep silence at bay, he did not mention it. And Annie was grateful. He had talked about his business and actually made her laugh on a few occasions as he described some of his more eccentric customers.

He had reached out once and had taken her hand in his. She had stared at it.

"It's good to see you laugh, Annie. I like the sound," he had said.

They had decided to skip the movie and had taken a long walk around the neighborhood instead, stopping for coffee at Dugan's. He had sat close to her and, for a fleeting instant, she could picture herself happy again.

Maybe Daniel and I. . .maybe I'm not too old for a child. Maybe. . .I could see it. He and I could. . .I mean. . .stranger things have happened. I read about older women becoming mothers everyday, she remembered thinking.

The image had faded quickly as she thought of Chance and the enormity of what she had lost.

In the confusion of her emotions, she had let Daniel hold her hand, let him put his arm around her shoulders, and even let him kiss her good-night at her doorstep. It was a quick kiss, and she had barely reacted. She was sure it was simply a sympathy kiss and nothing more. He had smiled and thanked her for the evening, then slipped off into the dark.

She realized later that she had said barely a few dozen words all night, and at one moment actually fought back tears. *It was all too soon,* she had thought. *And here I am blubbering in front of Daniel. What must he think of me?*

He had not called again. She had not expected him to.

The idea of dating someone who was trying to raise a child by herself had thrown him, she imagined. And after the child was gone, he had no idea of how to react. She had no idea how to react, either.

In the stack of envelopes on her desk was one from Pastor Yount. It was not from the church but from him personally. It bore his West Goethe Street address and his precise handwriting. His card was much more religious—a copy of a medieval painting of the nativity. Inside, along with the Scripture verse, he had added, "I am praying for you."

She might have smiled before at his note, but now the words seemed like too little and much too late. She knew, in the back of her mind, that God was in control, of course. But she felt, at the moment, that He had let her life career out of control, like a car without brakes on a mountain road.

Does God allow the brakes to fail? Does He compensate for the failed brakes with a guardrail that destroys the car? Or does He simply allow the car to plunge over an abyss to certain death but reward the driver with eternal joy in heaven?

Annie hated herself for feeling so hard and brittle, but the questions were there in her heart and she could not usher them out. They had no place to go—no escape, except in her thoughts.

Friends from church stopped over to chat. Annie knew she was a regular notation on at least six prayer lists and the subject of many whispered, earnest discussions at the conclusion of a Bible study or prayer meeting. She knew that when they stopped by "to see how she was doing," they really wanted to know if she had knit her life back together again, or had the loss of this child caused the frayed ends to completely unravel? Did she, she was sure they wondered, need some "professional" help in dealing with the loss?

A rueful smile found its way to her face. *And who might that professional be?*

She looked out the window. The clouds grew darker. Winds were off the lake, unusual at any time, and were filled with the portent of snow.

They all mean well. I know they do. But how do I "get better"?

She sighed. The laundromat was deserted. She doubted if anyone would appear before evening.

She hadn't eaten lunch. She hadn't felt like it. While the depression was draining, it had also made her lose nearly fifteen pounds. Mrs. Alvarez routinely pinched her cheeks and told her that no man wants a sack of bones and that she needed a little meat on them. The next day the old woman would appear with something fattening—like a casserole swimming with milk and cheese and a thick layer of french-fried onion rings on the top.

"I put some ground-up potato chips in it as well. You'll like it, Annie. It was my husband's favorite."

It waited for her in the refrigerator. Annie slowly climbed the stairs. After helping herself to a small portion of the casserole, Annie sat down, alone. She felt the tears come again. She was so alone. The apartment was silent. And she was so very, very sad.

Rather than fighting the tears, she let them fall for a few

minutes. Like a cloud passing over a field, the grayness lingered. She sniffed once more.

God, I know You are still there. I am sorry for my anger. But I am so sad at my loss. Please help me return to where I was. Please help replace the joy in my heart. I do love You. I do want to do Your will. I do, God. I really do. But I need Your help. I need Your direction. Do You want me to serve at church? Do You want me to work in the projects? How do I make amends? How do I get my life back?

She kept her head bowed for a very long time. Part of her, as she prayed, knew that she would have to return her plate of food to the microwave. Yet she prayed on. Asking for forgiveness once more, she felt her heart slowly unwind, just a fraction of an inch.

Maybe that was the sign she needed. Healing could be at hand. What she needed to do was wait and pray and seek God's face.

She blinked her eyes open. The sky had grown more overcast, the color of slate. The barest whisper of snow had begun. She placed the plate back in the microwave and, as she was about to start the time, the bell from the downstairs door sounded. She hesitated, and the bell rang again. Then again—longer and more insistent.

Annie checked the clock on the wall. It was nearing five. She was not expecting anyone. If it was someone from the church, they usually came just after lunch or just after dinner, never wanting to impose on Annie.

Peering down the steps, she could make out a shadow—

287

a short shadow. But that was all.

Do I really want to deal with this interruption right now?

But as the bell rang again, she snapped on the light and made her way downstairs.

ꕥ   ꕥ   ꕥ

As Annie opened the door, she felt transported, as if lifted from her life and placed in some other world, where logic and reason were exchanged with happenstance and serendipity. She blinked her eyes and looked again. It was true—she *was* in a new world where truth and darkness and fact and light bounced around in a thousand new directions.

For standing there, in the gentle wisps of new snow, was Taylor. And there, by her side was Chance, holding her hand. He wore a red knit stocking cap and was sticking out his tongue, trying to catch snowflakes.

A thousand years of surprised silence exploded between the three of them. Annie's eyes flew between Taylor and Chance and back again.

She could not speak. She could not move. Her hand twisted in an involuntary spasm about the doorknob.

Chance pulled his tongue back in. He peered up at— Annie—hard, like an evaluating scientist. He moved his mouth slowly, his tender lips opening twice before he made a sound.

"Mommy?"

Annie's heart leaped to her throat.

"Mommy!" Chance called out. He ran to her and clutched her leg with the viselike grip of a three year old.

Annie saw the tremble in Taylor's lips.

"I'm. . .I'm bringing him back to you," Taylor said softly. "It's been six months. And when he looks at me, I know that he is looking for you. I can see it. It's not mean. But he's look-ing for you. He has dreams, Annie, and he tells me that in his dreams, his real mommy kisses him. It's not me in his dreams. It's you."

Annie's heart, accustomed as it had become to shocks and terrors, leapt and struggled wildly in her chest. *What does this all mean?*

"But Taylor. . .the court decided. He's your son. It will. . .I mean all of this. . .will just take time. You have to give it time."

Taylor shook her head. Her hand was on Chance's head. He was still attached to Annie's leg.

"It has been long enough, Annie. Just because he doesn't love me is not the only reason I'm here. It's more than that. It's so much more than that."

Annie looked up from Chance.

Tears were streaming down Taylor's cheeks. "I lied, Annie. I lied from the beginning."

By now the snow had begun to twist and swirl about them in more earnest gusts. No longer a dusting, a full layer was forming on their shoulders and heads.

"Please come inside," Annie pleaded. "Come upstairs. We'll have some coffee or tea."

But Taylor shook her head. "I don't want to go up there.

Too many memories. And I don't think Petey ever liked me."

Annie couldn't help but check about in case Taylor had been followed by an agent of the state. "Then let's go into the laundromat."

Annie hurried along the sidewalk and held the door. She tried not to even focus on Chance, fearing that somehow, if she did, he would vanish like a cruel apparition. She saw that he climbed the steps one at a time and, once inside, looked up at her. Evidently satisfied that it was she, he headed off to the small table stacked with children's toys in the corner by the front window.

Both women watched him run. Then Taylor stared down at her hands, hidden by a thickness of green mittens.

"I lied, Annie. It was Derrik. It was because of him. There was never going to be a cabin on the lake. His parents were never going to help. He made me do all of this because he thought we could get money from you or the state or his parents. Derrik is a jerk, Annie. He is just a jerk. I couldn't believe it. He said he wanted to be a father and all that. Then when we get back to Wisconsin with the baby, his parents tell him that he needs to get a job and support us. So then he says the boy is all my responsibility. He is such a jerk."

Annie had her hand on her heart, trying to calm it. "Taylor, he needs time. He said he wanted to be a father."

"Annie, he's a jerk. You know what his parents said? They said that if he was stupid enough to get me knocked up, then he has to be man enough to pay for his mistake. There was never going to be any money. There was never going to be any cabin on the lake. They told him that they would never give us a single penny. And Derrik just flipped out when they told him that. Then he blamed me. Me! Like I had tricked him or something. As if I had any say in how his parents acted. I mean, I think Derrik just saw me and Chance as an easy way to cash in—so he could stay at home with his stoner buddies and never have to work."

Chance continued to play, slowly and silently. Annie glanced at him, even though she knew it would hurt.

He got so big!

He did not smile at her but stared back. Annie wondered how much he really understood about the past six months. He picked up a Buzz Lightyear figure and maneuvered it through the air.

"Annie, I really love the little boy. But not as a son. Maybe as a brother or something. But not as a mother. I was never his mother. You were. He loves you. He knows you."

Annie, in her wildest flights of imagination, could never have guessed that what was happening would happen. She had no inner reserves to deal with the emotions, the logic, the frantic feelings of joy and fear and wonderment.

God, can this be happening? she both prayed and pleaded. *Have You just worked a miracle for me and for Chance?*

"I have this paper, Annie," Taylor said as she drew out an envelope from her winter coat. "I had a friend help me with it. She's real smart and went to school to be a paralegal. So she's almost a lawyer. She helped me write this up. I signed it. I made Derrik the jerk sign it. My friend signed it. Then we took it and got it notarized. I don't know what a judge might say about it—but I'm giving Chance back to you. It's all official. And this time I'm not coming back."

Annie tried to catch her breath. "But what about your dad? Or Derrik's parents? Don't they want Chance?"

Taylor scowled. "My dad is so-o-o in denial. He didn't even want to see Chance—or me. Said he no longer has a daughter. And Derrik's parents are almost alcoholics and want nothing to do with me or Chance. This is just fine with them."

Annie saw a vast pool of hurt in Taylor's eyes—the same kind of hurt she'd seen in her own eyes in the mirror the day after her father had yelled so harshly at her. The day she had finally broken her calm reserve and had screamed back. . . then fled, for good, from her childhood home.

"It's okay, Annie," Taylor said. "Some people have it worse, you know what I mean?"

Taylor put out her hand and Annie grasped it. Then she drew the young woman into an almost-frantic embrace.

"The paper is all I have to give you, Annie. I don't have money for a lawyer, but my friend said it was pretty much all legal. And no one will ever come back to try to take him away. I may not be real smart, Annie, but that is one true, cold fact."

Annie wiped at her own tears. "But Taylor, how can you? How can you just. . . ?"

Taylor's tough-girl façade quivered, then faded. Her lips trembled. Instead of a hard-edged woman, she reverted to what she really was—a terribly frightened teenager who had no one she could count on. No one but Annie, to whom she was entrusting her greatest gift—her son, Chance.

"Because I have to," Taylor tried to explain. "Because I really do love him. I know I can't raise him. You told me when I lived with you that I have to trust God. Well, I think. . . no. . .I'm *sure* that this is what God wants me to do. Today is the first day since he's been born that I haven't felt dirty or ashamed or on the verge of panic. This is the right thing to do. I really think that God is telling me in my heart that this is all okay. I think God is telling me that this is Chance's only chance. And it's the right thing to do."

"But Taylor," Annie whispered, "do you know what you're really giving up?"

Taylor nodded. "I'm doing this for Chance. He deserves more than I can offer. He dreams about you, Annie. All the time. I thought it would stop right away, but he dreams about you—almost every night."

Annie nodded as if she understood. She did not understand.

"I left Derrik. He is such a jerk," Taylor said with a sniff. "I mean, he was so stupid that he even flunked out of our community college. Who is that dumb anyhow? All he wants to do is sit around and get wasted and listen to metal. That's no life for anyone. Not me. Not Chance."

Annie tried to interrupt.

"No, Annie—listen. Don't even think of trying to talk me out of it. This is what I'm going to do. No one told me I should. I have decided this on my own. And I'm sure. I'm tired of being pushed around and listening to what other people tell me to do. My dad pushed me around. Derrik pushed me around. And I'm finally doing exactly what I want to do. And that's giving Chance back to you."

Taylor exhaled loudly. In an almost childlike voice she added, "It's what Chance needs. He needs you. He needs you so desperately. I can feel his pain in my bones, Annie. I can't take it anymore. I don't want to be responsible for messing up his life as well as mine."

Chance stood up.

"Chance, Honey," Taylor said, "can you do me a favor? Can you get that bag from the car? The green one?"

Chance grinned at the opportunity to help and ran to the door.

Taylor must have seen Annie's worried look. "The car is right there, Annie. He likes to help."

The screen door slammed. Annie had not replaced it in the fall as she always had done. Somehow it had no longer seemed important.

"Could you tell him that I really did love him, Annie? Could you do that? Tell him I loved him way too much to take him with me? Tell him that I loved him?"

Annie knew she would begin crying.

Taylor must have sensed Annie's emotional state, for she held up her hand. "No crying. I have cried more these last couple of months than I have cried in my whole life. I'm tired of crying. Just tell him, Annie. That's all."

"I will," Annie promised in a whisper.

"And you have to wish me good luck," Taylor said with a forced smile. "I have a girlfriend in Orlando. She works at Disney World. She said she could get me a job there. Maybe even in the Enchanted Castle. That's where she works. Can you believe it? In the Enchanted Castle! Just like I dreamed about when I was a little girl."

Chance clambered back inside the laundromat. He was dragging a battered green bag.

"It's the one they gave me when I first got him back. It was your bag, right?"

Annie nodded.

"I think I have everything in it that you put in. Some of the clothes don't fit anymore. So I stuffed a few new ones in with it. But I wanted to make sure you had everything."

Taylor bent down and unzipped it halfway. "Here's his rabbit. He really likes it. But the carrot fell off somewhere. Maybe you could get a new one?"

Annie nodded. "I think I can."

Taylor handed the bag to Annie. "I have to go. The weather guy on the radio said it isn't snowing south of the city, so I need to get out before it changes its mind and gets worse."

That's when Annie hugged Taylor fiercely, knowing that a lifetime of hugs would not be enough to express her thanks for this incredible gift. After a couple of minutes, Taylor broke the embrace and walked over to Chance. The child had hardly said a word since his arrival.

Taylor leaned down. "Remember I love you," she tried to say through a sob.

Chance wrapped his tiny arms around her neck. Even though his mouth was next to Taylor's ear, Annie heard his whispered words. "I 'member you forever. Forever and ever. And 'member Jesus loves you too."

Chance had remembered the *very* words she had said upon their parting! And now he was using the same words to comfort someone else!

Taylor squeezed him again, then stood. Wiping her face with her palm, she tossed her long blond hair back from her eyes.

"Chance," she said solemnly, "you be good for. . .you be good for your mommy."

Chance snapped a nod. "I be good. I be good for Mommy and I be good for Jesus."

Taylor blew him a kiss and hurried out the door. The screen door slapped behind her as she jumped inside a compact, battered car.

In a minute or so the windshield wipers had clapped off the snow. With a single beep of the horn, the car bolted forward. And in the time of a dozen heartbeats, Taylor and the car disappeared into the snow.

ʕ　　ʕ　　ʕ

No human-inspired words could describe the glorious wash of emotions that swept over Annie as she gazed at Chance.

Nothing that could be written or thought could come close to the avalanche of joy and gratitude that filled her heart and soul. She felt as if she could no longer be contained by her own skin. And all because she was holding the hand of a little boy with luminescent brown eyes. A little boy named Chance.

She drew a deep breath. "Would you like to go upstairs?" she asked.

And just what is normal for this sort of day? What is appropriate for having your life handed back to you? And just how do I thank God for this miracle?

By the time she was halfway up, she knew she would spend the rest of her life thanking and praising God for this greatest of all gifts. Chance's fingers intertwined with hers as if he had never left. . .as if the last six months did not exist.

When he looked up at her and smiled, her heart stopped and started again.

"Mommy, where's Petey?"

Just then the fat, lazy cat ambled out of the bedroom that used to be Chance's and stopped in his tracks. He peered forward as only a cat can do, then took off toward them at a gallop, his feet sounding like horses on the hardwood floor. Two feet before reaching them, the cat leaped into the air and landed in Chance's arms like a dog, sending both of them tumbling to the floor in a squealing, giggling, purring, furry tangle.

Annie, at that moment, believed she heard an entire celestial choir, singing out with heavenly gusto, praising

God. And her own heart burst in a vast shower of heavenly fireworks.

§   §   §

That evening, well after midnight, Petey the Cat finally stopped mewing and trying to climb into Chance's lap. Chance finally fell asleep on Annie's bed. When at last the rooms grew quiet again, Annie took the paper that Taylor had handed her. She laid it on the table and unfolded it carefully, with trembling fingers.

The letter began, "Because Annie Hamilton loved me and because she loved Chance more than life itself, more than anyone, I, Taylor Evans, declare that Annie Hamilton shall raise this infant child as her own."

Annie closed her eyes. Familiar tears formed, but this time they were the result of sheer and overwhelming joy. As she closed her eyes to experience the wonder, she felt God's tender arms about her, holding her close.

Walking to the window, she opened her eyes and gazed up at the heavens, up past the car headlights, past the street lights, up and into the clarity of the winter sky. She stared up at the moon and the stars.

And she quietly whispered, "Thank you."

Epilogue

ANNIE HELD HIS HAND,
even though Chance did not like it.

"I can do it, Mommy," he said as he tried to push her away.

"I know you can, Chance. But there's too much traffic here. I need to help you. At least today."

The light flashed green, and the two of them set off across the street. Chance was enrolled in the afternoon session of the Webster Avenue Church Preschool.

Before drawing attention to herself and Chance, Annie had phoned Nickolas Manos to review the document that Taylor had left with Annie.

He had whistled as he read it. "This girl a lawyer or what?"

"Her friend was a paralegal."

Mr. Manos had smiled. "A good one, I bet. This is pretty good. But I ain't an expert in these things. Let me take a copy and show it to a friend. He does lots of work with adoption stuff."

Two days later he had phoned. "It ain't airtight, but close, this guy says. You say the parents aren't coming back? Or grandparents?"

Annie told him again of Taylor's remarks.

"Then I think you'll be okay to take him to preschool. Unless somebody contests this—you having the boy—you're the official guardian. Both the mother and father signed off and appointed you. It's pretty official."

The next day Annie had Chance registered. And the day after that, Chance began to attend his first school.

He needs friends. He needs to learn how to learn.

And now, a week later, Chance considered himself an old pro. Annie believed if she would let him, he would have attempted to make the five-block journey by himself. She bent down at the door to the church basement.

"Kiss," she requested, and Chance quickly and enthusiastically replied, wrapping his arms around her neck.

"See you when you're done," she called out as he headed toward the church door. Chance stopped to wave back as he disappeared behind the door.

Annie hurried up the stairs and out into the chilled spring air, blinking in the bright early sunshine.

Then she nearly tripped on someone. It was Daniel Trevalli, and she almost fell into his arms.

"Sorry I scared you, Miss Annie Hamilton," Daniel said softly.

"I just didn't expect. . .I mean, I didn't expect anyone to be here."

Daniel focused on his feet.

Annie quirked an eyebrow. It was unusual for Danny Trevalli to be quiet, even for a moment.

"Miss Annie, I need to ask you something. And maybe apologize."

"Apologize?" Annie asked, surprised. "For what?"

Daniel shifted his weight from foot to foot. "I kept saying I was going to call, then I didn't—at least when I said I was. I know we went out and all that, but I knew you knew I was. . . well, I wasn't really being honest."

Annie shifted her bag from one hand to the other. "You weren't?"

Daniel did not look at her directly. "I mean. . .yeah, we went out, and I'm pretty sure you had a good time. I know I did. But. . .there's that commitment word. I was scared, Annie. I never let on that I really liked you. I never wanted you to know. I thought that if you knew. . .then you would expect me to be something I wasn't."

Annie remained silent.

"Can we start again? For real this time? Would you mind?"

Annie waited.

Daniel stood still and looked up, his smile pleading and hopeful. "What about dinner. . .and a movie?"

Annie knew she had to ask. "The three of us?"

Daniel nodded. "I heard all about what happened."

Annie smiled.

"Yeah, Annie. The three of us. Me, you, and Chance. Dinner. And a movie. A G-rated movie."

After a long hesitation, Annie finally replied. "You can call me, Daniel. That would be fine."

And Annie walked away, hoping that Daniel did not see how big her smile had become.

But she knew he did.

ABOUT THE AUTHORS

Jim and Terri Kraus have been writing together for nearly a decade and have produced two fiction series: *Treasures of the Carribean* and *The Circle of Destiny*. They live in the Chicago area with their son, Elliot, and Petey the Cat. They love to travel as a family. . .except for Petey the Cat.

Terri worked as an interior designer for twenty years before becoming a mom. Besides writing, she is the women's ministries coordinator at their church, hosts a monthly book club, quilts, plays piano, and is studying Italian.

Jim is a senior vice-president at Tyndale House Publishers. He loves riding his most recent toy—a black Vespa motor scooter. He teaches Sunday school, loves every kind of music, and finds the best time to plot out a new book is during his long nighttime walks.

You may write to Jim and Terri in care of Author Relations, Barbour Publishing, P. O. Box 719, Uhrichville, Ohio 44683.

Would you like to offer feedback on this novel?
Interested in starting a book discussion group?
Check out www.barbourbooks.com
for a Reader Survey and Book Club Questions.